CONFESSIONS OF AN
Assassin

Linda Heavner Gerald

LINDA HEAVNER GERALD

CONFESSIONS OF AN Assassin

TATE PUBLISHING
AND ENTERPRISES, LLC

Published by Tate Publishing & Enterprises, LLC
127 E. Trade Center Terrace | Mustang, Oklahoma 73064 USA
1.888.361.9473 | www.tatepublishing.com

Tate Publishing is committed to excellence in the publishing industry. The company reflects the philosophy established by the founders, based on Psalm 68:11,
"The Lord gave the word and great was the company of those who published it."

Book design copyright © 2015 by Tate Publishing, LLC. All rights reserved.
Cover design by Gian Philipp Rufin
Interior design by Honeylette Pino

Published in the United States of America
ISBN: 978-1-62994-322-0
1. Fiction / Romance / Multicultural & Interracial
2. Fiction / Mystery & Detective / General
14.12.22

To Don, Jordan, and Jenna Heavner,
who comprise a family built on love and loyalty.
You have been an inspiration to so many.

CONTENTS

1

LOOKING BACK

It all began so innocently. Looking back, it causes great sadness to think of the person I was at that time—young, full of promise. I thought of myself as beautiful, superior to the others. Now I realize just how foolish, off course I had become, even in college, from the young girl in Manhattan, New York. My parents were part of the Carnegies. Our heritage caused great pride in all of us, even though my family was considered "the bottom of the line." Father and Mother were labeled "rebels." Plenty of money and prestige, they were easily accepted at family functions. Yet they were considered different. Never did they put on airs as some of the more distant family members frequented. Socially, their friends were very diverse. Those friends would not have been accepted by the rest of the family.

I, on the other hand, was a snob, just like the distant others. Pure and simple, if people didn't meet my standards for beauty or style, I wasn't interested. I surrounded myself with shallow and contemptuous people. Easy to be happy when you are told only what is expected, never the truth. To my mind, they were true friends. Believing that they would always be just that, I wrapped myself in their lies. What a foolish and shallow person I also was. This reference is not to my circle of friends.

True friends, I had six of them. They remain my family. The contemptuousness to which I refer was a group. Not any group but a hallowed government organization to which membership was indeed rare. My inclusion caused great pride in the beginning. Later, I would see the depths to which they condescended to achieve their warped objectives. Until I die, I shall regret my frivolous notion that affiliation with them ever achieved anything more than the greatest loss of my life.

Now, I am an older woman at the proud age of fifty, but I am not proud. How I wish that I had taken a different course. If only I followed the principles of my grandfather. Faith was a cornerstone for him. I possessed that faith, but as I matured, I thought it "uncool." So I allowed my friends to direct my choices even though that small voice inside tried to give me the right direction. I made many mistakes over the course of my life until I suddenly figured out that I was a mess. Then I needed much correction just as a sailboat, which erred off course for a long time. Changing my life and cleaning up my mistakes proved difficult and costly. In fact, I find it impossible to remove the baggage, which I created.

The big regret of my life was allowing my country to dictate actions, which were despicable. For my country, I committed the unthinkable act. It happened so slowly, getting caught in the web of lies. My life seemed glamorous, more than I ever dreamed. My actions became more and more exciting. The thrill was like a drug. I required added doses. Mounting danger simply increased the rush, which I experienced. Yet I told myself that I was noble, doing the right thing. To this day, I am not sure of one act—that treacherous thing which rids me of sleep even now. Right or wrong, I know I have received forgiveness. God has forgiven me, this I know, but I can't forgive myself. I suffer daily. Sometimes, when I am lying alone in a cold bed, I remember the life that I once possessed—the love that I shared with a man whom I never really knew, or did I? They told me I misread him. He was not the man whom I loved. That is the saddest part of my life. The part that I still grieve, the loss I unwittingly created. That loss is sometimes still unbearable. I acted without regard to his love. Superiority never allowed me to question my actions.

"Just do what you are told. Act, don't react." Brainwashing created a lifestyle, a way of thought. After my loss, when regret overcame me, it occurred too late. Maybe I could never prove his innocence. No proof was ever given to me of the "terrorist actions" he supposedly committed. How could I know the truth about him? I couldn't. For the rest of my days, I would question if there was a chance that he was my love. Still, my mind was wired to believe them. Had he merely used me to fulfill his objectives? The beautiful life that I treasured and that I still miss, was it really a lie? Could he have been so devious and cunning?

The result of the life that I chose results in mistrust, concerning everyone. My solitary life is necessary for self-preservation. Things could change in a split second. They might come to the door or approach me on the street. They are all powerful, irrefutable. Therefore, I try not to create any news. My quiet life is my only choice. Now I live with fear each day, afraid that there may be a knock on the door and several men in suits will look blankly at me. I will know what is happening but not what awaits. Anything could occur. Such is the life I created. My choices killed my chance of happiness. Fear and loss consume my life now.

This is not what I once expected. If I don't travel or call attention, maybe they will forget me. I know better, but I live that way. Life remains sad and unfulfilled. To find myself becoming old is beyond my expectations. I never envisioned being such. To find myself older and filled with regrets is torture. Perhaps this is paranoia due to mental pain or old age, I am not sure. There is no one whom I can consult. Age has racked my mind prematurely due to the pain, which I carried for so long. Physically, I suffer from arthritis. My beauty is gone.

Never did I try to replace him. There was no one who came close to winning my heart. After my loss, I silently suffered the pain and loneliness, which I created. I didn't deserve to love again. Never would I know a life with a partner with whom I had grown old. There would be no grandchildren, no memories of travel in my golden years, just a void existence. The funny thing is although now I regret my choices, this is the very life of which I dreamed. All of this is before the knock on the door providing the evidence—the painting that set me free.

2

MY CHILDHOOD

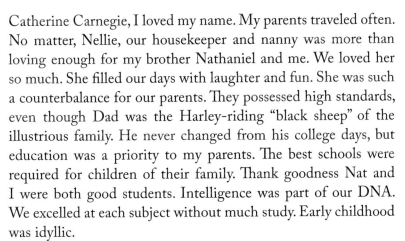

Catherine Carnegie, I loved my name. My parents traveled often. No matter, Nellie, our housekeeper and nanny was more than loving enough for my brother Nathaniel and me. We loved her so much. She filled our days with laughter and fun. She was such a counterbalance for our parents. They possessed high standards, even though Dad was the Harley-riding "black sheep" of the illustrious family. He never changed from his college days, but education was a priority to my parents. The best schools were required for children of their family. Thank goodness Nat and I were both good students. Intelligence was part of our DNA. We excelled at each subject without much study. Early childhood was idyllic.

Our teen years were also joyful times. Both of us were popular, so the social scene in Manhattan allowed us to come out in style. My debutante days still make me smile. I was a good child, which carried into my young teenage days. Filled with my grandfather's guidance, I stayed on the path of moral integrity. Then college came. I fell from grace. No longer did the light appear in my grandfather's eye. Instead, he looked pensive when I was around him.

"Oh, Cat, what are you doing? If only you could see where you are headed. I know. You see, I did the same thing. Knowing that you will not listen to me, I still can't help but try to instruct you. If you are wise, and I know that you are indeed, you will stay on the path you learned in Sunday school. Remember Miss Carol's words? Please come back to us before it is too late."

Smiling my most charming smile, I would laugh at him.

"Well, I'm following in your footsteps, I guess. Cut me some slack, Grandfather, I'm not very far away." Then I would prance out of his presence because he created an uncomfortable feeling in my soul.

My college days, the portal to adulthood at last, the time for making choices of my own couldn't arrive quickly enough. My family expected me to attend one of the Ivy League colleges as most before me had done, a university of which someone in the family was an alumnus contributing huge amounts of money to insure that the family children received preferential treatment. Secretly, I longed to be a Southern girl. After I read *Gone with the Wind*, my dreams changed. Thoughts of smelling the honeysuckle while walking under the magnolia trees filled my mind. Without a word to anyone, I applied to the University of Alabama. Well known for their sororities and party status, those young women would become the sisters whom I always craved. My parents shook their heads over years of dinners as a youngster when I answered their question with my best Southern accent. That progressed to constant dialogue. Even my "yes" friends told me I was being silly. What good would this accomplish in my life? Born Northern and bred with a pedigree, none of it produced pride. I longed to be Scarlet.

No idea of my treacherous act graced my parents. They had seen the applications to the "approved universities" but not this one. The day that I found the official envelope lying on the foyer table as I ran inside from tennis, I looked in horror. Surely Nellie had been instructed numerous times that when it arrived, she was to deposit it inside my dresser drawer. Grabbing it as though it was a ransom, I ran up the stairs.

"Your mama put it there. The one day that she picked up the mail. I'm sorry, Miss Catherine."

I was so excited that I didn't answer. My heart pounded louder than the heavy footsteps on the marble stairs. Clutching the long overdue reply to my request for admission this fall, I fell onto the bed.

"Please, Lord. please, let me get accepted there. I promise to do my best." About the only time that I prayed anymore was when I needed something. True to his promise to love and delight his children, God answered my prayer. Carefully opening the letter with shaking hands, happiness flooded my heart. All of those Southern dreams would be fulfilled. The gentile Southern women in Alabama would surely find me different but charming. Thinking of myself as capable of charming a mule, I would fit right into the daily social clamor of my dream university. Scarlet would pale in comparison to my wiles and softness. Margaret Mitchell created a disappointment for my family, but I would follow my own dream.

Dinner that night was the perfect occasion to explain my "soon to be disappointed" status, my fall from grace with my family. My brother was staying at Harvard. He was trying to gain acceptance into those sacred halls, but we all knew that was a given for him. His annoying behavior lately of trying to impress our father became sickening to behold. He possessed a different vision, longing to step into Father's footsteps. A carbon copy of the generations past, he would delight as much as I was about to disappoint.

"Well, there is no easy way to say this, so here goes. I have decided to go to the University of Alabama. Actually, the application was sent months ago. Finally, I received acceptance. My plans are to leave the end of August. It is my wish to pledge. This is my dream. Please be happy for me." Relaying this shocking announcement with great confidence even though my hands under the table were visibly shaking was a feat for me.

The looks of disdain told me no one was happy. I disappointed my entire family. Yet it was grandfather who I dreaded to face. Mother and Father would come around; they always did. Grandfather stood more difficult. My fickle Southern accent never amused him. Silence prevailed as I waited with a smile, knowing they would understand. How many times had my father been in the hot seat? So I waited for the longest time. Finally, they looked at each other. Nellie stood behind Dad with a casserole. She did not look pleased either. You really had to mess up to upset her.

"Catherine, you know this is not the path that we would have chosen for you. Still, you are a young lady now, so I feel inclined to allow you mistakes. I certainly have made plenty." His sadness was obvious, his displeasure certain.

"Your brother made us all proud by his worthy choice of Harvard. I guess one Ivy Leaguer is better than none. Right, Margaret, do you agree?"

Looking at my mother, he then softly asked, "What do you think, Margaret?"

Tears ran down my mother's checks as she looked at me. Softness in her eyes told me that she understood the desire to be different, maybe even to be shocking. She certainly shocked her family through the years.

"Yes, I agree. I'm surprised that you never shared the desire to attend a Southern university with us, Cat. That might have prepared us for this event, but I also understand your desire to be your own person. We can't stop you. I just hope that you will not come to regret your choice."

Running to my mother, I bumped into Nellie who spilled the overfilled bowl of vegetables onto the floor. Tears also ran down Nellie's eyes but for different reasons. Now she was forced to deal with the reality that I would indeed be leaving soon. I would be much farther away than she planned. She smiled her courageous smile, which I loved. Could it be this easy? Was I really about to embark on my seemingly impetuous dream? For a few more moments, there was silence and lowered heads. Nellie, dear, faithful Nellie suddenly grabbed me, hugging me so tightly that I almost choked on her sachet.

"I am proud of you, Miss Catherine. When you get to that dormitory, can I come to visit you? No one in my family ever went to college. At least, you are doing what everyone in my family only dreamed. Can't tell you how proud I am."

Still looking at my father, I mumbled, "Thanks, Nellie."

Then he looked me in the eyes. I saw his smile. The smile I reaped so many times when I thought that I was in serious trouble. His only daughter would not be labeled "renegade." He and Mom hugged me with such love. Soon, I cried with them. For the rest of my days, I remembered that moment. It was a moment of passage as though they were saying finally, *I was an adult*. Although I was responsible for my actions, they would be mine. In my head, I planned my drive down to Alabama. I had never even visited there. It didn't matter to me that I reached a major decision with little research. It must be as I envisioned—softness, manners, gentility, etiquette, and surrounded by my "sisters." I couldn't wait to pack. My luggage waited in the attic for Nellie to bring down. She would clean it, then help me pack.

Of course, I would need many new clothes. How would I decorate my room? Mom and I would have fun choosing those things. Now, how did I tell them that I wanted to drive myself? Last week was special, my parents bestowed on me a new BMW sedan for graduation. There would be plenty of room for all that I needed to take. It was equipped with GPS so I would not worry over getting lost. Of importance was the fact that I take this leap into adulthood on my own. Would they understand how vital for me to cross the Mason-Dixon Line alone as I found my new calling? How different would the Southern states become as I drove to my fate? Of course, we visited Jekyll Island and Amelia, as well as several others, but that was in my childhood. Now I was an adult. I needed to make this drive unaccompanied. It would be my passage into the person of my future. Excitement filled every pore of my being. Truly, this was adulthood. This was the new me.

3

NATHANIEL

Summer days quickly passed. There were forms to complete then mail. Shopping sprees, one after another, filled with joyous laughter and plans. Mom kept referring to "our" drive to the university. I only smiled. Her look told me that she suspected something was not right, but my newfound freedom kept her from inquiring. The only downside was my dear brother.

Nat changed into a real pain. Every time he entered the room, he was greeted with squeals of pride from Mom about her "Harvard man." Give me a break, with all the money they poured into that university, of course he gained acceptance. At least I had gotten in on my own credentials. Never did I stress that I was one of the Carnegies. The huge endowments were not given to the University of Alabama although plenty of funds were allotted. I was just an ordinary young woman who desired a higher education to the board there. Of course, I didn't need to worry about graduation or what career would still be lucrative by graduation or how much money I would need. All of those perks came with my birth. The fine arts degree was the only thing of interest to me. My love of painting was almost an obsession, so it only made sense to open my own gallery. My desire of offering help to the real struggling artist had been my dream since I remembered.

Nathaniel, on the other hand, became consumed by long sessions with Dad, planning what course he should follow once he was finally stationed in his storied place at Harvard. Mother would beam each time he entered the room. My reduction to helping Nellie serve him increased my disdain. Knowing that if I had assumed my destined role at such a prestigious, hallowed place, I would have received the same "rock star" treatment, did little at consoling me. No matter, I told myself, *A few more months until I was free.* So I bore the laughter at our July 4 party when Mom announced my college dream. The jokes were rude and insensitive. Still, I held my head high. Just knowing my dream was close allowed me to smile at their stupid banter. I was about to break out of their mold. *My world would be so much more palatable soon,* I told myself.

As time hastened to our exit from the family, Nat became exalted to a place of honor. I was tolerated as a silly girl who made poor choices. Soon, even I began to doubt myself. Yet I knew I could make any necessary correction. It would not be difficult to enter Harvard, Yale, or any of the other more "desirable" schools. My grades were better than Nat's, but my accomplishments no longer mattered to those whom I loved. Finally, the time of reckoning was upon us. To my surprise, my parents hosted a large party in honor of none other than Nathaniel William Carnegie. Everyone who was of any importance in New York was invited to attend. I just assumed that my party would be smaller, perhaps a week or so later. My party, however, never happened. The hurt was great. My parents didn't mean to cause such harm. They never considered the pain. They must have assumed that I realized my grievous error. Such behavior would not be celebrated. Those things may not seem like a big deal, but they were to me.

My grandfather hurt me the most. The light left his eyes at that point, never to return. Nathaniel became the light. I would watch my beloved's eyes follow Nat. When he looked at me, he lowered his eyes. He tried not to let me see the utter disappointment, but

I knew. Many times, I cried myself to sleep at my fall from grace. Was I really so off course? Perhaps, that is where I may have lost my way. If it was so easy to lose the love of my family, what did that say for the future? Was it necessary for me to play a game of plying them with promises as Nat did? I made a decision on what I believed to be right for me. Was that wrong? The pain, which I incurred from that summer, caused a callousness to cover my being. A false bravado seemed to follow me. After spending years planning this only to be rejected by those who always told me to "follow my heart." Had they lied? I decided to always look out for myself doing what I thought best for me. Let them celebrate Nat. My decisions were based on what made me feel good. Those very thoughts produced actions, which caused my additional fall from grace.

Grandfather never forgave me my impetuousness. Never would I see the light shine from those eyes, which were becoming dimmer. Forever after, I would miss our time. Our walks in the gardens and coffee early on summer vacations, he didn't invite me to join him any longer. Now he and Nat walked down the beach, arm in arm. I sat alone with my plans. No longer did I speak with my Southern drawl, which incited good-natured objections in the past. That now seemed silly and downright painful. Still, I maintained a stiff upper lip as I held my head high. A few more weeks, this would all be over. I was going to accomplish greatness.Now, I longed to do more than obtain a major in fine arts. I would do something noble. I would make them all proud. Regrets for deeming me foolish would result soon enough.

4

FAMILY FAREWELLS

Three days before my scheduled departure, I lowered the boom so to speak, but that boom backfired. When I announced at breakfast I had decided to drive by myself, the heated discussion, which I anticipated, did not ensue. Instead, my father calmly announced they deducted that I intended to drive myself. All of this was understandable since I was now self-sufficient. So they planned to go with Nat to Harvard and spend several days getting him settled. Dad scheduled many places to show him. He wanted to share some special moments from his time there. The excitement was penetrable. Nat looked at me with contempt. Now he became the golden child, while I was the misfit just like Dad before me. Yet Dad showed no association of like feelings with me. His son was now his world. Mom wasn't any more considerate. She still squealed with glee each time "her darling" entered the room. Deliberations filled my head about leaving earlier so that the three of them could start their celebrations.

The day before I was to leave, Mom announced she planned a special night for the four of us at the club. Well, that was something, at least. Finally, I looked forward to perhaps a mention of my achievements with great pride. They really should be proud of Nat after all. He followed the plan. I had chosen dissension. Now I must reap the results. How many times in my future would I repeat that statement?

Finally, the day arrived for the family dinner. Usually, I didn't primp, but tonight was different. Mom recently purchased my first Chanel, which I wore with great pleasure. The navy-and-white ensemble seemed perfect for this event. Nat looked like an Ivy League student in his navy Brooks Brothers jacket and khaki slacks. It surprised me when even with this choice. I was passed over for my brother. They glowed over their only son and how handsome he appeared. Dad winked at me. "You look nice also, Catherine." Well, so much for fairness in this family. Nat glowed as the comment was delivered.

We arrived at the club to praise for both Nat and me from fellow members. There were several other family gatherings for the same purpose. We all gathered for refreshments. Julie, one of my friends, yelled, "Catherine, you are the only Southern, ordinary student." Everyone laughed well naturedly, but it hurt. Again I raised my eyes to see Nat smiling. What was going on here? The rest of the evening was calmer. Dad toasted each of us, feelings soothed. Again, it was the family that I loved. Even Nat hugged me as we left, explaining how deeply he would miss me.

When we arrived home, I felt exhausted. Maybe I wanted to end it on a positive note, so I excused myself with hugs and kisses. The excitement made it difficult to sleep. Disbelief plagued me that I was heading on such a long, uncertain drive alone. They must really trust me, or was it just the perks of having a Harvard man were overwhelming? It didn't matter. Tomorrow was my swan song, and I was ready to sing.

5

LEAVING HOME

I barely slept the night before my departure for UA. All through the night, I felt racked with guilt for the disappointment I caused my family. No matter that my university ranked among one hundred public universities as one of the top, it just was the wrong location. Still, I reasoned I was fulfilling my dream; nothing could stop me. When the alarm clock finally sounded, I had been looking steadily at it for over an hour. Filled with excitement and longing, I bounded from bed. A quick shower helped invigorate me as I quietly pulled on the clothes lying on my chair. No makeup was needed. I would be driving all day with an occasional stop for gas. My goal was to take my time since I was leaving early, time was on my side so to speak.

The university facility took care of many details. Our attorney made some of the final arrangements as far as waving visitation. My arrival would be my first glimpse of my new home. Set for sorority visitation on Fall Formal Recruitment, plans were confirmed. The university sponsored eighteen of the national sororities. My family would not make the September family weekend yet I understood their desire to be with Nat at Harvard. No worries, there would be plenty of friends, I was sure.

Mom and Dad had always been early risers. When Dad rushed off for his commitments, Mom always was up with him.

Together, they planned their day over coffee and funny comments from Nellie. Now they had retired, most days, they slept a little later. Because of that, I didn't expect them to be up early for my send off. They surprised me by rising from their station at the dining table with their cups of coffee as I entered the room.

"This is surprising, seeing you both so early. You really didn't have to get up for me. My plan was to grab a cup on the road. I am really anxious to get an early start."

"That is nonsense. You sit yourself down and have a proper cup with your folks, or you will be sorry. You are all going to miss each other."

Nellie physically pushed me back into my chair and popped a cup of coffee in front of me. I wished my departure was earlier. Still, I smiled and picked up my cup from the saucer. Mom sadly returned my smile.

"Catherine, we are going to miss you so much. I know that we have made a fuss over Nathaniel, but you know we are just as proud of you." Having no such idea, I smiled and nodded just the same.

"Now, Cat, you must promise to drive carefully. You have plenty of time since leaving a little early." I didn't even realize that he was aware of my schedule.

He continued, "Please phone us along the way on our cell phone. We will be on pins and needles till you arrive." I doubted if "pins and needles" described the way that they felt. More sheer delight at "the darling's" Harvard-bound destiny.

I longed to be away from their anxious gaze. Gulping my coffee loudly, I stood to leave. Silence shrouded the room. Tears dropped from Nellie's large brown eyes. Hugging each of them, no word was spoken. As I walked to the door, I turned to see them huddled together. At that moment, I realized this was not just a rite of passage for Nat and me but for our parents as well. First, retirement signaled their aging, now watching their only two children leave the nest at the same time. Briefly, I envisioned the lonely rooms and quiet dinners with only each other and Nellie. The pangs of emotion pulled at my heart. Running back to them, I hugged each again, a stronger hug with profuse kisses and tears. Walking quickly, I exited my home of eighteen years then closed the door of my new graduation gift quietly.

As I drove from the long rambling driveway, out the gates, I stopped briefly. They were great parents. I had really been unfair in my constant criticism of them lately. I would miss them. I prayed at that moment God would keep them safe and be with me as I made my pilgrimage to UA. Yes, that was the moment of passage. My parents would always be loved, but I longed for a different sort of life. My desire was indeed strange. I desired a life of solitude. No one that I knew lived the life, which was beckoning me. It wasn't a noble calling. Just a desire to be alone. That desire may have had a very strong influence over the choices that I was about to make. A strange life but mine—that was what mattered most to me.

6

THE PORTAL

Today, I remember the two-week drive from Manhattan to Alabama with as much fondness as my memories of all the years, which I spent at the University of Alabama. It wasn't that I didn't love my time at 'Bama but in my mind, that drive was a rite of passage. A portal to the life that I always dreamed. The drive was the beginning of my new life. University life was never considered to be anything more than that experienced by every other student. The young age of eight started my obsession with all things Southern. My father told me that maybe it had something to do with the fact that our founding family members arrived in Henrico, Virginia. There were rumors of relations with Thomas Jefferson. I wasn't sure how true that was but decided that someday, when I owned my own art gallery with plenty of time on my hands, I would study my roots. How exciting to search through family records' gleaning bits of history. Having some family member tell me about their research just wasn't the same. I needed to see the accuracy of the search for myself.

At the age of thirteen, after completing *Gone with the Wind*, my obsession deepened into a pathological drive. I dreamed of someday being on my own with the ability of making choices for my future. In my mind, I referred to this time as "the portal." What I meant was the entrance not only into adulthood but the luxury of experiencing the Southern way. Living in the south, wherever I chose to live in an old, lavish Southern home surrounded by magnolias and crepe myrtles, which moved majestically in the soft, hot breezes each afternoon. That became a recurring dream. The beginning of this dream hinged on acceptance to the academic institution, which I chose then the town and house where I would live. Never did I dream of marriage or children. Those Southern things were my dream for the future.

Now, I had fulfilled two of the steps—acceptance to UA and making the drive to my new home alone. The excitement that filled my heart was beyond words. I obtained permission to arrive early at the dorm but was now thinking about going to some of the places along the way, which had only been dreams. If I tired, it would be easy enough to speed things up. There was no pressure now, just excitement.

Leaving Manhattan, I crossed the George Washington Bridge. Soon enough, I was on I-95, speeding happily along with the traffic. The thought formed it would be wonderful to visit Virginia. Oh, Virginia, the home of decades of old Southern gentility. Once conducting a test on dialects in various areas of the south, I had decided that out of all the states, the Virginians possessed the most beautiful accent. Theirs was "highbrow." Aristocracy oozed from their lilted speech. After years of practice, I was pretty good at it. To my professionally untrained ear, I sounded just as my beloved relations must have once sounded. That is before they left the south to live up north. What possessed them? Not me, maybe I would not have family, but I would live in the south someday. Living alone in the south did not fright me, but the ideas were a comfort. Actually I pictured my home frequently throughout my earlier years—sparkling white with large, dark-green shutters. There would be a spacious wraparound porch with shining floors of glossy gray. Antique white wicker furniture scattered in small groups. The ceiling painted sky blue as many Southern homes contained. My home must be old with an illustrious history, one where many families created lifetime memories. Perhaps a local home, which was registered with the historical society. Memories of past families would sustain my solitary life. I could do as I pleased. Frequently, I planned of rising early each morning to the finest coffee beans, which I would grind. Fresh French croissants would stock my freezer with the freshest of French butters. After a delightful breakfast, I would enter a room set aside for my art. Painted a sunny soft yellow, it would be the room where I spent my time. The old refinished floors protected with large rugs. My easel would always be setup. Paints stored with all of the essentials would sit on antique tables. That room would face east and allow me to watch incredible sunrises each morning with a cup of coffee and my paints. No ties; I would be free to paint all day if I chose.

My art gallery would be staffed with competent people. Located close to my home, I would only visit a few times each week. I would devote my time to genealogy, painting, and gardening. My small, intimate dinner parties would be the craze of my neighbors. Only the artistic, well-educated would be invited to those meals, which I would cook myself with the help of my trusted house assistant. I hated the word *maid*. Never would that be the description of someone whom I treasured as I welcomed them to my small family.

The food must come from the local market and be simple, artisan treasures coveted in the summers. Yes, it was all clear in my mind. Many more details were covered in my plans as well. My thoughts were on all of those long awaited dreams as I drove out of New York. Maybe my vision was selfish, but I planned on doing great acts of benevolence in the future.

The first night, I arrived in Richmond, Virginia. It surprised me to find that I wasn't at all tired. The drive, far from being draining, was exhilarating. It proved simple finding a room at one of the local hotels. Especially given the fact that the University of Richmond also welcomed hordes of students and family, finding a room so easily was a pleasant surprise. I only hoped that the remainder of the long drive would be so simple.

At one time, I considered seeking admission to this private university but declined that thought. Immediately leaving the solitude of my room to walk with other students, companionship was needed. When I saw the campus, I felt ill. Perhaps my choices were a terrible mistake. This was an acceptable university. Most students appeared extremely friendly. A group of just-arrived freshmen girls invited me for a local Italian dinner. We walked carelessly to the cool, dark restaurant. The air inside was freezing after the scorching heat outside. Immediately, we ordered ice tea. I knew enough about the south to order sweet tea. Any good Southerner knew that to be the only way to drink it.

Offering very little to their good-natured bantering, I mostly listened. This evening was lighthearted and filled with disbelief that they were finally on their own. Everyone was thrilled to be a part of this beautiful scene. Wishing desperately that I had conducted more research, confusion targeted my plans. To be a part of this dream only made sense. This was where my ancestors originally landed. The only reason that I failed to decide on this possible school was I thought it too close to my New York home. Mom constantly would have visited. Once again, I was being selfish, but I had not wanted that. I craved a solitary existence.

Whenever speaking that long-ago evening, I used my best Virginian accent. It was important that I appear as a local. My plan seemed to work. Everyone assumed I was from the area. Several girls questioned me about the city. I just made things up. Now I realize this was a way for me to maintain some control over a "completely out of control" period. Those memories always make me smile.

The next day, I drove to Monticello located in Charlottesville, the home of the third president of the United States. The possibility that I may be related to him created longing to learn of this scholarly and innovative person. Monticello rates as the epitome of Southern charm. The architecture was beguiling. The eleven thousand square foot home was actually designed by Jefferson from Italian Renaissance architect Andrea Palladio. Situated on a summit of eight hundred and fifty feet in the Southwest Mountains, everything about this home was designed for beauty and functionality. Monticello means "little mount" in Italian.

The furnishings appeared simple but beautifully in tune with the dimensions and period. I loved everything about it. Each room was studied with a decorator's eye. That would be my pattern for my home someday. The landscaped grounds were another example of quintessential good taste. I made note of each shrubs and flowers in a journal, which I carried everywhere as I did my sojourn. That day passed much too quickly.

Exhaustion crept over me as I headed to find a hotel in the late-day traffic. Things yesterday had been so easy. I hoped that I would not have a problem finding lodging in yet another college town. Charlottesville, the home of the University of Virginia, was one of the most beautiful places I ever visited. Even today, I am called to return there. The university was designed by none other than Thomas Jefferson himself in 1819. It was beautiful beyond words. The initial board of visitors comprised of Jefferson, James Madison, and James Monroe could not have been anymore stately. Beauty surrounded the site, which was mostly farmland belonging to Monroe. My heart ached once again to think that I might have attended there. I would be "home" now instead of facing another exhausting drive.

The University of Virginia always ranked at the top of the national university ratings. It would have been an honor to be a part of such a prestigious school. Again, I questioned my decision, wondering if I may transfer there someday. Plagued by doubts as I drove in the hot late-day traffic, feelings of loneliness and fear overcame me. Fortunately, I was once again able to find a small local hotel. Now, too tired to go out to dine, I ordered delivery from a local restaurant suggested by a young student working the front desk. After eating, I didn't even shower. Instead I fell into a deep and much-needed sleep.

Arising early the next day, I headed out of Charlottesville with a heavy heart. I just knew that I had made a colossal mistake. Would choosing the wrong university wreck my college days? After a breakfast at a local IHOP, I felt rejuvenated, committed to my original plan. No, I couldn't have made a mistake. My dream loomed so clear. I was young and unsure of my ability to make choices. Those were my faults. Yet that indecisiveness would be a trait following me throughout my life. Later, the doubts from inability to make up my mind would consume me.

Just hold onto your original dream. Yes, Charlottesville would have been perfect, but there must be a reason that Alabama was your goal. I would not despair but resume my drive, feeling somewhat confident. Much sooner than I thought, decision time about my driving route to Alabama confounded me. The idea formed that it would be delightful to take the Blue Ridge Parkway as far as North Carolina. Hours of my past had been filled with reading information about that scenic drive, a forty-five mile per hour route of some of the most beautiful scenes one could ever imagine. Yet as much as I longed to experience the peace and beauty, was I up to traveling slowly for so long?

My body made the decision for me. Turning off my planned faster route, I now found myself on the Blue Ridge Parkway. This turned out to be the correct choice. The peace, which flooded my soul as I gazed upon the Blue Mountains bathed in white puffy clouds, reinforced my thoughts that I was capable of making wise choices. A slow speed was not at all dull but allowed me to enjoy the beauty without an accident. I arrived in Blowing Rock, North Carolina. There I was treated to luxury by the staff of the Inn at Ragged Gardens. Delighted by a gourmet dinner, I felt at home. The elegance of such a beautiful room was buffeted by a rustic feel, which made it perfect for this small mountain town.

Although I never returned, I often remember with plans to revisit that part of "the portal."

Leaving Blowing Rock, I drove only minutes before assuming my route. The remainder of the drive seemed pleasant without event; however, those were the highlights. Soon enough, the fateful day arrived. I would enter my new home, my new Southern life. Located in Tuscaloosa, Alabama, my arrival was eminent. Only hoping that I would not regret choosing the University of Virginia instead of UA, I put on my brightest smile. Watching for signs of the university, I was shaking. Following directions from my GPS, wet, trembling hands created difficulty. Then I saw it. Large red brick buildings, as well as the President's Mansion painted white. There were huge expanses of well-maintained green lawns. It was as I imagined. The books and photos over which I pondered did not do justice. Maybe it was not rated the most prestigious of universities, but it worked for me. Immediately, I felt at home. Following the instructions, which our attorney gave me, I arrived at my dorm.

The rest was pretty much as any other's college days. My experiences were positive. I received a great education. Also, I developed many friendships. Three of those remain cornerstones in my current life. Linda Hughson, Margie MacKay, and Rhonda Wilson are still best friends. The kind of friend whom you don't need to contact often to feel connected. Each time we are together, the connection is alive. They are my family even today, just as I planned so long ago. I chose them for my relations.

After graduation, we flew to Abaco, Bahamas. Margie's family owned a gorgeous home on that magical Caribbean island. Two of my friends already had plans for the future. Rhonda and I were the slackers. My only plan remained finding that large white house with green shutters. It was out there; I just had to locate it.

7

MY DREAM HOME

The time in Abaco was truly a dream. My parents spent a great deal of time in St. Bart's, as well as most of the Caribbean. Hilarious times on yachts with friends delighted Nathaniel and me throughout the years over dinners. The MacKay home presented the same sort of lightheartedness. A typical Nassau colonial mansion graced by large white columns, the palatial home delivered a statement of refinement. It was painted chocolate brown with sparkling white trim. The interior boasted all French slip covers with overstuffed cushions. Mementos of travels filled the inside, hiding treasures from all over the world. The design was not "beachy" but shabby chic. It worked well.

Each of my friends gathering to celebrate our graduation was a strong Christian. Margie and Linda had stayed devoted, but Rhonda and I were a little off course. To my family, I was way off course. Realizing that I was denying my true convictions, I maintained my faith while living a little wildly. Keeping one foot founded in morality, I planted the other in the world. Yet I knew that God was there and that my salvation was sealed years ago. *I would clean up my act on down life's road*, I told myself. Rhonda and I would take time from the other "good" two and club hop.

Rhonda was a beauty. She loved beautiful clothes with an impeccable sense of style. Beautiful inside, as well as out, created someone very special. Margie remained moral and focused. Already engaged to the man of her dreams, she was so in love. John was getting the best of us. We all knew it. Linda appeared to hold tremendous talent. She would be the least critical of us, always able to help. Married already, she would never falter. Sam and she married the last semester of university in a simple wedding. Abiding love in their eyes was what most young women dreamed. While I was delighted for them, I maintained my dream for a solitary life of various studies.

Helping me find my dream home filled our daily conversations. Each of my friends thought they had the answer. As soon as we left the Bahamas, I visited Chapel Hill, North Carolina with Rhonda. She was certain that I would find the third part of my Southern dream. Then I scheduled to arrive in Northwest Florida with Margie. Her family waited to greet us. There, she stressed that her fiancé's family could convince me to make the coast home. Finally, Linda displayed confidence that Sam could show me the dream home in Alabama. That really made sense because I loved UA so deeply. Those honeysuckled dreams waited for me. I just needed to make the choice.

Leaving the Bahamas presented problems. Now we truly would embark on our adult lives. Our storybook time at college magical, but reality was waiting. Each of us obtained a great education, now time to put it into play. We caught Bahamas Air to Miami. Then we flew into Raleigh/Durham airport. Rhonda's car was waiting. She had been correct on her descriptions. University of North Carolina at Chapel Hill was regaled for providing a wonderful education, as well as fun social life. Rhonda and I floundered a little unlike our other two friends. Their futures were focused and planned. We reverted back to our college days, where we spent most of our time in clubs, having a great time. Rhonda attracted more boyfriends than the rest of us put together. She seemed to be a magnet, a really engaging one at that.

Yet nothing impressed me at the university. The beautiful old white house in my mind never surfaced, although we did not look with great zeal. When I left Chapel Hill, Rhonda had devised about as many plans for the future as I. Her father recently passed away, so her mom seemed happy to have her company. I knew that she would marry soon. She already had received several proposals. Her life as a school counselor could wait.

When I arrived in Florida, I was hopeful. Living there would be the Southern way of times past. The quiet daily flow, as well as the gentile locals, would appeal to any Southern belle. Yet to get the crowds to support my art gallery, I would need to live in Tallahassee or Panama City. Since I wanted a small town, this location would not work. My heart was on the Forgotten Coast, but the town was not ready for my plans. I left Margie and John, envious of their love and devotion. Their plans were already underway for the wedding of the century in their small town.

Lastly, I visited Linda and Sam. I knew at once that the rural town would not support my little art gallery, but Linda assured me that their idea rested on a place called Eufaula, Alabama. The name was appealing. I hoped the town would dazzle. Could my beautiful dream be close?

The day after my arrival, we set off. We allowed two days for a serious search. Sam's family welcomed us, but I felt more at home in a local B and B. My solitary longings did not bode well with family arrangements. The next morning, as Linda and Sam arrived, I had a strong feeling that this would be the answer.

— — — — — —

Eufaula was the answer to my prayers. Walking down one of the streets early the next morning, I was delighted as I witnessed pages from my Southern vision. Many of the buildings were listed on the National Register of Historic Places, just as I dreamed. The historic town was typical of Southern legends, which told of land once owned by various tribes of Indians, land that was confiscated and developed by rich Southerners. The wealth of Eufaula was the result of being a major shipping and trading point for the surrounding counties in Georgia and Alabama. The location of Eufaula would bode well for my art gallery. Barbour County hosted all of this, the largest city in its jurisdiction. Strangely, to a Northern girl, the town was originally started by an act of the New Jersey legislature on March 24, 1869. My parents would love the history of this dreamy town. Many remaining antebellum homes testified to the glorious past of this beautiful place. Located on Lake Chattahoochee, everything seemed perfect. Still, a beautiful town was not what I wanted. I needed the house.

Sam and Linda arranged for us to meet with Seth Greene, a friend of the family. They described him as real estate agent extraordinaire. Personally upon meeting him, I had my doubts. The town was definitely causing a yearning in my soul, but would I locate my home? It happened easier than I ever dreamed.

Planning on a day of house hunting in the humid exhausting weather of mid-August, we all carried bottles of water while looking at each other with resolve. What wonderful friends to support my search. Linda, I understood, but Sam just met me. I was learning the true Southern spirit. Mr. Greene was very Southern. A long-ago transplant of Charleston, South Carolina, his lilting speech dauntingly was reminiscent of Virginia. He was pure class.

Arriving in a neighborhood of new homes, which were supposed to look like old ones, I was devastated.

"Mr. Greene, what is this? Remember the hour that we just spent in your office discussing my dream home? These homes are not historic. They are beautiful indeed, but not my dream." I was almost in tears.

"Well, not so fast, missy. I am showing you these only to make you appreciate the difference in detail between the newer versions of older homes as compared to the real older homes. Money."

"What? What in the world are you referring to? Money?" I was beginning to think that Linda and Sam were very off in their praise of Mr. Greene's extraordinary abilities.

"Yes, Ms. Carnegie, money. You had better have plenty if you plan on throwing money down a bottomless pit. Now these beauties are good for years with an occasional paint job and just a little maintenance."

"Dear Mr. Greene, money is not my problem. I am more than prepared to spend my money on a bottomless pit rather than allow some historic, beautiful home to languish because the market has taken a hit. You see, I have the funds. I need the home." I found myself yelling to the horror of my manner-laden friends. They would never allow such behavior. They all lowered their heads in shame for me.

After apologizing to all, I explained how important this home was to my future. Looking at me with a look of embarrassment for my meltdown, as well as lack of manners, Mr. Greene smiled.

"Well, then, let's head over to the historic part of town. Your dream home waits to be shown. The owner passed away about eight months ago. None of the family is interested in moving here. All of the children reside in the New Jersey area, so the house will be sold. It is a beauty."

Once again, we all piled into our host's car. He was not so happy with me, refusing to even look at me now. His gaze was always upon Linda and Sam since my earlier meltdown. Obviously, I committed the unforgivable error of Southern etiquette—I raised my voice. I felt awful. Up north, yelling was a way of life. No one was offended or shocked. I still had a ways to go on being Margaret Mitchell's protégé.

We drove just a few miles. He parked in one of the few remaining shady spots on the sunny street, and we once again dove into the summer heat. It was one of those humid days without a spot of wind. Perspiration was running down my face. In fact, my entire body was wet from the assault. Thinking that I was about to cause heat stroke in these gentle folks, I decided to suggest that we call the search off until later. Since the house that he wanted to show me was unoccupied, what difference would it make when we viewed it?

"Um, Mr. Greene, should we wait until this evening to look at the property?" I asked in my softest Southern drawl.

"Now, why would we do that?" His tone had changed. Forgiving and forgetting was not easy for this man.

"Well, why don't we just visit some of the other homes, which you have scheduled and which have owners? That way, no one is put out."

Thinking myself to be showing kindness and compassion, I was shocked when he sternly stated, "I have not scheduled any others. I have the perfect home. You better make a speedy offer. It will not be around long."

Now, I was not a real-estate tycoon, but the house had already been on the market for eight months. I strongly doubted if it would sell during this day. Mr. Greene may be more of a salesman than I had earlier given him credit.

"In fact, we have arrived at your new home. There it is." Pointing to something behind me, he looked up with great pride. I realized that I had not been paying attention to our tour. Turning, there stood the home of my dreams! It was breathtaking, everything that I wanted and then some. It looked so large. The new paint was gleaming white. An "in your face sort of white" with large workable dark-green shutters, neatly arranged groupings of old wicker furniture, which had also received a coat of paint waited for their future owner—me. Without planning, I grabbed poor Mr. Greene, hugging and kissing him. Now, he did look at me.

"My goodness, maybe you should see the inside. No telling what sort of response I may receive. Should we go inside?" The gleam in his eye told me that all was forgiven. Maybe he smelled the heavy commission waiting for him.

As we entered the home, the coolness from the air conditioner wrapped us in a feeling that all was right in the world. The large entry foyer contained highly polished dark mahogany floors. A large round table held a crystal vase of crepe myrtle and magnolia branches from the front yard. What more of a sign could I expect? This was just as I dreamed. I already knew this was my home. Linda's small hand touched my sleeve. The smile on her face told me she knew that our mission was accomplished.

The shutters were slightly closed to keep the bright light from damaging the antiques, as well as cool the home. The smell was fresh paint and heavenly freshness as flowers greeted us in each room. My home consisted of a formal living room, which was a soft-green color. The sofa and chairs, as well as the tables, were old Southern classics. The less-formal den painted a darker green, which projected casualness. It gleamed with slip-covered furniture. Most importantly, the kitchen maintained old attractiveness with new appliances. My master bedroom was a soft rose and reminded me how drained I was from all of this. There were four bedrooms and three baths upstairs. Each room was as I would have designed. When we entered a sunny yellow room facing east, I actually cried. It would be a shame to set up my easel, but I planned on protecting the floor with rugs purchased from the local consignment shop. The room was packed from floor to ceiling with large shelves, maybe it had once been a library, but someone lightened the tone by adding satiny white shelves. It would be perfect for my studio. Providing plenty of room for books on art, as well as tubes of paint and necessary supplies, I knew that I was destined to live here.

"I'll take it. Can you draw up the contract? When can I move in?"

Mr. Greene, now used to my impetuousness, was totally rattled. "You must see the rest. I have never heard of anyone purchasing a home, especially an older home, without seeing the rest."

"The gardens, I need to see the gardens. Then let's return to your office and sign the contract. I'm ready for lunch. Any takers?"

Mr. Greene looked at my friends with a slight shake of the head. "Who am I to advise such a wise lady? Let's look at the gardens." Was he being sarcastic? I could not care in the least.

The gardens were up to standards set by the rest of my property. Someone worked for years, establishing a proper English garden. Large box woods surrounded my new home as a fence might. Inside of the dark-green shrubs was planted row after row of plumbago. The soft blue/purple was the desired color missing from most gardens but not mine. There were beds of old tea roses with fragrance, which only they could provide. Beds of lilies, purselane, and many others of my favorites were now bobbing in the delightful breeze, which suddenly arose, breaking the misery of the humidity. I longed to sit on the front porch with a glass of sweet tea and study the beauty, which someone else had graciously spent hours planning and working. Now some of my mornings would be spent in my garden with my gardener giving me advice. My family would love the splendor of this home, as well as the history.

I did agree to complete the tour. We returned to my hero's office, writing the contract. The listing was fairly priced. I only offered a slightly lower amount. The four of us attended the area's premier restaurant to celebrate my accomplishment, compliments of Mr. Greene. After returning to my room, I received the expected call. Excitedly, Mr. Greene relayed the fact that I now owned the prettiest home in Eufaula. As I rested the phone into the cradle, I realized that maybe I could get back on course now. How could I not after being blessed so richly? All of my dreams were now realized.

8

LIFE IN EUFAULA

Life in Eufaula proved slow and easy as did the moving process. I owned few possessions. Most of my college mementos were simply stored in the large attic. All I needed, I just purchased as a package. Constantly, finding myself walking around my new home lovingly touching several of the exquisite pieces of furniture, my heart overflowed. Surprisingly, my dream was realized easily and perfectly. To say that I loved my new life was an understatement. Each day greeted me with joy.

After moving into "Tara," that dream home which filled my nights with images of a large structure framed by a shady porch tucked inside the heavenly fragrance of wisteria and tea roses. I would spend my remaining days enjoying my southern reverie. I phoned my parents to invite them for a visit. I wasn't surprised when Nellie explained that they had gone for some time around the world on a cruise with friends. They did not plan for return any time soon. That was my parents—free spirits to the chagrin of their family. Well, it was just as well. My call wasn't out of loneliness but guilt. Truly, I did not feel anything approaching the need for visitation. In fact, I abhorred the idea of being responsible for entertaining them. No, I just wanted to extend the invitation.

Each morning, my routine was as I imagined for so many years. Bounding from bed, I headed for the Cuisinart, which was programmed the night before. Pouring my coffee, I would smile at all that I accomplished. Never did I think of giving God the praise. I had done this without any help. How arrogant and stupid I was. Then I would carry my bright yellow cup onto the front porch and rub the plaque, which announced that this home was registered with the National Register of Historic Places. Each morning, I selected a different chair in which to read the local newspaper. Eufaula was a busy place. I definitely selected the right small town to host my art gallery. This was a crossway for traffic from other counties and states.

That first morning, I posted my need for a house person and gardener both with the local paper, as well as online. Why not take the rest of the week to rest and enjoy my new home? Next week, I would find my small house staff. After that, it would become necessary to locate the site for my art gallery. All of this would take months of hard work painting and decorating. Already, I collected plenty of art, which I asked Nellie to begin sending me so my displays could be started. It shouldn't be difficult attracting new artists to hang their art as well. Life was good, and Eufaula was now my home.

The next morning delighted me when I noticed my AD for help at the top of the list. Checking my computer, I was again surprised that I already received five resumes for house person and one for gardener. Calling the first lady listed, Jean, I was pleased with the softness of her voice. Yes, she lived in town not that far away and could come for an interview today. We made an appointment for 11 a.m. Great, things were progressing ahead of my schedule.

Right on time, the doorbell chimed later in the morning. Opening the door, I was pleased to find a lovely young woman in her midthirties. Her accent was heavy, not polished as I liked, but she possessed the look of an honest woman. With pleasure,

I welcomed Jean into my home. Her credentials were infallible. She recently moved back to Eufaula so that she could nurse her mother. Unfortunately, facing her now was settling the estate with the passing of her mom. Inheriting her childhood home improved her financial picture greatly, but she now needed weekly income. Hiring her on the spot after calling her last employer who gave her glowing references seemed like the right thing. Her demeanor was peaceful. I liked the fact that she wasn't a talker. She fit perfectly into my home. Before Jean left, I mentioned that now I needed a gardener. Her husband, Albert, was also in need of employment after returning with his wife to care for her ailing mother. Immediately, I phoned his last place of employment. The rave reviews he was given were compelling. Jean explained that he studied landscaping and loved everything about working outside. He could arrive tomorrow with Jean. My staff would report for instructions. I couldn't imagine giving instructions to anyone, but I was about to become an employer. Life kept changing.

The next morning, the doorbell chimed at eight. Before me stood the rest of my new family. They were perfect. Jean was pale with brown hair. She wore no makeup but had a scrubbed glow. Wearing a white dress, she must have been instructed to dress so for her last employer. I explained she did not need to wear a uniform, but Jean insisted she felt more comfortable. She was lovely. Albert, a tall strapping young man, entered beside his wife. He appeared a little younger than she. The years of hard work outside in the humid heat tanned his skin a deep brown. His eyes were amber, almost yellow. Together, they were indeed a handsome couple. I would be proud to have them working for me.

Showing them around the house with explanations of my likes was easy. I did not feel pretentious or odd. Outside, Albert really knew his stuff. Ably, he identified each shrub and flower. Wholeheartedly, he approved of my garden plans of not making any changes. He thought as did I that we should just maintain and plant an occasional shrub. I had not even noticed the small green house located behind the main one when I purchased it. Hidden by very large English Hawthorne, Albert appeared delighted at the find. It was in great condition as was the entire house. We were both happy to find a large sink inside the greenhouse where Albert could wash his hands and water flowering pots of plants. For years, I would discover wonderful treasures in my home, which I didn't realize existed when I purchased it.

Soon, Jean began preparation of my dinner. I had given her "carte blanche."

"Just cook anything you like for a while. I am not picky. Cook enough for yourself and Albert as well." She was pleased.

Entering the sunny yellow art studio, I gently closed the door, turning on the stereo to one of my favorite operas. The soothing sound familiarly calmed me in this unfamiliar home. Yet, there was a feeling of comfort about the home. It had been my dream for such a long time. Gently depositing a large canvass onto a favored French easel, I collected a few brushes from an ample collection and mixed soft colors together on a small board. Instantly, I was lost in "my" world. For hours, I painted with delight to the wonderful smells entering as vapor under the door. Yes, life was good. I could spend the rest of my time here on earth doing just this. Indeed, I was clever.

Around three that afternoon, Jean and Albert headed home from their first day with me. They seemed as happy as I. Realizing nothing had been ingested since early morning, I raised the lid of the dark blue pot simmering happily away on the burner. Delicious pot roast surrounded with fresh vegetables teased me from a heavy sauce. Grabbing a bowl and ladle, I filled it with this delightful concoction.

Then I noticed the red light on the oven door. Opening it revealed flaky homemade cornbread waiting peacefully. It was wrapped tightly in aluminum foil. Carrying my find onto the front porch, I returned to the kitchen and poured a glass of Cabernet. I turned up my favorite opera. This would remain my pattern for many months until my life changed once again, learning that the carefree life of an adult was not so carefree.

9

LIFE AS I HAD ALWAYS DESIRED

All week, I pinched myself to be convinced that I wasn't dreaming. Life could not have been more perfect. Time spent with my small house staff proved extremely satisfying. The solitude allowed me to paint some of my best work. Working in binges, I may not paint for a few days but suddenly be inspired. Then finding it impossible to drag myself from my easel, I painted obsessively. Jean expressed concern for my lack of appetite, but I assured her that I had always been so. Many evenings before leaving, she would set dinner on a tray in front of my closed door. I suppose she reasoned that the delightful smells may entice me, but they did not. Nothing could sway me from creating until suddenly, I would lose the desire. At those times, I would work on my genealogy or gardening with Albert. Both Jean and Albert worked out well. Jean was not exactly a gourmet cook. She wasn't nearly as versatile as Nellie. Still her simple, rustic meals seemed the right thing in this Southern town. Frequently each week, she would head out to the local farmer's market, returning with delectable treasures from local growers. All of this proved delightful. Albert transformed the gardens. They looked even more beautiful. I could not find a weed. How did he work his magic?

One week passed quietly as I settled into my new life. Friday evening, early in the twilight, I was startled by the door chimes.

Not expecting company, this was a surprise. To my absolute delight, there stood Linda, Margie, and Rhonda. They each carried a small bag and a large bag.

"We knew that you would never invite us once you embarked on your solitary retreat, so here we are! It is a surprise, but we hope that you don't mind." I was delighted. After a long tour, which included the gardens and green house, which Albert had made into a small apartment for himself, we entered from the hot, humid day into the quiet of my new home. We all were dehydrated, so we each filled a large crystal glass with ice water.

"Now, where do you want to go for dinner? This is our treat for 'room and board,'" Rhonda asked with her sweetest voice.

"Don't be silly. You girls go on upstairs. Get showered and settled. Report down here in one hour, where I will have a simple meal with wine waiting." The silence was profound.

"Are you well? What in heaven's name has come over you? Cat Carn cooking?" Margie looked shocked.

"Oh, go on. I can cook. Actually my new assistant, Jean, has taught me a few secrets. She didn't officially teach me, but I have been watching her. The Southern way of cooking with fresh, simple ingredients is not difficult. Where else can we go and relax with such beautiful ambiance? Now, go on! Hurry back. We will have a wonderful time."

They left the room mumbling about my sudden interest in cooking. Margie's earlier reference to me as "Cat Carn" had begun almost immediately at UA. I was unable to remember who started it, but one of my sisters shortened my name from Catherine Carnegie to Cat Carn, which stuck. It seemed likely that would remain my name for the rest of my life.

Opening the fridge, fresh vegetables waited. Jean never disappointed. Preparing a simple salad with a few homemade sides would be easy even for a novice such as me. My desire to cook was surprising. My mother never did such a thing. Maybe once or twice in my entire life at home I saw her grace the kitchen for such a task. Dad enjoyed cooking on the grill, but Nellie had always done the rest of the meal for him.

By the time my three friends returned, the music was playing, and the wine poured. Everyone except Margie grabbed a glass. Marvin Gaye was crooning on the stereo as I served my offerings for the evening. We enjoyed the best time. The rest of the evening filled with laughter as I prepared my first dinner party, which had been merely a dream for many years. Feeling relaxed and happy, I could not believe my new life. Never had I even considered preparation of a meal, but to pass on dinner out at a restaurant, something had changed. My enjoyment for such a simple pleasure was surprising. The indescribable warmth and comfort of my new home created a desire to remain close to it.

After dinner was completed, everyone helped clean up. In no time, we were outside on the front porch. Mesmerizingly, the soft hissing sound of the night insects relaxed us. I felt a million miles away. Gently, a Southern breeze blew our hair as we looked into the heavens covered with thousands of twinkling lights as diamonds. Nights in Eufaula were very dark, which accentuated the heavenly bodies above us. Way in the background, I could hear the haunting *hoot* from a barn owl.

"Cat, you have outdone yourself. This is just what you talked about all of the time we were at college. How did you know that this would happen just as you described?" Linda's eyes glowed in the soft light from the streetlamps.

"I didn't. It was simply a dream. Believe me, I know how blessed I am. I'm surprised that Sam allowed you time away. Everything okay?"

"Oh, sure, things are wonderful. Actually, he firmed up some plans with his dad, so this weekend was the perfect time for me. He asked me to express his delight at your new home."

"Well, if it hadn't been for the two of you, this may not have worked out so perfectly. How can I ever thank you for enduring the heat that day?"

Looking at my friends, I realized how precious each of them was to me. They were my family now. Mom and Dad were still on their cruise. I hadn't heard a word from them or Nat, but that was not surprising.

It did surprise me when each lady left the porch without a word. As I sat alone, I wondered if I had offended them somehow. Just as I decided to check on them, they all returned carrying a large package.

"Well, we feel a little stupid, but this is our housewarming gift to you. Honestly, we never thought about you actually cooking, so this is sort of a joke on us. Anyway, here it is." Margie frowned.

Pushing the large box at me, I was surprised at the heaviness as well as the thoughtfulness of the gesture. As I ripped the elegant silver paper away, I knew that Linda had lovingly wrapped it. It was easy to spot her many talents. Nestled inside of the large box was the biggest, blackest frying pan that I had ever seen. It glistened with oil.

"Everyone in the South has one. This is my great grandmother's pan. She left me two. It has been seasoned for years. I will explain the procedure later. You must have this pan. From this ugly pan, you will be able to prepare the best meats and sautéed veggies ever." Linda looked so proud that I didn't have the heart to mention that one just like hers came with the kitchen. In fact, that might have been the reason my dinner was so tasty. Not realizing that it was special or that it needed special handling, I gratefully listened to her disclosure.

"Not so fast. Don't throw the box away without looking inside again. Did you think that Rhonda and I were not contributing to your present?" Margie was looking sternly at me. Tearing away more paper, I noticed an envelope laying at the bottom of the box. Opening with care, I found an official statement. Rhonda and Margie had spent hundreds of dollars purchasing a month's worth of dinners at the premiere restaurant in Eufaula. Their generosity was overwhelming.

"We didn't realize that you would obtain a staff so quickly. Even more surprising is the fact that you now cook. We assumed that you would starve. Our bad." Rhonda looked a little shocked.

"Don't worry. These will come into good use. Jean and Albert plan to visit family soon. They are leaving at the end of next week. It will be wonderful having a few gourmet meals. This is perfect. You must possess ESP," I said with a smile.

Quickly, our time passed. Rhonda and Margie traveled great lengths to visit me. As I hugged each one good-bye at the end of our weekend, I felt certain my life was on track and pleased with myself for all of the wonderful things that had occurred. Once again, I never thought to thank God for blessing me. I decided control of my life was mine. Credit for this wonderful life belonged to me. Having no idea how quickly my solitary life was about to change, I would regret the folly of my actions.

10

MY ART GALLERY

I painted like a woman possessed for days while Jean and Albert clucked over me like chickens. Already, they felt responsible for my well-being just as Nellie had for our family. That was a comforting feeling. Honestly, I hated to see them leave for their family visit. Since a child, I possessed an innate ability to tell when something was about to change. It wasn't necessarily a bad thing. Sometimes, the event that was on the horizon proved a happy one. Still, I always hated it when that creepy feeling came over me. It seemed likely that my feeling must pertain to my house staff. Without causing alarm, I warned them over and over to be careful. They would be traveling to Nevada for the family visit. From what I observed of them, they were always in a hurry unless they worked at my house. There, they were focused and careful. Later, I would learn that my house staff possessed the same trait as me. The alarm bells going off for them were attributed to my well-being. We were all on edge. They were concerned for me, and I was worried for their safety. At the end of the week, it was almost a relief that the time of departure arrived. At least, whatever was about to happen would soon occur. A few days later, I would remember my sense of relief at that time with tears. Yet there was nothing that I could do to prevent the inevitable.

After Jean and Albert left on Thursday evening, I felt so alone. Feeling pretty pleased with my abilities, I tried to tell myself that the anxious feelings, which I experienced, were from paranoia due to so many changes lately. The feelings would not abate however. At that point, I decided it was time to take on the challenge of locating an art gallery. Months of work getting the building just the way I envisioned would ensue. As well as locating artists, which I found interesting and wanted to feature. Everything had been easy about buying my home. I felt pretty confident that locating my art gallery would be just as simple.

Sleeping in the next morning, I thought that these family trips, which Jean and Albert would need to take occasionally, were not so devastating. They would allow me to sleep in and enjoy the peace of my new home. When they were present, I felt a need to withdraw, which necessitated closing the door of my studio and painting. Now I could take my time and enjoy my new home. After a late morning breakfast, I drove downtown to search out an empty building or lot on which to construct the building, which I saw so plainly in my mind.

Driving around the small town, I located two possible sites. Then hunger overtook me. I stopped at a local diner for a sandwich. To my surprise, there sat Mr. Greene. As he turned the page of his newspaper, he looked up right into my face.

"Well, if it isn't my favorite real estate buyer. How is the new house?"

Explaining that I was the happiest in my life, I thought for the first time about asking for his help. Even though it would involve a commission, I had not really seen anything that was suitable for my needs. After explaining my wishes, I saw "the" light that I had seen as he pointed to my house that day.

"Actually, I just listed the perfect property. Enjoying a bite of lunch before I return to put up the sign, looks like that won't be necessary. This property is perfect for you." He smiled his smile.

I was elated. Mr. Greene sure made my life easy thanks to Linda and Sam. Mr. Greene left the room.

Enjoying time out alone at a restaurant before my search with Mr. Greene, it delighted me to have several locals introduce themselves as they welcomed me to Eufaula. Mr. and Mrs. Boyer even invited me to a small party the next night. They were expecting the mayor and several other notable citizens of my fair town. All of the attention allowed me to experience a feeling of connection with my new home. Grateful for the invitation and looking forward to returning an invite, my induction into town seemed complete. Soon enough, Mr. Greene strolled leisurely into the dining room. It was apparent that he earned respect from the town. We left their presence as he excitedly told me about the property. It did not sound anything like what I described.

To my amazement, he pulled in front of a small warehouse. The outside was covered with brick painted a pale gray with a dark-gray canopy covering the door. Outside, it was fine, but inside, it was nothing like what I desired. The walls were all red brick. Some of those had been whitewashed. The result was a rough look not the elegant ambiance of which I dreamed.

"Mr. Greene, this is not what I described earlier. We are not on the same page at all." I frowned at his lack of connecting with me on my description. My earlier thoughts that he seemed to always know the best now seemed absurd. Yes, he had been right once, but not now.

"Oh, I think that you are so wrong. This has the potential of appealing to everyone. Think about men looking for art. They do not want some pink fancy room where French canapés are served at receptions. This room will make even the men feel like you considered their needs. It will encourage them to come to your events. The roughness of the walls, which you see as a defect, can in fact be used to great advantage. Think how easy to hang your art in the mortar and patch it easily when paintings are sold or added. The different dimensions will not cause all of the patching, which sheet rock may need. Look up at the direct lighting, which shines already onto the walls. At night, the hue will be dramatic. Light will be on the paintings, not in faces. The women will love the fact that they glow instead of looking washed out. Now, inspect the floors, they are unbelievable."

Suddenly, I saw his vision. Although it was not at all like mine, it was very appealing. Looking down at the floors, I wrinkled my nose in disgust. They were covered in deeply stained old carpets.

"Mr. Greene, you may need to have your glasses changed. These floors are nothing if not shameful. The carpet will have to be removed since I hate it. This is not a possibility."

"Lift up the corner there." He smiled because he knew that I saw the vision.

"I am not touching that nasty carpet. You lift up the corner."

He smiled. Once again he proved correct. He knew much more about real estate than I. As he took his time obviously enjoying my feeling of defeat, he walked to the edge, pulling back the smelly, nasty covering. To my great surprise and absolute delight, there laid old parquet flooring, the sort laid years ago—heavy beautiful patterns of expensive dark parquet. It was exquisite. I could not believe my good fortune.

"I'll take it. Draw up the contract. What is the price?"

Victory shone on his face as he shook his head. "Now, you know that I am not going to allow you to be so careless. We will go back to my office. We will discuss the price. You will think about a fair price, then we will contact the seller. He is a friend of mine. Come on, I'll buy you a cup of coffee. I need it each day about this time. It is difficult for me to get through the rest of the day without my caffeine charge."

"Coffee, are you kidding? In this heat, I don't think so."

"Well now, missy, we are not going to sit outside. I do have air conditioning at my office, you know." I was becoming very fond of this Southern gentleman.

As we entered the coolness of his office with our coffee in hand, I thought of how quickly I became a part of this friendly, gracious town. He was right in the way that we studied the contract. He allowed me time to think about a fair price after showing me a few comps on the downtown area. Leaving me for a short time provided the ability to arrive at a fair offer. When he returned, he called his "old" friend. In no time, I was the proud of owner of not one piece of real estate but two in Eufaula. The feeling of pride was great as I hugged Mr. Greene. The owner said that we could close as soon as the inspection was completed.

Walking back to my car, I passed the restaurant where Margie and Rhonda presented me vouchers for free dinners. In fact, they were still in my purse. What a nice way to celebrate. As I entered the cool dark dining room, the soft music and delectable smells were enticing. The doors of this trendy establishment had just opened. I was the first customer, which suited me since I would be dining alone. The waiter seemed sensitive to my slight feeling of awkwardness, so I was seated toward the back in a corner. Immediately ordering a glass of champagne, I felt ready to relax.

Glowing with happiness at how well things had gone for me, I felt such contentment. What a great dining spot even boasting a gourmet chef. It would be a treat coming here occasionally, although I appreciated Jean's meals. The waiter asked me to join him for dinner later in the week, but I declined. I loved my life and didn't need a man to make me complete.

I drove back past my new art gallery knowing once again, I made a wise choice thanks to Mr. Greene and, ultimately, Linda and Sam. Parking in the garage, I heard the unfamiliar sound of my phone ringing. No one had phoned me in such a long time. I was unaccustomed to the sound. Now running to reach the intrusive box, I slipped on the rug still able to answer it before I lost the call.

"Oh, good, Miss Carnegie, is that you? Cat Carnegie, I believe. Is this you?" The voice sounded gruff but official. My heart was pounding in my chest. This would not be good news. I thought of my premonition. Poor Jean and Albert. It must be related to them.

"Yes, this is Cat Carnegie. How may I help you?" The loud, beating of my heart was deafening. I had trouble understanding the caller.

"Miss, we have been trying to reach you all afternoon. We even came to your house. You need to sit down. Do you have family close?"

"No, I am fine. It is Jean and Albert, isn't it? I knew this would happen."

"Miss, I don't know of a Jean or Albert. This concerns your parents. Your father asked me to call you. It seems that your mother sustained a pretty nasty cut while sailing. They tried to treat it but were miles from hospital. The cut became infected with some sort of super bug. They have taken her to hospital in New York. You need to call home. I think that you need to hurry. It sounds very dangerous. Your father is beside himself. So sorry—" I dropped the phone and collapsed.

When I awoke, the phone was beside me. My face was covered in tears. With trembling hands, I phoned home. Nathaniel answered. I knew as soon as I heard his voice that it was too late. Mom was gone. Nathaniel told me to pack some clothes then drive to the local airport. He would make all of the arrangements. I should be home as soon as possible. Dad remained at the hospital.

"You need to hurry, Cat. He is really bad off. I don't think that he can handle this." Gently, the line went quiet.

11

IN THE WINK OF AN EYE

It amazed me that I slept on the plane. I guess knowing what awaited me was not going to be pleasant contributed to my depression. Father was always in control. I had no idea what it would be like to watch him struggling. Although my family never appeared close, they were my family. I loved them in my own way.

When I arrived in New York, our driver was waiting. He whisked me as quickly as one can be "whisked" in New York traffic. The ride provided no conversation. Mom and Dad always emphasized the staff were employees not friends. That was with the exception of Nellie. Nellie was different. In our minds, she was part of the family. We all unloaded on that dear, gentle woman.

Upon arrival, I realized that I had not brought the key. This resulted in my waking the entire house, not what I planned. Of course, Nellie came to the door, but lights turned on all over the house. Thank goodness that Nat did not come downstairs, which seemed a little strange.

"You had better get a good night's sleep, Miss Catherine. There is more going on here than you know." Nellie looked very tired.

"What does that mean, Nellie? What are you not telling me?" Now, I was wide awake even more worried.

"Please, Miss Catherine, I am tired and just don't feel that I should discuss this. You will see for yourself soon enough. Don't worry, it is nothing to do with your dad."

"Well then, this obviously concerns Nat? Nellie, don't keep me hanging."

Nellie just shook her head as she picked up my small bag. She walked me to my room but refused to comment further. Suddenly, I felt exhausted again. Maybe Nellie's refusal to communicate was best for us both. Tiredness washed over me like a heavy martini.

My room was just as I left it. The faux paint in shades of deep gold and burnt amber caused me to remember long ago when Mom and I changed my room to that of an adult. I was sixteen years old and delighted Mom considered me old enough to make the decision for colors. The dark mahogany wood of the furniture glowed next to those rich, bold colors. Nellie purchased fresh flowers, my favorites of paper whites, in a pot to match the colors of my room. By my bed was a picture of Mom and Dad with Nat and me on our last cruise. They chartered a yacht in Mustique. We spent the entire summer on that boat and in the Cotton House Inn and dining room. That was the most wonderful time I ever experienced.

Nights were intoxicating at Basil's Bar where we rubbed shoulders with rock stars and celebrities. The island was more interesting to me than St. Barths's. My parents glowed in that photo. They were in their element, so to speak, because they loved the islands. I don't think there was an island left in the Caribbean that they had not cruised. I wondered where Mom had sustained the injury, which claimed her life. Had she suffered? I guessed it didn't really matter now. She was at peace. It was as though I could feel her presence in the quiet of my room.

Standing there, holding that dear photo, I realized the fleeting element of time for all of us—the daily cycles of birth, aging, and death with the occasional loss of a child before a parent. That must be the hardest to bear, especially a very young child. Yet the loss of a loved one to death is never easy. Sure, my mother enjoyed a long and very happy life, but I was not prepared to lose her. My faith gave me comfort. I believed in an afterlife. Just knowing that someday I would see her and recognize her made this entire process bearable. Maybe I had fallen from grace and maybe I was not where I should have been, but my God already sealed my eternity. I couldn't do anything to change it. How did atheists live? Handling the loss of a loved one without knowing you would see them again, that would be unfathomable for me.

As I walked around the room, a sense of comfort overcame me. I found myself kneeling by my bed as I did so long ago. As I prayed, that old familiarity came rushing into my soul, "Dear Father, forgive me for not talking with you in such a long time. Please know that I love you and really need your presence. My mother lived a long and blessed time, thank you. Father, would you please tell her that I love her and will always remember her. Thank you for letting me know these dear and peaceful souls. Amen."

Now, I felt in touch with the spiritual side, which is in each of us. We may deem it "uncool" or even become so arrogant that we think we have accomplished greatness on our own, a sign of an unknowing person. The tiredness that washed over me was a blessing. I stumbled into bed without a shower and slept the sleep of an innocent child. Little did I know the challenges waiting for me the next day.

The next morning, I knew that God answered my prayer. I was overcome with a sense of his presence. I knew that I could handle whatever awaited me. After my shower, I walked slowly downstairs to find Nellie holding a cup of coffee, staring outside.

"Good morning, Nellie, how are you?"

As she turned toward me, I noticed the large circles and swollen areas under her eyes, which were not apparent last night. Sure signs of sleep loss for anyone. Her smile was slow and sad.

"Good morning, Miss Catherine. Hope that you slept well." Just as I reached for a cup of coffee, a young woman walked into the room, dressed in a bathrobe. As I looked at her, I realized that robe was one of mine. Now I felt totally confused. Was this a friend of Nellie's? She did not appear to be one of my mothers.

Walking toward me with a gnarly snare, she quickly changed to a fake smile. Holding out her hand to me, she loudly said, "You must be Catherine. How nice to finally meet you. I hope that you and I don't have any problems. It is wonderful that you own your home in that little country, southern town of, what is the name of that Godforsaken place?"

As she stood smiling at me, I felt repulsed. Who in the world was this? Why would she come to our home at the worst possible time? With great resolve, I looked at her but did not return her smile or handshake.

"Excuse me, but who are you, and why are you wearing my robe?" I was distressed by her lack of manners.

"What? This old thing? I thought that it must belong to Nellie here except that her rather large rear would never fit it." With that, she laughed.

Nellie turned to leave, but this character wasn't finished with her onslaught of insults.

"Nellie, I want my regular breakfast. Yesterday morning, I sat here for over fifteen minutes before you came to check on me. I expect your inquiry as to my desires as soon as I enter the room. You may have the rest of this family fooled but not me. That will soon change once Nathaniel and I are married. When our child is born, you may be replaced. My reason for telling you now before I move here is because Catherine can duly note our conversation. She probably feels the same but just didn't have the nerve to tell you. Now, hurry on and bring me my breakfast. I am feeling a little nauseated this morning. I need to lie down for a while." Then she smiled as she walked down the hall to the powder room.

Nellie and I looked at each other for several minutes. Her hands were shaking. She looked very pale.

"Miss Catherine, I don't think that I can continue on another minute. After the funeral today, I will turn in my notice. I hate to leave your father in this mess, but my nerves can't take anymore. I hope that you understand."

"Nellie, you are not going anywhere. Dad needs you more than ever. Who is that ridiculous person?"

"Her name is Ginger Smith. She is Nat's fiancée. They are expecting a child. Two weeks ago, she showed up with him. It seems that he has taken over the company with your father's blessing. He was doing a great job until she showed. Now he gets drunk each night. It is a mess. Your father did not realize all of this was going on. I overheard Nat and her talking a few nights ago. He plans on buying your share of this house in order to raise his family here. Miss Ginger is bringing one of her friends in to decorate. If only you could see what she has chosen. Your mother would never allow such a cheap, hideous ensemble in this home. Miss Catherine, I can't stay here. I am old. This is my time to exit. She hates me. She refuses to be kind to me."

"Has Nat seen how she treats you? I can't believe that she would dare do so in front of him."

"You are right. I was surprised that she was rude to me with your being here. I don't know what that was about."

"Nellie, I do know. She was staking her territory. If she and Nat think that I will walk away from here leaving you with that predator, they are very wrong. Maybe I will buy him out."

It took much convincing to assure Nellie and get her agreement to remain until Dad returned home. Out of love for him, she did agree to remain until after the funeral when dad was settled. My heart broke to see her endure such tragic treatment. We always treated her with love and respect. She quietly left the room to prepare the monster's breakfast.

As she was almost to the door, Ginger came prancing back into the room. "What, still no breakfast? Maybe you should pack your things. Why not leave now?" She smiled sweetly at me.

"Nellie, you go on. Prepare Miss Smith's breakfast. We need to have a few words." Ginger now looked a little nervous.

"You know how you have to treat hired help. I'm just letting her know who is in charge." Ginger held her head high but would not look at me.

"Yes, I do know how to treat our staff. I'm afraid that you have no idea. Just where are you from, Miss Smith? Tell me about your household staff. I can find out anything I need in about five minutes on the Internet, so don't lie to me."

Ginger walked toward me and smiled. "You want the truth? That is fine. I am from the mountains of Georgia. My parents had one child, me, because they were so strung out on drugs. They couldn't have any more. We lived in a mobile home, where I was unkempt and filthy. I barely graduated from high school, but I did. Nat and I met in a bar where his friends came looking for a good time. My job involved making sure those rich boys came back. They were good for business. Unfortunately, the timing stacked against your brother. He was the one who got me pregnant. Don't worry, all of the paternity tests have been done. Darling Nathaniel is the father of my, our, child. I will soon be his wife because he has such high standards that it was unimaginable this child remain with the likes of me. I threatened to abort it, but he would not allow it. So here I am. Love me or hate me, I'm not going away. At least not until I give birth. In the meantime, I thought that I would leave my mark on this sad place." With that, she looked contemptuously around my home.

Just at that moment, Nellie entered the room with a breakfast large enough for a lumber jack. Ginger sat stuffing her mouth so full that she could barely swallow. After Nellie left the room, I grabbed Ginger by the sleeve and pulled her up to my face.

"Now, you listen for a moment. In this house, you do not give orders. For as long as this charade continues, you will show respect to Nellie. I may buy this house right out from you and Nat. Life can become a living hell because of me. Get it? Your behavior will be exemplary until after the funeral. When my dad comes home, you are out of here. Nothing about you interests me except the child that you carry. Do you understand?"

She sat back down, continuing stuffing her mouth without comment. Just as I turned to leave the room, Nat entered.

"Oh, good, Catherine, you have met Ginger. I'm sure the two of you will be great friends." He looked so innocent. I felt sorry for him.

"Nat, what have you done? I know the entire story. At least your friend did not lie. I want her out of this house. You don't know it, but she has been rude to Nellie. There will be absolutely no changes done to the décor of our home. Do you understand? Now, leave quietly, or I will be forced to have a little talk with our father. You know that he can't deal with this now."

Nathaniel looked shocked, but he nodded his head in agreement. The look he gave Ginger told me he was beginning to understand. He left the room in a hurry. She continued to stuff food into her mouth until her plate was cleaned. She smiled again, running behind him.

They did not attend the funeral. Dad remained in such a state that he didn't seem to notice. I held his hand and brought him home. He instantly went to bed. Nellie slept in his room. Two weeks later, he died.

Again, we attended a funeral. By now, I was numb. Nellie left our family's employment with my blessing. I returned to Eufaula. Three weeks later, documents from the family attorney arrived. They outlined Nathaniel's desired to purchase my share in the family home. The proposal was more than fair. I agreed. The arrangements were made. I planned on returning to New York in one month when I would sign the necessary forms.

12

HIM

For the entire next month, I thought of Nathaniel. Why had he married Ginger? He was a very smart man. Not just book smart but there always had been a street smartness about him as well. During the month, my heart softened in regard to Ginger. Even though she appeared rough and mean spirited, there was something about her. At the appointed time, I returned to New York with a bit of excitement and intrigue about seeing the two of them again.

When I arrived in New York, there was no driver waiting. How quickly things changed with the death of our father. I hailed a taxi. Actually, I enjoyed the feeling of normalcy. My arrival at the family attorney's office found Ginger and Nathaniel waiting patiently in the lobby.

"So sorry that we were unable to send the family car, Cat. Ginger experienced a close call with the baby. All is well now." Turning to Ginger, her appearance seemed different than the morning of our meeting. Her hair was brushed off her face. She removed the hideous makeup, which she wore early in the morning at our home. Now she appeared fresh, almost childlike. Her faint smile seemed unsure. Where had the cockiness of earlier gone? She shyly held out her small hand, which I took. It was moist. I smiled.

The attorney, Mr. Williams, ushered us inside his spacious office. I had forgotten the incredible view of the city from his bright office so high in the sky. He shook all of our hands then proceeded to business. He was well known and busy. All of the documents were as we agreed. Everyone signed. The entire transaction was over in about fifteen minutes. Now I felt a little awkward.

"Catherine, would you like to have lunch with Ginger and me?" Nat looked tired and unsure of himself as well.

"Sure, I would love that." I smiled at both of them.

As we walked on the street, out of nowhere, the family car appeared. Charles drove us a few blocks. Quickly, we arrived at Nat's favorite lunch spot. The famous Monkey Bar was abuzz with diners always in a hurry. Truly this was the place of legends. If only the walls could talk. An old New York haunt, which Nat and I loved since we became of age. Dad and Mom frequented here so often that everyone knew them. Looking around the room, I remembered when I had been a part of the New York scene. I did not miss the fast-paced life at all. In fact, I longed to return to my safe haven in Eufaula.

That lunch was the moment Ginger and I became friends. Tremendous change occurred in this young girl. Now she was soft and gracious. Her manners were impeccable as I remembered the day when she stuffed her mouth with no regard to her rudeness. Smiling often, she would place her hand lovingly on her stomach. She told me how excited she was at the birth of their first child. It would be a boy.

With excitement, I contemplated the fun ahead for all of us. My nephew, never had I given the baby much thought. Ginger described the new nursery. She carefully explained only that room would be changed. Now she loved the house, appreciating the beautiful decorations my mother thoughtfully placed there. What a change. Had Nat sent her to manners school? I longed to spend time with them.

While laughing and enjoying ourselves, Rhonda phoned me on my cell. I forgot to turn it off. I excused myself, walking to the front entrance. She excitedly rambled. Apparently, she was in Washington. My presence was desired at once. She had phoned Nat and knew that I was scheduled to be in New York at this time. I agreed to fly as soon as possible, meeting her that night. Hugging Nat and Ginger, I excused myself as lunch ended. Still carrying my small bag with me because Nat had not invited me to stay with them, I planned to stay at the Hotel Elysee for one night. Since no reservations were made, things were simple to change. Instead, I caught the first plane to Washington, hoping to find the cause for such excitement.

Once I landed, I remembered my last visit with my father to this city of excitement and history. My trips to Washington always proved exciting. The taxi took me to the Willard Hotel located just one block from the White House. Without a reservation, I booked a room. I phoned Rhonda. All the plans were confirmed for our meeting at 7 p.m. Rhonda had a new friend. Dining was planned at his favorite restaurant—the Siroc Restaurant. We hoped to enjoy great Italian cuisine. Relatively new, I had read some reviews. Rave reviews indicated a great place. Rhonda claimed it as her favorite also. I couldn't wait for the evening.

I came prepared. One of my little black dresses and Jimmy Choo heels were neatly folded and lovingly packed by Jean in my bag. All of this drama was too much for me. I questioned why I was needed by Rhonda is such a mysterious fashion.

Sleep descended on me. Several hours later, I awakened from a nap. How had I slept so long? I hurried to our designated meeting spot. Upon entrance to the popular room, noise reverberated from each table. Rhonda's restaurant was abuzz with Washington's finest. Quickly, the hostess escorted me to our table. There she sat absolutely glowing. Seated beside her was a very handsome man, Barrington Bourge. He introduced himself with a kind smile. Rhonda was up to something; I knew *her* look. Almost as soon as I was seated, she held up her hand. Shining in the candle light glowed a large platinum diamond.

"Can you believe it, Cat?" She hugged Barrington who smiled again. They both looked happy, which made me think of Margie, John, Linda, and Sam. Suddenly, I was the only one of my small group without plans to wed. That did not bother me in the least. I loved my life. Now I delighted at a chance of closeness with my brother and family. Their son, my nephew, would fill any void.

It seemed that Rhonda and Barrington planned to wed in Paris. I listened with joy to their plans. As she and I shared moments from the past with Barrington, he impressed me with his ability to listen and ask questions over the smallest detail. Rhonda had a keeper. No doubt they were perfect for each other. This prominent attorney in Washington allowed her the life of which she dreamed. Rhonda appeared elated at the chance of becoming part of that social scene in a difficult city to find acceptance. At one point during their dialogue, I happened to look over at the bar. There sat a very handsome man, watching our table intently. There was familiarity about him. Somehow, I knew I had met him but could not imagine where.

Smiling, he walked over to our table. As he approached, he apologized for any interruptions. His smile seemed directed at me as he questioned, "Cat Carn, how long has it been? You probably don't remember me, but I attended UA with you. We actually went on a double date one time." As he refreshed me on the details, I did remember vaguely the evening he now described. A casual friend insisted I have dinner with him and friends. Even then, it all seemed so strange. I barely knew Michael.

The evening long ago had gone well. His friends had been this man Frank Adams and a woman whose name I could not now recall. After all of those years, that evening remained in my mind as a strange event, which made little sense. Frank had asked me many questions about my personal life. He seemed almost obsessed with me. After that, I spotted him around campus often. He frequently appeared at meetings, of which he was not a member. Everything about him seemed peculiar. Nothing came of his actions, so I forgot about him. Now he excitedly told me he lived in Washington. He had met with Rhonda and Barrington on their arrival. He explained that one of his first inquiries concerned me. Rhonda had explained that I loved Eufaula. Why did he still maintain interest in me?

"Frank insisted that I phone you to share in our happy news. Weren't the two of you involved?" She smiled at me with a suspicious look.

"No, Rhonda, we barely knew each other, but we're friends." I had added the last remark when I saw the disappointed look in Frank's eyes. *What was going on?* I wondered.

After he was invited to join us, he spent the rest of the evening barely speaking. Instead, he watched me with such intenseness that I soon became tired of his stares. Eventually, I excused myself after thanking my friends for a wonderful evening. The Siroc had not disappointed. The meal was indeed wonderful. Returning to my hotel, I dreamed terrible dreams all night about Frank. Once again, I experienced an uneasy feeling. Something important was about to happen. What happened was important. It changed my life forever.

13

JILL

The next morning, I booked an early flight. Longing filled my heart to return to the safety of Jean, Albert, and Eufaula. The taxi delivered me to the front door, where Albert met me. Lovingly, he carried my small bag inside over my objections. He and Jean babied me, but I loved all of their attention. Jean excitedly told me several people inquired about my recent posts for employees at the art gallery. I named it Carnegie Hall. I thought that humorous. Perhaps it would inspire interest from my small town. Immediately, I felt rejuvenated, ready to work. It was good to be home.

Upon entering my sunny art studio, I felt deep joy. My current painting of a street scene in downtown Eufaula awaited me. It was good. Now I couldn't wait to begin hanging my treasures on the old walls of my gallery. The floors shinned after a deep buff and polish. In fact, a crew cleaned it from bow to stern. Before leaving for New York, I assembled what I considered my best works from all of my stash of art. They were wrapped by Albert while I was gone. Now they waited, ready to be transported downtown. Deciding to phone a few of the contacts awaiting response to my post for an assistant in Carnegie Hall, I called each one with excitement. After phoning several then pulling up their resumes, one was so highly qualified. I could not believe she resided in my small town.

Answering on the third ring, Jill excitedly reiterated her qualifications. Recently, she had lost her husband to cancer, stating her need to be busy. She had never worked outside her home. Due to the change in her life, she longed to use her college education in the arts working at my gallery. Sharing excitement at the name of Carnegie Hall, we agreed it should spark interest. Salary and hours needed to be discussed, but I had the feeling she would work for free. However, my offer was generous. She accepted immediately. Once again, in my impetuousness, I hired on the spot. That decision eventually empowered my life. An appointment was arranged to walk through the gallery. After explaining that one hour was not rushing her, the call ended. I quickly showered. Albert loaded his truck with my paintings. We were off to hang paintings before Jill arrived.

Albert and I only hung two of the paintings. Typically, we disagreed on location. I relished the fact that he spoke his mind. Never did he tell me what he thought I may desire to hear but always the truth from his perspective. The chime on the door reminded me I had not locked it. I turned with irritation. Albert and I had accomplished so little. Before me stood the perfect assistant. She was well coiffed. Extremely beautiful, her long auburn hair expertly pulled off her face into a sweeping style with diamond hair comb. Her mauve dress and pearls would have been perfect in New York, but she looked even more impressive in Eufaula. The residents would appreciate her sense of style. The smile she presented beamed warm and friendly.

"Well, Jill, welcome to Carnegie Hall. I hope that we are able to help many local artists. In the meantime, Albert here, my handyman and I are hanging some of my art so we can open our doors. Albert just explained that many crates have arrived from various towns. I can't wait to open them so that we see what sort of talent awaits us." The two shook hands as they smiled.

Jill looked around the warehouse, which had been transformed into a most impressive gallery. "It is beautiful. Where did you come up with the idea in this little town? I can't tell you how much I need to work. Can't think of anything that I would rather do except see my husband again?" She lowered her head. I thought that I saw a tear slide down her cheek.

I squeezed her shoulder and waited for her to compose herself. Soon she did. We walked around the room as I described my plans. She surprised me by adding many excellent ideas, which I never considered. Our union would be successful, I could feel it.

"Cat, why don't you go back home? Allow Albert and me to open the crates. We can hang all of the art. I bought a pair of jeans and shirt in the car just in case. I must work. You go home. Complete more paintings to help us fill all of the space." Yes, this was what I hoped to find. With that, I departed my gallery feeling confident that it rested in capable hands.

14

RECEPTION AT CARNEGIE HALL

For two months, I worked with incredible zeal. Days were spent opening crates. Beautiful paintings were suspended on the once bare walls. Carnegie Hall appeared alive. Evenings were spent alone in my studio. Jean's meals kept me packed with energy. The creativity, which I possessed, was staggering. Painting after painting tenderly were completed. Albert retained a unique ability. How could one man own so many skills? His ability to frame each work of art so professionally deeply impressed me. He carefully hauled each framed masterpiece to my gallery. There, he and Jill squabbled over location. At the end of those two months, the walls shimmered with exquisite paintings. It really looked like a gallery. Jill and I decided on little black dresses with black heels and pearls for the opening evening. Local caterers would serve champagne or sparkling water, as well as canapés. I couldn't help but remember Mr. Greene's earlier warning. Would our event be interesting enough to attract male residents of this fair area? I wasn't sure. Jill insisted that I needn't worry. We advertised our opening two months in advance.

Excitement crowded the air as I dressed for my big gala. Waiting at Carnegie Hall, I was delighted to find Jill looking radiant, as well as Albert and Jean polished as I had never seen them. Pride of my staff enforced my confidence. We toasted our adventure with a glass of champagne. My hands shook, but Jill glowed, poised and controlled.

One hour later, the lights dimmed as the four of us stood proudly, looking at the walls. Perfect lighting gently streamed on polished frames. It was beautiful. Our first customer was none other than Mr. Greene. He instantly picked out four of our paintings then headed back to the champagne. Jill wrote the invoice as I giggled with Jean over his decisions. Each painting was painted by me. I felt so proud, but admittedly, dear Mr. Greene appeared to have consumed several glasses of something. It didn't matter. I would gladly refund any monies tomorrow if he wasn't happy.

Shortly, the mayor arrived with his wife. They chose two paintings by local artisans. Things were going better than planned. Couple after couple arrived not just to see the new addition to our town but also with serious desires for locating new local talent. Jill was busy writing invoices. A small line formed. Jean was soon assisting her. Albert entertained the patrons with his gardening stories as he helped remove and wrap art before carrying it to waiting cars. I realized our next reception would require more employees. Easily, two more sets of hand were needed. Even the caterers made purchases with relish. Maybe I underpriced some of the pieces, but it seemed fair earlier.

Classical music softly played as I circulated around the room. Finally, I relaxed, loving my exalted status as "art expert." Linda, Sam, Margie, and John all attended, leaving with several invoices each. Albert would stay busy for a long time delivering local paintings, as well as packing some to be mailed. I definitely needed more help. What a wonderful situation. Filled with anticipation at the prospect of helping more people discover employment in Eufaula, contentment flowed. Then I saw him. Standing alone with his eyes glued to my every movement. Frank waved and smiled. I wanted to run the other way. Instead, I walked slowly, returning a smile. He softly kissed a double kiss, squeezing my arm a little too familiarly.

"Cat Carn, you never disappoint. What an amazingly talented woman. Frequently, I recall the way you kept us all laughing with your different Southern accents back in college. You sounded so real. Hard to believe that you were not born here, Virginia, or wherever you decided at that moment. Honor student as well as in just about every club, how did you do it all? Now what a coincidence that you are here in Eufaula. This happens to be one of my favorite places to retreat, really uncanny, don't you think?" He smiled at me again as I had that feeling something was about to happen. The moment did not feel threatening or scary, just strange. Frank reached for another glass of champagne from the silver tray carried expertly by a young caterer. She smiled at him with a flirting look, which he ignored. He seemed only to have eyes for me, or was I being silly? Maybe the success of the evening had swollen my head. He did not try to hide the gold band shining from his right hand.

"What a shame that you didn't bring your wife. She may have enjoyed this evening." Now I smiled smugly at him.

"What? Jenny? Oh, she refuses to leave our new baby. Robert Alexander is five months old today. You know how new mothers are hesitant to leave that first time." I had no idea but nodded.

"Anyway, I will bring her soon. You will love her. Everyone loves Jenny. You remind me of her. Maybe I should say that she reminded me of you when I first met her. I must tell you that I have always found you to be a most attractive woman, Cat. Please tell me that you are not offended at my admiration. You, Jenny, and I will be great friends. I understand that you enjoy the local gourmet restaurant? A friend of mine owns it. He says that Rhonda and her crew purchased several nights of meals for you. Isn't that a great place?"

Once again, something just wasn't right about him. I turned to see Albert wrapping a painting. He was watching me. Nodding as if to let me know he was close. What was it with Frank? I wanted to like him because Rhonda said he was a close friend of Barrington's. Yet his demeanor always caused such an uneasy feeling. It was almost as though he did it on purpose. Still, I lightly touched Frank's arm.

"Sure, that would be lovely. If you are ever able to convince your wife to leave that new baby, just let me know. I would enjoy your company." I smiled my sweetest smile as I walked to Albert.

Loudly stating, "Albert, you are my body guard. You are always watching me." Albert looked slightly confused but raised his thumb in agreement. Feeling a little paranoid, I turned to see Frank smile. With a look of amusement, it was as though he enjoyed seeing me squirm. My little performance had not been taken seriously. The champagne created sleepiness. Jill sweetly hugged me.

"Cat, go on home, everyone is almost gone. Albert and I will close after the rest leave. I don't think anyone more will purchase this evening. Besides, the refreshments are almost gone. That will be the kiss of death." She laughed as I thought gratefully how important she became to the success of my venture.

When I arrived home, the ringing of the phone greeted me. "Guess who just phoned us to tell us of your huge success this evening. Cat, I'm sorry we missed your opening. We will attend the next one. Barrington and I need massive art to fill these big old walls. Anyway, Frank says you are a big success in Eufaula. We didn't know he loved that old town so much. That is great. It will definitely make the two of you close. You will love Jenny. Everyone loves Jenny. You must be tired. Go on to bed. Call you later. Bye now."

The line went dead as I thought how strange all of this was becoming. I didn't want anything to threaten my happy home, but this Frank character seemed weirder by the day. I would probably never see him or his wife. He just needed to occasionally get away from that new crying baby. None of that rang true, but I refused to think about it anymore.

15

CHANGE OF ADDRESS

After our successful gala, I enjoyed the status that I now obtained. When I walked into the local coffee shop, another patron would recognize me and purchase coffee or scone for me. There were other such examples. After feeling swallowed into the mass in NYC, this new fame felt welcomed. Life settled into a peaceful pattern. The heat started dissipating. All of us looked forward to fall. Sweet fall in the south, at last I could resume my work with Albert in the gardens. I could learn a great deal from him.

Now, I collected enough art from local potters as well as artists. Their work resulted in Jill and me planning our next big event. We slated our featured guest artists. I could envision the income, which they may produce. How wonderful imagining these tireless artists receiving payment after hours of creating beautiful works of Eufaula or garden scenes. Talent in the area was surprising. I could picture Jill and me dressed in long jersey mauve dresses with low heels, the heat softly humming behind the cold guests. We would add hot chocolate to our menu with the chilled champagne as served before from silver trays. Much culture resided in this small Southern town. Our contribution seemed warmly welcomed.

Albert began checking the fireplaces at home. On the first frosty morning, fires would glow throughout our peaceful abode.

There stood a fireplace in almost each room. Looking forward, I pictured large Christmas trees in my home and gallery. Soft Christmas hymns and holiday tunes playing in the background as I painted at home or sold art in the gallery. All of my friends were happy. Nathaniel and Ginger expected their baby boy soon. Christmas, I would have a nephew for whom I could make exciting plans.

Jean really blossomed in the kitchen. Planning large pots of homemade soups, she asked if she may be allowed to serve soup at our next art event. That couple were trusted members of my family. I missed my parents. I knew this Christmas, in spite of all of the joy, would contain moments of sadness, remembering a wonderful Mom and Dad. Yet never did I feel lonely or melancholy. There just wasn't enough time for such thoughts.

One morning, weeks later, as I enjoyed my morning coffee, the phone rang. I never remembered to carry it to the outside table, so once again, I was running toward that hideous box. Rhonda's ramblings were difficult to understand. I caught enough to know she was in a panic. She needed me to fly to Washington as soon as possible. That was about all that I could understand with her hysteria. I booked the next flight, packed some clothes, then left a note for Jean and Albert who had not yet arrived.

When I reached DC, miraculously, there stood Frank at my gate. He looked alarmed. Now I was concerned. As he drove me to their Georgetown residence, he explained the situation, which was not as dramatic as I expected. Last night, Rhonda and Barrington attended a state dinner. On their return, they discovered someone had broken into their home. Strangely, nothing had been taken as far as they could tell.

"Just wait till you see their lavish new home. It would take forever to tell if anything is missing. There is so much of everything. Her jewelry is extensive. They keep saying that nothing is missing, but they don't know. The police think that the break-in had just occurred as they returned. Thank goodness the perpetrator left at once."

We turned into a driveway lined with pavers. Boxwoods surrounded the large lot. He was correct in his description. The driveway meandered gently. Soon enough, a stately red brick home with large white columns came into view. It was dramatic. Frank parked in front. His familiarity with their home stuck me as a little uncanny. When we entered, he even turned the alarm off. Rhonda was in such a state. She demanded the alarm be set each time someone entered. I looked at Frank questioningly. He only smiled and shrugged. *He must be a really close friend*, I thought. Soon Rhonda came running down the stairs.

"Have you heard of the dreadful thing that happened? You are a lifesaver, Cat. Where are your bags?" She stood, staring at my small brown leather bag, which Frank sat on the old wooden plank floors.

"What bags? I only bought enough for one night."

"One night? Weren't you listening to me during our conversation? Cat, we are scheduled to visit Barrington's parents in Martha's Vineyard. We must go. They would be devastated. We will be gone for one month. We need you to house sit. I can't leave my home without someone being here. What if the burglars return? Barrington keeps a registered gun by the bed. Don't worry, you'll be fine. Oh well, you can use my clothes. I guess I have plenty." She looked uncertain of her last statement.

"Gee, Rhonda, I don't know. The house has just been burglarized. I know nothing about this area, as well as never having stepped into your home. That is a pretty tall order. The gun thing doesn't really help me relax."

"Oh poo, you know Frank and Jenny. They aren't that far away and have already volunteered to look after you. You will be just fine. Well, Barrington and I must go. Our plane leaves soon. Frank can answer any questions. Love you, thank you for doing this. You'll have a great time." With that, she kissed me lightly on the cheek.

"Now, you look after her, Frank. Come on, Barrington. Let's run before she changes her mind."

Barrington came running down the stairs. He gave me a look of sadness but continued to rush pass me. He turned at the door, smiled, and they were gone.

"I don't believe this. I planned another art reception soon. There are many things for me to do. I could not understand her on the phone. Nothing was ever discussed about me staying here for one month. I have my own home to watch over."

Frank just shrugged. "Well, I'm sure you will work it all out. You'll be fine. Jenny isn't that far away. Actually, we will take you out to dinner tonight. Then I'm away for an undisclosed time on my job. Sorry, I think Rhonda spoke out of line making you feel like I would be here. I won't, but Jenny is close although she has her hands full with the new baby. Well, got to run. We'll pick you up at seven tonight. Be ready for a great meal. It's the least that I can do." He ran out the door as I stood in the grandiose home, feeling very much alone.

Looking around at my grand surroundings, I could not picture Rhonda here. As I walked around, it was sad to realize that there were no mementoes of her past nor did I see anything personal of Barrington's. It was a little sad as though she was trying hard to fit into a social scene, which she would never understand. Everything was indeed splendid. Finally, I found a guest bedroom, which would do nicely. I entertained the idea of checking into a hotel. I would have felt more comfortable. This would be a long month. Already, I fought such anxiousness that I felt tears in my eyes. I wanted to return home. With that thought, I phoned Jean.

When I heard her voice, I softly began to cry. Jean listened patiently to my plight. Then she suggested that she and Albert fly up to stay with me. That seemed absurd. At least he could help Jill prepare at the gallery, as well as get the house ready for

Christmas. All of the drama lately of losing my parents and in a way my brother, filled me with loneliness. I explained all of the things that I wanted them to accomplish at home. Jean made a list while promising to phone each evening.

After washing my face, I continued to walk around the house. The master bedroom and bath were posh. I was surprised that they would choose this home, but it was beautiful in a showy way. Unable to resist, I entered their closet, which was a large room. As I lovingly touched her designer clothes, I noticed a small picture. It was the only personal item I noticed. It was sitting with her shoes. I realized that she must see it a few times each day. Beaming with smiles larger than life were Rhonda, Margie, Linda, and me. I held the photo and cried. Having always dreamed of being in charge of my life, my wish now seemed like a mistake. I never dreamed becoming an adult would be so difficult.

I cried just looking at the carefree, happy faces in our college photo. In just a short time, everything changed. Before arriving here, I felt proud of my life. I longed to go to my childhood home, but it was no longer mine. The home in Eufaula now seemed like it belonged to someone else. This home was not my friend's taste. Only Margie and Linda remained stable. Sitting down on the worn old floors, I lovingly thought of generations who lived here. Had there been other tears of loss shed on these floors? Although the rest of the home was over decorated, whoever finished these floors maintained the beauty of the wood. Scratches and scars from the past only made them more beautiful. The rest of the décor seemed garish compared to these beautifully refinished floors. All at once, I thought of Ginger.

Once having felt so critical of her, now I respected the changes she had made. I longed to spend time at my home again. Confusion ebbed through my mind. Where was home? Even my beloved Jean and Albert suddenly seemed unknown, surreal. As I held the photo, I cried again.

Finally, no more tears arose. I returned to the room I had chosen earlier. Was this the room that Rhonda meant for me to use? I didn't want to do anything to cause her more pain. She also experienced great change. Making my way back to the room, it dawned on me I had not seen the kitchen. Returning back downstairs, I eventually found the bright-yellow room. Yellow-and-blue tiles decorated the back splash. This room maintained a French ambiance.

Walking to the appliances, I was unable to turn them on. After all, my cooking abilities were novice. I would not be able to cook my breakfast without possibly causing Rhonda further problems. I sat down on the floor. As I stood, wiping my tears, I observed a note with my name on the front. Rhonda informed me she did have a staff, but they were given the entire month off. Everyone worked hard helping her move into the house quickly. Since they planned their holiday, it seemed a good idea to give the staff the same time away. She had no idea that she would be confronted with a break-in.

Now she regretted that decision but couldn't change it. I was not to worry though because they hired a guard who walked the property several times each night. Again, she informed me that

> You will be just fine. I have purchased an entire month's coupons from the local Starbucks. Your breakfast and coffee will be waiting each morning. There are plenty of salad fixings in the fridge. The restaurant where you, Frank, and Jenny are dining will also host you for dinner every evening. You can expect a driver to pick you up each evening at 6 p.m. early the way you like it. Get some rest and have fun.
>
> Love,
> R

I clutched the note to my chest as I made my way back to my room. It would be a long month, but I would survive. Entering the room, I noticed shelves of books on the side by large windows, which looked onto the street. I selected *The Great Gatsby*. I wanted to read it again. Settling into an overstuffed chair in beautiful Scalamandre fabric, I began to hungrily read. It had been a long time since I had curled up with a good book. As I started to relax, the gentle sound of large raindrops began to hit the roof. Maybe this would not be so awful. The only thing that I could do here would be to relax.

Hours later, the soft rain had become a deluge. I wished that I could remain here this evening. Jenny and Frank would arrive soon. Rhonda had purchased a basket of my favorite soaps and perfumes. Even my "hard to find" shampoo peeked at me from the large white basket topped with a pink bow. A wonderful shower head provided rejuvenation. I searched through her clothes, pleased that at least during my stay, I would be the best-dressed woman in this well-dressed town. Exactly at seven, the doorbell chimed. Frank and Jenny rushed inside as they kissed me twice each. Jenny shined radiantly. She was beautiful. Frank looked better than I recalled. Pushing a bottle of Cabernet in my face, he quickly walked to the kitchen.

"Let's have a glass of wine and relax." Sounded like a great idea to me. Things were going well until I casually asked, "Frank, what do you do for a living?" He looked as if I threatened him.

"Why do you ask? What business is it to you?" He no longer seemed so charming but abrasive.

"I didn't mean anything. You seem to have so much time on your hands. I just wondered. Never mind, it is not important."

"It may appear that I have excess time, but I am always working. My position is the most interesting job anyone could ever want. Since graduation, I have worked for the State Department."

Without meaning to meddle, I couldn't help myself, "Which branch is it?"

He looked at Jenny as he smiled, but I could see the irritation on his face. "Well, if I tell you, I may have to kill you." They both laughed. I did recall some old joke with that punch line. I felt uncomfortable, suddenly aware that I was alone with a group of strangers.

Standing, he pulled Jenny gently up to his side. "We need to be going to the restaurant. I can't be late for reservations there. They are extremely difficult to obtain."

Pulling in front of a large bright building, we waited in the valet line for a short time. Everyone seemed to know Frank, catering to him. The table we were given was "his" table. Once again, things seemed weird to me, yet I was determined not to be on edge. This was going to be my evening. Thoughts of returning home to a place I didn't know in a town where I knew no one was frightening enough.

The food was wonderful, then Frank managed to ruin everything. Each time I looked up, he watched me with keen interest. Jenny seemed oblivious as though this was typical behavior for him. The lack of conversation quickly hastened the end of the evening. My host became pensive. I was driven home. Escorted to the door as I turned, they were gone. I stood alone, really alone.

16

MY FIANCÉ

Frank and Jenny drove away. My hands shook as I unlocked the door, turning off the alarm. At least I left lights on all over the house. It seemed to take forever turning them all off. Just as I completed my task, the phone rang. The shrillness of that sound in the quiet house caused me to jump. I listened to Jean's soft voice telling me how she and Albert missed me. As she talked about all of the activities at "my" house, strangely, I felt it wasn't mine at all. A feeling of disassociation from my inner core developed, a weird feeling that I didn't belong anywhere. Listening as she completed her call, I tried sounding normal and friendly. I did not feel that way. As I hung up the phone, I noticed my hands shook again.

Making my way up the grand staircase, I thought it odd that Rhonda had not phoned. She was probably having a wonderful time at Martha's Vineyard. The tears started again. What in the world was wrong with me? Perhaps I should see a psychiatrist. I cried for a number of reasons—the death of my parents, the loss of my childhood, the loss of Nat as he once had been to me, my new life, and fear of this place. My list was long. It seemed a long time before the tears stopped. I showered then slipped under the luxurious covers.

Each time I almost fell asleep, I heard a suspicious sound. All during the night, I ran to the window or downstairs to check the alarm. Finally, at 6 a.m., I arose and dressed. There was absolutely nothing for me to do on this dark morning. I looked over at my almost finished book, *The Great Gatsby*, with relish. Before I tackled that, I decided to follow Rhonda's earlier advice and walk to the nearby Starbucks. The early-morning darkness did not frighten me. It was the darkness in the evenings, which filled me with dread and foreboding.

Walking down the brightly lighted street was wonderful. This was exactly what I needed. It was delightful walking down a new street. The lavish homes blushed beautifully in the early-morning light. Starbucks was located conveniently. In fact, it was too close. I would have enjoyed a longer walk. So many patrons at this early hour surprised me. Folks were already dressed for a day at the office. Others dressed casually like me. I grabbed a local paper, taking my coffee and scone to the back of the restaurant. Reading the morning paper remained a morning ritual for years. That was how Mom and Dad always started their day.

A sense of normalcy comforted my battered nerves. I smiled spontaneously. Lost in my world, it surprised me to hear someone speak my name. This intrusion was unwelcomed. Turning, I noticed the best-looking man flirting with me. He was tall and muscular. His dark hair and brown eyes gleamed in the light of the room. His smile revealed perfect teeth. In fact, he was too perfect. Yet there was something charismatic. I desired to know everything about him. To my surprise, I cooed, "Please, sit down."

The handsome stranger smiled again, seating himself before I could catch my breath. He explained Frank phoned last night telling him all about me. He slowly talked in a beautiful voice with absolutely no hint of an accent. Apparently, we had a great deal in common—good friends with Frank, Jenny, Rhonda, and Barrington who was his *connection*. I thought that an odd choice of word. Still, it was refreshing having someone interested in me. He worked with Frank, he guardedly stated.

"Look, I can take as much time off as I want, how would you like for me to give you a tour? We could maybe eat lunch, then go to my favorite park if you would like. Pretty soon, the cold weather will strip me of my time there. What do you say?" He was beautiful. I found it impossible not to stare.

"You know what I would really like to do? Could we just walk around the neighborhood? I enjoy studying the architecture of these homes. Many of them are old, but there are some modern." I smiled my most dazzling smile, although I had not paid attention to my teeth in days. He must have been greeted by a "less than sterling" smile that didn't matter. Being with this person was easy.

He nodded in agreement as he extended his large hand. "Hello, I'm James Brown, not related to the singer. My friends call me Jim." I laughed at the joke.

"I live around the corner. Walk with me back to my home. I'll change quickly, then we are off." Again, the large smile. He reached for my hand, pulling me gently onto my feet. I found myself walking out of the establishment with this complete stranger, feeling slightly alarmed at my actions. I didn't care if I was being reckless. The loneliness of the past few days overwhelmed me. I needed some fun, so we walked in the early morning. I found Jim witty, as well as interesting. He had traveled everywhere, it seemed. Much too quickly, we walked up a steep hill to yet another large home but not nearly as lavish as Rhonda's. This was more to my taste.

The home appeared to be very old. Red brick with square posts holding the ceiling of an ornately carved rambling porch greeted me. The staged wicker pieces reminded me of my home in Eufaula. Suddenly, my heart ached to go home. Still, I was enjoying my new friend. He unlocked the door. I followed him inside as though I had done this a hundred times. The starkness of the furnishings after Rhonda's fully stuffed mansion appeared shocking. I must have looked startled for he explained he had not lived here very long.

"In fact, I could use the suggestions of a beautiful woman." He grinned.

"Is that an invitation for a job?" I lightly touched his arm.

To either my shock or delight, I wasn't sure. Quickly, he grabbed my arm. He pulled me into his chest as he kissed me so passionately that I felt lightheaded. Everything happened quickly. The loneliness of late, the lack of confidence, something caused me to react in an alarming manner. I kissed him back with abandonment of caution. He lifted me in his arms. Obviously, we were headed for his bedroom. I didn't object. The voice in my head tried to be reasonable. I refused to listen. In moments, we entered the darkened room. The bed was unmade. Fragrance soothed my nerves. I thought the sheets smelled too clean. Had he sprayed them with cologne? Nothing mattered to me. I needed someone in my gloom. We clung to each other as we made love. It wasn't foreign but seemed natural. I didn't want the excitement to end. Jim was strong and caring. Clinging to him, he continued holding me long after we finished our act of love. I felt faint again. Soon, we both fell asleep. The earlier exhaustion from lack of sleep washed away.

We must have slept for hours. The ringing phone caused us both to awaken with a start. Alarm at what occurred filled me. Did he regret our actions? Would he have an excuse to rush to the office with never a thought of me? I didn't think I could handle such behavior from him.

"Yes, things are fine. No, really, right on schedule. I'm actually amazed." He laughed a gruff laugh. Then he glanced at me but turned his eyes quickly away.

"Don't worry, you know me." Again the hardened laugh. He put the phone back on the cradle and gently pulled me to him.

"Would you be very disappointed if we stay right here? We can walk tomorrow. I have just returned from a trip overseas. I am exhausted." He smelled of soap and shampoo.

"That would be wonderful. I'm pretty tired myself." I explained about Rhonda's trapping me to house sit, but before I could finish, his deep breathing told me that he was asleep. I thought of his explanation of being exhausted. If he was exhausted, I didn't think I could handle him rested. I smiled.

We must have slept all day. Gently, I felt him kiss my neck. "Come on, Cat, let's go get some dinner."

How had he known that my name was Cat? Earlier he had stated that Frank had told him my name was Catherine. Still, I reasoned that many people with my name shortened it. Nothing was going to come between Jim and me. I needed this strong man in my life. Now I couldn't live without him. I longed to take him to Eufaula as soon as possible. My future would be built with him. Instead of rising, we repeated our earlier actions. My body craved him in a way that I never experienced.

Helping me out of bed, Jim walked me to the shower with his arms cradling me. We showered, repeating our lovemaking with great intensity. I was not accustomed to behaving in such a way, yet I didn't care. After our shower, he gently dried my skin, applying Chanel lotion. I recognized the fragrance. Right then, the alarms in my head should have been addressed. Why would a single man have Chanel body satin? Again, I denied anything strange. Maybe an old girlfriend left it. Could he be as lonely I? Was meeting our destiny?

"Jim, I don't have any clothes except my jogging suit."

"Well, don't worry. I have a closet of clothes, which are just your size. I think that you will find something. You see, my wife and I just divorced." Again the smile was so convincing.

Reason in my head nagged, *If he just moved here, why would her clothes still be in the closet?* Once again, I reasoned that they may have divorced after they moved here. Maybe they thought that the move may make them closer? It was ridiculous but slightly possible.

Without a single question, I dumbly followed him to the largest closet I had ever seen. The closet was larger than Rhonda's, filled from ceiling to floor with high dollar designer clothes. Any woman would have been shocked. Not me, it could be possible. Anything he told me, I would not question. It seemed as though I was drugged. My feelings were both numbness and elation. I dressed quickly.

Walking out into the reds and oranges of what must have been a gorgeous sunset, I desired to see each sunset in my future with him—my dream man whom I never really dreamed of meeting. I always desired a solitary life, but not now. Holding hands, he told me a little of his life. He traveled extensively, which caused his marriage to dissolve. The fights that occurred between him and Connie were horrific. Still, he missed not having that special person.

"I loved being married, even though I knew it wasn't fair to be gone so much. My job is demanding. I love it."

"What exactly is it that you do?" I smiled up at him as he looked at me in disbelief.

"Why do you care? I make a great salary. You will never want for anything. You see, Cat, I'm lonely. I miss my wife. This may seem like a preposterous statement. Although we haven't had enough time to fall in love, real love, I believe we are right together. Without a doubt, I know you can make me happy. Do you think I have the potential, if I work hard, that I could please you? We are not ordinary. There are some people in this world who are capable of knowing what they want. I want you. You would make a wonderful wife and mother. That is clear. What I'm trying to say with great difficulty is that I think we should be engaged. I'm asking you to marry me. Let's get the ring then plan a beautiful, simple wedding. What do you say? This is the way I do things. It is important to me that you trust me. Do you?"

"I can't believe this. Are you joking with me?" I truly wanted to be his wife. Jim was everything I could want. Yet this was a little fast even for the jet set. I heard about movie stars who dated once or twice then married. We were not that. Later, I would realize the folly of my actions, but it would be much later. Now I wanted to know the joy Margie, John, Linda, Sam, Nat, and Ginger already knew. My plans for a solitary life seemed foolish, not my rush to find love. It was shocking that I even entertained the idea. Why not get engaged? We would take our time to be sure. He was correct in that we were not ordinary. All of these thoughts ran through my mind. I was infatuated with the possibility that I might find love. As I hesitated, he became finicky.

"Do you mean that you don't desire me?" He looked hurt.

"Are you kidding? Of course I find you desirable as a lover, husband, as well as father. We just don't know each other at all. Do people do this? I mean rush into something so important? Do we run out purchasing a ring? We don't need to buy a ring. The commitment is from our hearts." Even to me, the words sounded hollow.

"I know a jewelry store, a very good one, which is close. Maybe you will find one that you love. If we find out that we have made a mistake, it is not irrevocable. Come on, live dangerously. Let's go buy you a ring. What do you say?" He turned, and once again, I followed him. As we entered the garage, I noticed that there were two cars—a black Mercedes as well as a white Jaguar. He opened the door of the black one. "Your carriage, my love."

We did not drive very far until I spotted the store. The proprietor knew him instantly. I wandered around, feeling a little foolish but determined to pick out a ring. Should I search for a really large one or be considerate and pick out a smaller stone? I was at a loss and feeling more foolish by the moment.

"What about this one, Cat?" Jim was pointing at something in the glass case.

Mr. Stahl smiled as he stated, "Now, that is a beauty. It would look lovely on your lady." They smiled at each other. As Mr. Stahl removed the twinkling stone, I gasped. It was a very large platinum-encased stone. It reminded me of the one that Rhonda wore with such pleasure. Could this really be happening to the woman who always wanted to live life alone?

The ring was a perfect fit. Jim handed Mr. Stahl his American Express. The transaction was quickly completed. The thought entered my mind that I was insane or maybe we both were. Still, I craved being normal. Everyone thought marriage was necessary for happiness. Why not try it? As I entertained a dozen thoughts, Jim drove to the restaurant instead of walking as we planned earlier. I seemed to be floating, ignoring the voice in my head telling me how foolish I was behaving. Later, I learned I acted exactly as I had been profiled. Although I swore to want a solitary life, I wanted to be loved. I had never known the love of a man. My behavior predicted by the experts.

Driving to the same restaurant Frank took me last night did not make sense. "Are there not any other restaurants in this city? Rhonda gave me a month's worth of free dinners here. Frank brought me here last night."

"What, you don't like my choice? Sure, we can go anywhere you like, but this is the most convenient, as well as one of the best." Suddenly, my perfect man seemed a little irritated.

"No, of course, this is fine. I really enjoyed being here last night." Just as we started to leave the car with the valet, the phone rang. Jim looked annoyed but answered it immediately.

"We are just going into dinner. Mind if I phone you later? Look, don't worry so much. Everything is better than you will ever believe. Cat is starving. See ya."

"Jim, that was odd. It sounded as if your friend knows me. How could that be?"

"Yes, he knows you. It was Frank. We are really close friends. I told him earlier that we are hitting it off incredibly well. He wants me to be happy again. Come on, I'm famished. Get used to dinners here. We will come here on a regular basis. Both Frank and I have our own tables reserved while we are in town." So many things didn't make sense, still I was with my future husband. What sort of future did we have if I started questioning everything that seemed odd to me? It seems hard to believe I was so desperate for love. Yet I would repeat my impetuousness in the same way later in life. Yes, I was right on cue for the next chapter in a sordid triangular mess. Clearly, I was in love with the idea of being in love but did not have any experience knowing how to proceed.

17

MISTAKE?

"Catherine, I think I will take this entire month off from work devoting it to you, my love. We will take a trip, if you want. Anything you would like, that's what we will do." He kissed my neck early the next morning. We were staying in Rhonda's house.

"That would be wonderful. Thank you, but I don't want you to get in trouble. I am accustomed to a certain lifestyle, you know." I kissed him back and wrapped his dark hair around my finger, something I started doing. He had the most incredible head of thick dark hair. He smiled back. I thought for just a second about a life of solitude. I now stood on an abyss, about to change my life to that of a married woman with husband and children. What about my beautiful Southern home and life in Eufaula? Was I so desperate for love that in just an instant, I would throw all of my dreams away? Apprehension filled my mind as I became cognizant I was making a colossal mistake. My need for love put me out of control. I seemed unable to stop my spiral down. Lately, all that I wanted to do was stay in bed. Not in a sexual way but sleeping all of the time. Was it depression or something else?

"There is a beautiful hotel in Asheville, North Carolina that my former wife and I sometimes visited. Have you ever heard of Biltmore House? The hotel there is European in charm. We could ride horses or hike or swim, the list is endless. Are you a spa girl? My wife loved the spas."

"No, not really, that scene has never appealed to me. I am too careful with money, I guess. My father taught us frugality, which is engrained in me. That does sound great though. When should we leave?" Jim looked surprised.

"That is a different trek. I thought that you wanted to hang around this house being Rhonda's house guard." He looked remorseful that he had made the recommendation.

Dressing for our sojourn to Starbucks, our morning ritual, the day outside looked dreary. Determined to be the most wonderful wife to Jim, the weather wouldn't daunt me. He followed such a demanding schedule. It meant a great deal that he was taking time off. As I entertained those thoughts, the phone rang. Rhonda's voice on the other end sounded distressed. Now what?

"Cat, is Jim there close by?" Rhonda was whispering. My friend was definitely the drama queen.

"Of course, I'm happy to report." I tried to sound carefree so that Jim wouldn't become suspicious. Something was wrong.

"Cat, listen to me very carefully. Be very guarded in your feelings for him. I can't say much because he and Barrington work together. If Barrington finds out that I have said anything, I would be in serious trouble with him. My life is wonderful, just the same, some very weird things are happening."

I understood her sentiments. We talked briefly. It was hard to hear her whispers. My faith in my friend restored if she would take a risk with her relationship to her husband for this call. Now I knew all of the bells and whistles were correct. I was behaving as a fool. Still, there resided that voice, which I chose to believe. It enticed me that perhaps Rhonda was the foolish one. Filled with doubts, now I longed to go back to Eufaula. One thing was becoming clearer; Eufaula was my home.

"Maybe I should make our reservations for Biltmore now? What do you say, pretty lady?" That dazzling smile, which once seemed so gorgeous, now looked like the mouth of a shark. His teeth were ragged, not so beautiful.

"Who was on the phone? You don't have a secret lover, do you? You know, Cat, I am a very powerful person in the government. I don't like games."

I had about all that I could take. His gruff tone sounded very much like a threat. What had I gotten involved in? What had Rhonda? Still, being the impetuous opinionated person that I was, I couldn't help myself. "Jim, are you threatening me?"

He smiled right in my face. "Maybe. What are you going to do? Call Rhonda? Not a wise idea, Barrington is my boss."

"Oh, really? I thought you worked with Frank, and that Barrington was a hotshot attorney." The lies were becoming transparent.

"Darling, you are way over your pretty little head." He walked to the phone with his address book to make the reservations. As he waited for the desk clerk, he watched me with interest. After the clerk picked up and the conversation started, I amazed myself by walking to the phone with a smile. Putting my finger on the disconnect button, I hit it as hard as I could. This action took Jim by surprise. He sat there holding the phone with a dazed look.

"I no longer want to go anywhere outside of Washington. Really, I don't know what I was thinking. Rhonda would kill me if I left her house unguarded." Instantly, I regretted my choice of words. It crossed my mind that killing was a possibility with Jim.

"Sure, I understand. Let's get our coffee and think about things." He did not look happy. I was feeling very discouraged. We walked the brief way without a word. Only one more week then Rhonda should return. At least I had stayed most of the time. Formulating a plan of exit, I fell off balance by Jim's arms coming around me. Out of the blue, he pulled me close with a kiss.

"Please forgive me, Cat. I was way out of line. When you get your way most of the time, I guess it is hard to deal with dissent.

Sorry if I was hard on you. You are my love, about to be my wife. I would do anything to make you happy. Just look at that big ole ring. Do you love it?"

Looking at the ring, I simply nodded. Starting the day off with an argument was not my desire. After our small breakfast with a nice caffeine jolt, news fix from the *Washington Post*, I felt a little better. Rhonda's phone call created distrust. The former voice of encouragement for Jim and our relationship started once again in my head. The decision of how to handle this was suddenly clear. With only a week until Rhonda's return, I would observe Jim as objectively as possible. Maybe then I could determine if I needed to run as the voices in my mind and heart declared.

We spent the rest of the day at the Smithsonian. It had been years since I visited the museum. Walking around the cool halls, Jim's brilliance became clear. I never knew anyone so well informed. How could anyone be so diverse in their knowledge and skills? He must find it difficult dealing with average people such as me. No wonder he appeared on edge often. At one point, I kissed him as we walked past a relic from the past. He looked annoyed, surveying the people around us. No one seemed to notice, so he relaxed.

"Does that mean all is forgiven? I am sorry about that incident this morning. Obviously something upset you, right? It wasn't your fault. Who was on the line?"

Since my childhood, honesty had always mattered to me. Telling the truth was the right thing. Seldom had I ever resorted to lies, so with difficulty, I mumbled, "It was Jean. Problems at the gallery. I'll have to work on it."

We looked at each other. He knew that I lied. Something changed at that moment. Never would we even pretend again. When Rhonda returned, I would be out of his grasp. We spent the next week walking around each other. He was nice. I remained cordial. No more promises of our undying love. We tolerated each other. Whatever happened, it had been a mistake.

Passion clouded my mind. Never had I been deeply involved with a man. I had mistaken the strong feelings of desire with love, but what about Jim? He was a sophisticated man of the world. Why would he portray himself as having fallen head over heels for me? There was something of tremendous value going on here. Was I the prize?

Four days before Rhonda's scheduled return, Jim announced he must leave overnight. He would be back for Barrington's return. Quickly packing a small bag, he avoided any sort of eye contact with me. As he pecked my cheek, I looked into his eyes. He looked tired. For the past several nights, he received late-night phone calls on the line downstairs. Something was bothering him. I walked down the stairs with him to a waiting car and driver. He explained that he wasn't sure where he would be staying tonight. There were several "fires" to put out. He apologized for seeming distant. With that, he was gone.

I felt like dancing. The terrible charade ended. Still, I found it hard to walk away from the most gorgeous man I ever knew without more than a hunch that something was wrong. Spending the rest of the day with *Gatsby*, I finished the book. When I awakened from a long nap, it surprised me to see darkness outside. I had slept for hours. The phone was shrilling at me.

The voice on the other end sounded vaguely familiar. A woman with a soft Southern accent began giving me directions to a bar/restaurant across town. It was a legend in Washington. I wrote down everything she said. Changing clothes quickly, I did as she instructed. She emphasized that if I would hurry, "All will be revealed."

"Thank you, Lord," I whispered. I could feel that it was almost over. I called a taxi as I ran down the stairs.

18

THE TRUTH

The taxi driver smiled as I asked him if he knew the spot. "Lady, if I can't find that one, I should stop driving." I smiled back. Immediately, my mind began to defend Jim once again. Maybe things weren't so bad. Could he just be a habitual liar? Such a theory, created all sorts of problems. Next, I considered perhaps he was waiting for me with a fabulous dinner and a great excuse. I knew that was not what waited for me. Confusion remained the only certainty.

Washington traffic was a mess. It took so long to reach my mecca, the place where "all would be revealed." Lover or maniac would soon be disclosed. "Don't be so naïve, Cat, you know the answer," I sadly stated to myself.

"Are you calling me naïve, lady? Wow, I haven't ever been called that. Thank you, I guess." All of the lies and games were almost over. I only smiled at the driver in the rearview mirror.

He pulled into the requested spot. "Can you just park? This shouldn't take long."

"Lady, are you insane? No one gets out of that place without a long wait. I can't afford such a place, but you will spend a lot of time, as well as all of your money. I can't wait for you."

"Believe me, I won't be long. It will be worth your time." I didn't want him to leave me. Fear was overcoming my former bravado.

"You don't have a gun, do you? I mean, you are not going there to kill some cheating weasel, are you? Believe me, I don't want to get involved with that sort of thing. I am a law-abiding citizen with a wife and two kids."

"I promise you that I do not have a gun. It won't take long for me to see what I need to see. Please don't leave me." My plea worked. He nodded as he winked at me. It felt like he had been in this situation before as a woman needed to see what she "needed to see."

The loud laughter and bright lights of the entrance were a bit of a shock. The beautiful people of Washington filled the establishment. This did not look like the sort of place that someone would cheat. Yet Jim knew that I was a homebody and would not come here alone under any circumstance.

"Excuse me, do you have reservations? I'm sorry, but reservations only this evening. Not a single table has cancelled." The stylish young woman looked at me sympathetically.

"Not a problem. I'm just meeting a friend for a drink." She smiled and nodded. Walking toward the dark noisy room directly behind, I found myself alone in one of the busiest bars in Washington. How many important, life-changing deals had been casually conducted here? I didn't want to know. After scanning the room, I thought this a mistake. Someone had sent me on a wild goose chase for no reason. I was becoming angry. This garbage was not helping. Again, I looked around the room. This time, I checked more slowly with a great deal of care.

"Well, hello, beautiful. Can I buy you a drink?" Turning, I was looking into the eyes of a younger man who appeared to have already bought too many drinks. I smiled.

"My husband is tall and angry. I don't think he would like your suggestion." My new best friend slinked away.

Something attracted me to look way back in the darkest corner. The man facing the bar looked familiar. He was laughing. Even in the darkness, his teeth flashed a brightness that was hard to ignore. Carefully, I walked to the couple hiding in the darkness behind other patrons. As I slowly approached, the man laughed loudly. Now, I stood very close.

"She was probably the dumbest ever. Where Frank gets these broads is beyond me. Come on, engaged in one day because she slept with me. I knew that I was good, but that is more than I ever knew." The lady laughed loudly.

Jim sat holding a drink as he gazed into the eyes of a really beautiful redhead. He never looked at me that way. This was the person that he loved. It became so apparent. Why would he play with my emotions hurting me like this? It didn't make any sense at all. I did a favor for my friend. If there had ever been a victim, it was me. Then the flash of light from the bar caught the gold band on the women's finger. As I looked again, Jim was now also wearing a matching gold wide band. He was married? Rage filled me. What he had done to me was unnecessary. What sort of perverted monster was he or for that matter was she? He continued to tell her personal moments between us. Her laughter encouraged more details. Betrayal of the worst sort made me feel ignorant. I was "the dumbest one so far." Well, I would just show them both how dumb I really was.

Walking up to their table, I leered, "Darling, I don't think that I have met your wife." People turned around to see what was happening. They looked uncomfortable. The area around us became quiet. Washington was used to this scenario, but even here, discomfort resulted from betrayal.

"Matching bands, well, I should probably show her my big, ole diamond. Isn't that the way you described the dumbest of them all? You are right. I was dumb, but the game ends now. "

Jim watched in disbelief. He played me all wrong, never considering that I would show up and confront him. The woman looked outraged.

"Go home, honey. He is mine." She looked at me as if I were a country bumpkin. My New York attitude arose from deep inside.

"Yours, really, honey? Well, you can have him. Who wants him? He is lousy in bed. I tried not to hurt his feelings, but he is the worse. I have seen many, none this wimpy." I lied, but it came out easily.

"Yes, he is yours, but I wouldn't claim him so loudly. You have him, and you have this as well." To my absolute amazement, I picked up her martini and threw it into her face. She screamed. Jim, rat that he was, actually smiled at me. He recognized something at that moment as did I. Never had I known that I possessed the ability to play a game. The ability to inflict pain came easy for me.

Turning, I marched past the horde of shocked patrons. "Who was she? That was amazing. That man must be a lying scum, probably they both got what they deserved." Yes, Washington's finest all right.

Walking out the door, not a person tried to stop me. The taxi driver saw me exit. Quickly, he came hurling toward me. Opening the door for me, I jumped inside. We drove away rapidly.

"Did you see what you needed to see?" He looked concern.

"Yes, I saw it. Now I need to go home. Will you take me to the airport, please?" He nodded.

"Wish I could have seen what just happened. I think that I would be talking about it for a long time."

"Yes, you are right on that. So will most of those." Our eyes met briefly in the rearview mirror.

"You are a fighter, right? Sometimes, you got to do it."

It took most of the night for me to get a plane back to Alabama but, eventually, I did. Early the next morning, another taxi took me home to Eufaula.

19

HOME AT LAST

When I was finally able to insert the key into the lock of my door, my hands shook so dramatically. Intense tears ran from my eyes. I could barely accomplish the task. In the safety of my home, I was overcome with shame and fear. I felt like I was deep in a black hole. My beautiful home, which once brought me such joy, now only deepened my pain. What had I just done? My once perfect life seemed shattered. Was I really so desperate for love that I would sell myself like that? Always, I craved solitude, now why would I risk my reputation and beliefs to act as though none of it mattered? After a long hot shower, I did not feel any cleaner. Somehow, I felt soiled, used. It was a dreadful feeling.

Eventually, sleep did arrive. Later in the day, I was awakened by a gentle knock. I didn't think that I could face Jean. She seemed to have it all together. The love she shared with her husband made her loom in my mind as perfect. Jean would never sleep with a complete stranger as I had so easily done. After several soft taps, I went to the door. Jean gasped when she saw my badly swollen eyes. She looked shocked.

"Miss Cat, what is it? Has there been another death?" Only someone innocent could deduct that death was the disaster, not poor choices, which landed me into a myriad of evil.

"Oh, Jean, I have made so many mistakes over this past month. I became involved with a married man. I didn't know he was married, but still, I am so ashamed." The tears ran down my face uncontrollably. If only I could return to my confident, happy self. That time seemed a lot longer than a month ago.

Jean entered without an invitation. She motioned for me to get back in bed and gently covered me with the sheets. Sitting across from me in a damask wingback chair, she smiled. Very softly, she told me her story. One that was different than I would have imagined. Her tale was one that I needed to hear.

It seemed that my "perfect" assistant had once been a prostitute. Actually gasping, I found it difficult to breathe as she shared her life. Never had she told anyone about her ordeal. Dear, sweet Albert found her one night in a bar. Drunk and strung out on drugs, she was contemplating ending it all. He carried her against her will to his simple home. There he nursed her through the withdrawal of alcohol and cocaine. She told me how she begged him to kill her to end the pain. He read the Bible to her eventually convincing her that she was a child of God.

Assuring her that God loved her, she came to understand she was important and of value. His explanations of how we, as God's creatures, could never do anything to stop the love, that God possessed for each of us. With time and Albert's care, she became clean and whole. Together, they attended church. They worked in their community, tirelessly helping others who felt unloved and of little value. When her mother was faced with cancer, they rushed to her side. Leaving behind what little they possessed, with no regard to their own futures, they took care of her mother.

"You see, Cat, we are all flawed. No one is perfect. In fact, none of us are as we seem. Sure we clean up pretty well, but each of us bears the scars of mistakes and failures. Please, don't be so hard on yourself. You are still young. It is fine to recognize that maybe what you thought you wanted so badly is different from what you decide that you need later. Maybe, you really want to be in love. Is that so terrible?" Jean smiled compassionately.

I returned her smile. Suddenly, life did not seem so sad. The thing that I did not share with Jean as she squeezed my hand and left my presence was the fact that I felt something sinister was happening in my life. There was a force at play that I didn't understand. It was as though I was being used, but by whom? Surely, Rhonda would never be part of a group who meant my harm. Jim made it sound as though Barrington was in charge of him and Frank.

So was Barrington somehow setting me up for some sort of catastrophe? It didn't make sense. None of these people even knew me except for Rhonda. I couldn't accept that my sister, Rhonda, could be involved in this lying scheme. Someone who knew me, as well as anyone else in my life, someone whom I loved. Rhonda's timing was uncanny. The phone rang loudly. Rhonda's voice seemed softer than usual. Her compassion was obvious.

"Cat, are you okay? I heard Jim talking with Barrington. They were laughing about how naïve you are. I feel just terrible to have played any part in your being used like that. Thing is, I don't understand what is happening. It seems that Barrington is much more than an important attorney. He is head of some sort of government agency. Really, I only get bits and pieces of conversation. Then I am eavesdropping because I need to understand what is happening. Apparently, you are really important to them. Do you know why? Are you working with them somehow? I know that this is a legal group because I know Barrington. He would never be involved in anything that was not above board. Cat, he is the most honest and genuine person whom I have ever known except for maybe you. You must know that I would never do anything to compromise you or hurt you in any way."

Since I already decided that earlier, I assured her that I trusted her and loved her as a sister. Rhonda continued by telling me that she believed that the break-in, which had occurred at their home, was not real but staged so that she would invite me to Washington.

"The night that it happened, I told Barrington that I would ask Margie and John to house sit, but Barrington insisted I phone you. I thought it strange, filing that in the back of my mind. Now the entire episode seems staged. Why would there be a break-in but nothing was taken? Without a doubt, if Barrington suspected that someone tried to burglarize us, he would never have left for Martha's Vineyard. The entire month, he encouraged me to phone you and find out how things were developing with Jim. Barrington and Jim spoke several times each day. He would talk with Jim briefly then leave the room and close the door. Cat, what is going on? I love my husband and would never doubt him without good reason. I am developing an uneasy feeling that things may not be as they once seemed."

Well, great, my worst fears just confirmed. Why would I be of importance to the government? Then I remembered a group of us at UA discussing what we would like to do with our futures. At that moment, I remembered with chills that Frank said, someday he would be in the CIA. Almost as a joke, I stated I wanted to be a spy. It was all a joke. Now I wasn't laughing. Fear spread over me with a deep suspicion that my life was about to change. Once again, my feelings would prove to be correct.

20

LIFE ON EDGE

In a few days, life was back on track. There remained a feeling of edginess. No longer did things seem so carefree. I tried to appear normal, but I felt that someone was watching me. Everywhere I went, I looked over my shoulder. If it seemed that someone looked at me too intently or for longer than necessary, I tried to get away. My friends did not seem to suspect anything. Life continued as though the entire bizarre episode in Washington never occurred.

Fall of the year arrived in Eufaula with Albert building fires in each of the fireplaces. Jean cooked large pots of mushroom and potato soups. Jill had done an incredible job of attracting talented artists and displaying their art. Carnegie Hall echoed beauty. Many paintings sold and were delivered. Albert continued to amaze me with his many talents. Life was filled with excitement but not the same.

Jill and I hosted another art reception. We featured two very different artists. The night was as perfect as our first soirée except it was much larger. There was a line wrapped around the building. Entry coveted. It seemed that this small town starved for something more than an everyday occurrence. My vision of Jill and me attired in long jersey mauve dresses was a reality. We were a hit. My parents would have been proud of me.

Nat and I talked frequently. Ginger was the perfect wife and mother. He told me how proud he was of her. They hoped for another child in about a year. He even discussed running for Congress soon. Yes, our parents would have really been proud of us both.

Soon, I relaxed a little. The sting of that month in Washington passed. I had begun going out. On this particular day, dreariness shrouded the local restaurant. Mr. Greene's humor had brought roaring laughter to the entire diner. He had just left as I contemplated our friendship and all that he had contributed to my life. As I looked up, there stood Frank. I heard myself gasp.

"Well, hello, Cat. Fancy meeting you here. How are you? Jenny and I discussed calling, but we are pretty unreliable friends, I guess. You look great. Nice to see you enjoying yourself with your little real-estate friend. I've been waiting for his exit."

Not knowing whether to play along with him or just walk away, I relied on my intelligence to handle the situation. He looked normal. Maybe he had never really been a threat? I wasn't sure, but there was something intriguing about this strange charade.

"Well, Frank, back in Eufaula, I see. How are things in Washington?" I looked bored, although my hands were damp, and my heart was pounding.

"Oh, the same ole routine. You know Washington." He sat down at Mr. Greene's used spot. He smiled warmly. It looked to me like the smile of a crocodile. I didn't trust him at all.

"How are Jim and his wife? I'm amazed that you would approach me as though we are friends. In my world, friends don't let each other get caught in such a lying scheme. Does he still laugh at my naiveté? He probably loves telling your government group of how easily he scored. Did you really make CIA? Wow, that is incredible. I'm still waiting to be a spy for my government. Can you help?"

Laughing, I looked into his face to see that he turned white as a ghost. The smile was gone. He looked totally freaked out.

"Cat, you shouldn't make jokes like that. I'm surprised that you even remember that discussion so long ago. You always acted superior to me. I knew that you were making fun of me, but I was attracted to you. I didn't care. You were never aware of the effect that you had on most men. It is a shame that you didn't pursue your desire to work as an agent. You would have been perfect." Looking up from my paper with a smirk, I was met with a gaze that was not joking. Frank now appeared very somber. Maybe my past feelings were not so out of kilter from reality. Could a joke from college be following me? Was I being pursued by my own country? There was a fascination in what was happening.

"Cat, did you enjoy Washington? Would you like to meet me there again? I have a proposition for you. You may enjoy what we are about to present to you. It will be a great deal of fun, as well as lucrative for you. We do realize that you don't need the money, but use it to help others. If you are interested, you will be part of something so intensely large that it will change your life. There are things at play in this world, which involve extreme danger. Are you up to a challenge? If you are not and ever disclose this, you will be made to look foolish and flippant. However, if you are interested, we promise you can make a difference and do something that matters. Something that matters not only for your country but for the world. I need you to be serious, not your usual impetuous self." His entire countenance changed. It seemed as though he carried the entire weight of the world on his shoulders. I felt a connection. It was as though in those moments as he waited for my response, I was about to meet my destiny.

"Tell me where and when. I will be there." What had I just done? Perhaps that long-ago joke was about to become reality.

21

THE CALL

Months passed with no word from Frank and his "organization" or whatever they were. In my mind, I could picture the laughter as he disclosed our "secret" discussion and the fact that even now, I waited to be contacted. I went so far as to think that maybe "my love," Jim, was telling them intimate details of his scam.

"Now, that one is dumber than dumb. Hope that you have more like that, Frank. I'm still reeling over her stupidity." Briefly, I would feel flooded with regret, doubt. Eventually, I pulled myself out of self-pity and shame. Someday, they would get their just reward.

My simple life continued as more artists were helped through Carnegie Hall. As Thanksgiving approached, I received a call from Nat inviting me to visit with Ginger and him. I was elated.

- - - - - -

Thanksgiving with my family would deliver me from inner doubts. High expectations for their future surrounded the young family. Ginger had matured. They replaced Nellie.

"We called her, Cat. Ginger offered her job back, but she is enjoying her own life now. She is well and sends her love. Our Nellie is different. It seems that she has become quite the seasoned traveler. Her son took her to Europe for Thanksgiving. Isn't it wonderful after years of waiting on all of us, she is being cared for? I miss her, yet I'm happy that she is enjoying life." Nat looked like a little boy with his unruly cowlick sticking up on the back of his head, the same way it had when he was a child. Nellie and I spoke often, so I knew all about her. In fact, I sent her money for a Christmas present so that she would have extra for her trip to Europe.

"Some very important people are pushing me to run for a congressional seat, which I am considering. Ginger is behind me but a little afraid that her background may hinder me. I say, bring them on! Try to beat up a lady who is doing her best. The country won't stand for it. Right?" His occupying father's seat seemed strange. He carved the turkey with a steady hand as though he had done so a hundred times.

"Nat, I don't know anything about the government. Do you know anything about the CIA?" I hoped that he didn't catch my large swallow upon asking.

"The CIA? Well, no. No one knows much about those guys. You're not dating one, are you? I really don't think that you want to get involved. That is one very different group."

"Well, are they dangerous?" I was sounding a little panicky. Nat put his knife down and was now staring at me with alarm. Ginger looked down at her plate as though I was in deep trouble.

"Of course they are dangerous, if you cross them or are on the wrong side. Cat, for goodness sake, are you dating one of the agents? I sure hope not because I can guarantee that they know everything about Ginger and me, as well as our entire family." Looking at Ginger, he smiled.

"Not that I care, we have nothing to hide. Don't you worry, honey. No telling what Cat has gotten involved with, but we are fine." He seemed to relax and return to his carving. I changed the subject. It was never discussed again. Still, I had an uneasy feeling that I may have gotten involved in something way over my head.

After my return to Eufaula, Jean, Albert, and I started making Christmas plans. Nat and Ginger were going to Georgia to visit her family. Her entire family had not been together in a very long time. Her brother now lived and worked in Louisiana where he owned his own company. She seemed excited to think that her family would be a part of the baby's life. Things were really working out well for them.

One evening, as I was reading a Suspense/Thriller about a CIA agent who was killed by her own, the telephone startled me. Thinking that it was Margie, whom I phoned earlier in the day, I didn't check the number.

"It's about time that you phoned me. Do you and John want to join me this year for Christmas? Rhonda is gone to who knows where. Linda and Sam are going to his parent's home in Arkansas. I really want to stay home and celebrate."

"Well, bummer. I thought that you may be interested in flying to Washington. I have a meeting set up for you, if you are interested. You still interested in joining our illustrious group and making a difference?"

I had thought of little else since our last conversation. Still, second thoughts plagued me. Frank's long lapses of communicating with me were hard to bear. If they needed me, then shouldn't their contact be in a consistent manner? I became irritated with the whole mess. Nat's comments at Thanksgiving hadn't help soothe my fears.

"Oh, yes, I am ready to hear your presentation. Do you have the dates?" Was I truly insane? That was not what I had planned to say. There were a million details that needed care if I was to have all of the Christmas trees decorated the way I planned.

Frank seemed as though he knew without a doubt that I was ready to sign on and do whatever they told me. It was as though they were reading my mind. I wrote down the flight number, the hotel, and the time and place for our meeting. Unfortunately, it was scheduled four days before Christmas. This would completely decimate my plans. Like a robot, I wrote down all of the information without a single question. The conversation ended as I sat there feeling, once again, like a fool. I seemed unable to stand up to these people. What was wrong with me?

22

WASHINGTON

I cancelled all plans for house guests and informed Albert and Jean about my trip. They always supported me, and never did they question me about my private life. A week before my scheduled departure, I called the airlines. Yes, all arrangements were confirmed, as well as hotel reservations. I would be staying at L'Enfant Plaza Hotel. We were to have dinner that night in the dining room, which was where "the" meeting would occur.

Excitement began to build as I considered the fact that my country wanted me. I was needed to do something really important, something that may affect the security of America. I felt useful and proud. Constantly, I read books about the CIA, FBI, and the government in general. When I walked down the street, I made a point of checking details about my surroundings. I trained myself for my new job in surveillance. Yes, Nat may be a congressman soon, but I was about to be drafted in the CIA. Dad must be turning cartwheels in heaven. I laughed as I pictured that sight.

Finally, my big day arrived. I wasn't even nervous. I thought that I must be a natural for this line of work. The flight was uneventful. Frank had not mentioned that a driver would pick me up, but surely, someone as important as I must rate a driver. I walked through the gate with a confident smile. I had to show that I was in control. In my mind, I thought of Ginger. Her attempt to appear in control of Nellie proved futile and foolish. Surely, I was not behaving as foolishly as she.

Looking around, there was no driver. In fact, no one waited at the gate. Well, surely, when I walked outside of the airport, he would be waiting. Probably the "higher ups" concluded they did not want to attract attention to me. Smart. Yes, I was working for a very intelligent group. I would have to compliment them on their wisdom.

Walking out into the winter day, a sharp blast of wind blew my dress up to my waist. Great, I didn't think I was supposed to attract attention to myself. I read that in one of my books written by an ex-CIA man. Looking around, again, there was no sign of anyone waiting for me. Well, they made a mistake. They were only human, after all. Now I would work closely with them advising them how to meet new agents.

L'Enfant Plaza Hotel was my dad's choice for accommodations way back in the 1970s. I remembered well the fun, as well as good meals. It seemed appropriate I would be starting my new career in that same place. As I exited the taxi, I noticed that the hotel had aged well. Many renovations occurred throughout the past. Located in Southwest Washington near the Smithsonian and the Metro, it remained a popular destination for travelers and businessmen. I rationalized that the proximity to Capitol Hill made it the choice for government agencies. It was also located near the National Mall, so I was in the heart of Washington, right where I needed to be. My country needed me. I would deliver.

Expecting to be booked into one of the executive suites, slight disappointment caused me to frown. I found myself standing in an ordinary room of the three hundred seventy-two rooms and suites. Wow, my country really did need me. Another mistake. They should be reprimanded. I would wait until my job was more secure. Yes, I was in control. My reservation called for two nights in Washington. Then who knew where they may need me. Maybe

I would be whisked to Iran or some other "hot spot." Once there, I would be able to expect a suite. All of this spy work was draining. I decided to lie down briefly.

The phone softly rang unlike the shrillness of my home phone. Frank's voice sounded slightly irritated, "Cat, where are you? It is fifteen minutes past the time for our meeting. Come to the dining room at once." The line went dead.

I was not off to a good start. Punctuality had always been one of my best traits at least until now. Running a comb through my hair, quickly I changed into the dress and shoes, which was packed for the meeting. Upon leaving my room, I slid a piece of tape on the bottom of my door so that I would be able to tell if anyone entered my room. Hastily, making my way to the elevator, I looked in each direction just in case someone may be casing me. Just another example of the books read in preparation for my career as surveillance expert.

Walking into the lovely dining room, I easily spotted Frank alone in the back. This was not going well. I was late. Where were the others? What did that say for the professionalism of "my" group? I really needed to be a wise leader.

"Good evening, agent Frank. Hope that you are well. Where are the others?"

Frank looked annoyed. "Cat, what are you doing? You never refer to me as 'agent anything.' As far as 'the others,' what are you talking about? It is just us. You and me. Got it? Now, have a seat and relax. Would you like a drink?"

"Yes, sir, sir. I would like a vodka martini. Stirred, not shaken, of course." I gave him my best smile.

"Oh, I get it. Just like James Bond? Right? You are a funny girl."

I really didn't think that he should make reference to my hero, James Bond, who was really Daniel Craig. Still, I would not begin to make suggestions until I was hired and part of the team.

Frank was scanning the room. I turned to check out the other diners.

"Cat, please turn back around. Never turn and look around the room. Now let's enjoy the evening a little. Then we will get back to our discussion." We did enjoy our time. I soon started to relax. Frank was just like Jim in that he was smart and witty. We had a wonderful dinner. Since I was famished, I ordered a large filet mignon. Then we had another drink. Yes, this spy business was agreeable.

By the time that we finished our meal, the room cleared. I noticed that the background music played louder. They probably were accustomed to meetings like ours. They knew that there would be eavesdroppers. This was a very good tactic. I pulled out a notebook, which I had begun to keep on points to discuss with "my" group.

"Cat, what are you doing? Why did you bring a journal?"

"Oh, right. Like you don't know about the importance of keeping a journal. I have been very busy preparing for this new career. One of several books, which I read by ex-CIA operatives, informed me of the importance of maintaining proper records. Don't worry, I will not use your real name, George."

"Cat, you never write things down. You will need to use your brain. Stop reading those books immediately. Not a single decent government agent would resort to journals. They would never do that."

I was certain I read it just the other day. When I returned home, I would get rid of that book for certain. I looked at Frank intently.

"Now, Cat, I think that if I tell you why we are interested in you that may help you understand the scope of what we need. To begin, when you made that decision to buck your family's choice of university that was impressive. In fact, that is the thing that we need—someone who is able to think outside of the box, so to speak. That drive from New York to Alabama all alone was very impressive. Your infatuation with the south, the uncanny ability, which you showed in changing your accent so easily and believably was impressive and duly noted. Are you following me?" I was not only following but was shocked that they knew so much.

"When you and I met in Alabama, I was infatuated with you. Now, you see, that is extremely important because we need a man magnet." He smiled.

"A what? A man magnet, you say? What exactly is that?" Now I was not following.

"That is a woman who can attract men. You have that ability. I doubt if there are many men who could resist the likes of you. Jim was a test. You passed that one, hands above. He said that you were great in bed."

"Wait a minute that was a test? He slept with me to see if I was any good in bed? That was in preparation for my job as government agent?" These guys were beyond "bad"; they were ruthless.

"Cat, no one ever said that you are going to be a government agent. Okay? Your role will be one to do as you are told. You will be used as needed. Got it? Now, the thing that really impressed us was the way that you tracked ole Jim and his wife confronting them. That was a step above what we expected from you. You must not be afraid or at least not show it. When you threw that drink in his wife's face, well, that was incredible. Jim knew then I was right in my assessment of your abilities. They weren't sure about you until that moment. Are you following me?"

His constant asking if I was following him became increasingly annoying. Did he think I was an absolute idiot? This was not brain surgery.

"Of course, I am following you. Now, some of what you are saying is impressive, but some of it is not. For example"

"Remember, you do as you are told. You do not make recommendations. We don't care to know your feelings. You do as you are told. First and basic rule of what we need from you. Are you following me?"

It became apparent that he was enjoying his superiority over me, but I was not worried. I expected to exceed him soon. He probably scored low on the ladder. Surpassing him due to my intelligence should be easy. My grades in college were highly superior. Still, I just nodded yes that I was following him.

"Cat, the thing that you did that most impressed us was tossing the drink in her face. Apparently, you have the ability to inflict pain. Don't think about that statement. You have a little natural ability. There is no point in overanalyzing this. You will never understand it, so remember, do as you are told. You can't go wrong. Does what I say make sense to you, and are you up to round two?"

It sounded to me as though they may be looking for a hit man with the reference to inflicting pain. Still, I would do what needed to be done to help my country.

"Yes, sir, sir. I am ready to continue." I really wasn't sure, but what else was I going to say?

"Great. Good to hear it. Breakfast tomorrow morning at 7 a.m., and then we are off to get some info. Let you meet a few other people. Get a good-night's sleep." Before I knew what happened, he was gone.

23

I JOIN THE GROUP

The next day is now a blur. We ate an early breakfast. I barely slept the night before. Questioning my sanity and the actual events of late, I started to think that perhaps all of this was just a sick game. Maybe none of it even occurred? Why would my country go to great lengths to add me to a group when there were so many highly educated college graduates? Surely in all of those, there was a "man magnet." It felt foolish even saying those words.

Frank seemed more relaxed and treated me with respect as it looked as though I was about to join his ranks. The bizarreness left me feeling as though I watched a silly movie. I wanted to laugh out loud or yell, "This can't be happening."

Instead, I continued listening to his pitch and acting interested. Several people were waiting in a highly polished modern office of glass and steel upon our entrance. They all looked professional, not at all part of a sinister plot. If they were insane, they did not look the part. Relaxation flowed through my tight body. In fact, if truth be told, I wanted it all to be true. What if for years, some group gathered information on me because there was something about me that no one else could provide. Could it be possible that I, Cat Carn, actually contained deep intelligence? Maybe I was good for much more than painting and conducting lavish galas. Such tempting thoughts titillated me. Just as I so badly wanted Jim to be a part of my life, I desired this adventure. Also, I wondered if others who were drafted or whatever this procedure was called, did they feel disconnected?

Everyone stood when I entered with handshakes and welcomes. It was very impressive. Frank told them at one point that I thought I was needed as an agent. They all looked at me laughing good-naturedly. One of the young women told me that she trained for her position for years since college but still ranked with little importance.

"Believe me, it is not easy to be an agent. Most of us just 'do as we are told.' There is no danger as you see in the movies, at least not in what we do." She smiled as she looked around the office at the young faces, which surrounded us. As I studied the group, it appeared that most of them were beautiful young men and women. Did they possess the same trait as I? Perhaps this group simply existed as "man or women magnets?" I smiled as I remembered the term.

The amount of information they stored on my family and friends was unimaginable. All of my close friends and family were now part of my "file." If my rank was of little value, why so much work? When I entered the building, I had not seen a sign identifying it, which I thought strange. Still, *do as you are told* became imbedded in my thought process.

Tremendous paperwork waited for me. Soon, I became tired of the process, yet I was now a part of whatever this involved. Several documents had been signed and resigned. Explanations reiterated I was not a part of the CIA, followed with, "Do as you are told, and all will be well."

Over and over, I repeated that I would do anything for my country. That seemed to be the most important thing I contributed during the hours invested that day. Later in the evening, a dark car transported me back to the hotel for a brief change of clothes. Only to be picked up by a small group of the same folks and taken to a different hotel. Once there, we shared a celebratory dinner. Toasts raised several times to the "new staff member." Apparently, I had been hired for just a normal job. No explanation was divulged as to my role nor were any descriptions of what my job entailed. At the end of the evening, many pats on the back and handshakes were offered as I was walked from the room. The others merely turned their backs to continue their meeting. Another dark car delivered me to the front door of L'Enfant Plaza. Once again, I remained alone.

The next day, I took a taxi to the airport only to fly back to Eufaula without any idea as to when I may be summoned again. Without a doubt, this happened, but all was so shrouded in mystery, I found it hard to believe.

Later in the week, it was as though, once again, none of this had occurred. To all of those whom I loved, nothing changed. Christmas was very quiet. The one tree, which Albert placed in the foyer, twinkled with hundreds of bright white lights. I remained too tired to think of decorating. Jean and Albert hovered over me as though suspecting that something was wrong, but they never inquired.

Christmas morning, they presented me with small gifts. Albert constructed many beautiful frames for the art, which we hoped to collect. They were varied sizes and colors. Jean baked Christmas candies and cookies. Their love and devotion ranked as the best gift anyone could desire. My gift contained a large bonus for each of them, which delighted them. It was a Christmas of quietness filled with love. That evening, we sat by a gentle fire, sipping homemade eggnog, which Jean also prepared. The sweet Christmas tunes gently playing in the background gave us all hope for the coming year. I wondered what these dear friends would think if they knew what I had just done?

Margie, John, Linda, and Sam all phoned. I had not talked with Rhonda in weeks. I was prepared that Barrington may insist she avoid me once he heard of my involvement.

The softness of the evening allowed me to think about my new role. Without a doubt, I joined something very important. This instilled a feeling of pride in me. All of the craziness warranted if I could make a difference. It didn't really matter the degree of my role, just that I was part of something important. My solitary life now seemed to be the most confusing part of the puzzle. Frank knew my plans yet never explained how my life may change.

Several weeks later, Frank called late one evening as I painted in my studio. I turned down the music, delighted to hear his voice. We chatted casually for several minutes.

"Now, Cat, are you ready to go to work?" That was it? Just like that, my career would begin. After all of the games and lies, I felt totally prepared for anything.

"Yes, I am ready." *Don't share your feelings. Do as you are told.* All of the drillings of those facts came to my mind. I simply waited for more facts.

"You are going to love this. You and I, Cat Carn, are going to dinner. A package will arrive by special courier. You are to dress to kill."

It would have been much easier if he didn't say those things. Since I was just a "man magnet" I was no longer worried about being a hit man or any of those ridiculous thoughts, which I once entertained. I knew what he meant.

"I'm not sure what to wear. How formal is this event?" I innocently asked.

"That is what I just explained. A package will arrive with instructions and clothes that you are to wear. You need to provide underwear. That evening at your hotel, a stylist will be sent to arrange your hair. You do not have to worry about anything, follow directions. By the way, your phone line has been checked. It is totally fine. Still, never discuss anything, just the way that you were instructed."

"I remember everything. You no longer have to worry about me." I was aware that I felt like a Barbie doll, who only did as told and was not to make any decisions. Yet it was not a condescending feeling. *Anything for my country*, I reiterated in my mind.

Three days later, a package did arrive by special courier as soon as Jean and Albert departed for the day. Inside a large sealed box laid the most gorgeous Vera Wang black dress with matching heels. The dress fit perfectly as did the shoes. I stood in front of my mirror, feeling charmed. This was going to be so much fun. Never would I do anything of importance, they told me. I was merely to do as told, and I would be paid nicely. I never dreamed that I would be paid to dress in such incredible clothes with exquisite accessories. Later, I learned that the jewelry was not real, just as the ring from Jim. Any clothes were to be returned by special courier the next day. Oh well, this was all for my country, right?

24

MY FIRST ASSIGNMENT

I followed the instructions perfectly, explaining that I must visit Rhonda again. My staff was not surprised. They began to expect these crazy calls from my friend with her bizarre expectations. After all, what sort of friend would expect someone to stay for a month in a home, which had just been burglarized? My group knew what they were doing. They arranged things so perfectly that it all made sense to everyone close to me. I was following Frank in my head for sure.

L'Enfant Plaza Hotel was selected again. If the hotel had any clue what was happening, it was never revealed. I arrived to an ordinary room. Never was there a suite or anything grand. The rest of the day of arrival was mine to do as I pleased. Nothing was left to chance. They even directed me when to shower. A knock on the door told me that my hairdresser had arrived. On my first assignment, she provided me with a manicure and pedicure. Most of the time, just my hair was styled. Immediately, I dressed. The phone rang from Frank. He just arrived in the lobby. We shared a drink in the bar. It was obvious that we were supposed to look as if we were having an affair. I played alone. It was fun and exciting. Then we attended a special function where we were to work that evening. Frank advised me that we must appear to be a couple having an affair, which was going badly. I saw the looks of some of the married women as they clutched the hand of their husband whenever I approached. Anxious looks were replaced with smiles when I hugged them, offering a double kiss. This was Washington and not unusual at all. There were no offensive remarks as to my morality or Frank's precious wife, Jenny. The game was safe with these calloused, worldly people.

When I returned to Eufaula the next day, Jean and Albert never appeared suspicious. After they left, a courier arrived for the gown. The sealed envelope was returned in another sealed envelope, which was provided. Never did I feel the slightest hint of danger. Simply doing as told, I experienced a wonderful time.

Each assignment was entirely unique. Often, there would be small dinner parties at Washington's finest homes. Those events proved a little harder to pull off. I felt sorry for Jenny. Her husband was doing his job, but I could imagine the conversation the next day between some of the wives. Still, he was greeted as though he was royalty by the very women who must have despised both of us. I continued to convince myself that I was doing all of this for my beloved country. That made it palatable for me. I guessed for Frank as well.

My life gained a new and exciting edge. The art and galas were constants at my home. My respected status in the community increased. I planned my own small dinner parties. Sometimes, I invited Frank and Jenny. If she feared anything about my relationship with Frank, she never mentioned it. We were good friends.

The calls started off infrequently, increasing over the years. My life never involved dating, although I did receive several requests. The solitary life I craved remained mine, well sort of. I now had a private life, which no one suspected. My friendships with Margie, John, Linda, and Sam stayed secure. My friendship with Rhonda changed. We seldom talked then only superficially. She never mentioned things as I suspected would occur. She followed Barrington's instructions, I knew. Of course, she must.

Ginger and Nat's precious child, Maxwell Patrick Carnegie was so beautiful. I spent over two weeks with them. He beamed a beautiful boy with thick red hair and blue eyes. He became the child that I never had. Our relationship stayed close from the time that he was born. He was the light of my life. Ginger and Nat appeared happy. Soon they were blessed with a little dark-haired girl named Natalie. Although she and I were close, it wasn't like the relationship that I shared with Max.

Nathaniel's dream of a congressional seat was also realized. His election was overwhelming by a landslide vote to office of House Representative of New York. I knew his dream had just started. His goal was much higher. He changed from a young boy dominated by his father to a man just like him. Dad would have been amazed by his only son.

After returning from a visit with Max, it surprised me to hear the doorbell. I had just begun to unpack my bags. I never had uninvited guests, so I was indeed shocked. Checking the window, there stood Linda and Sam. What a welcomed surprise. They entered to hugs and kisses. Explaining that they were on their way to visit family, they were just passing through Eufaula. It thrilled me. No, they couldn't spend the night or have dinner. Just a quick visit with a glass of Jean's delicious sweet iced tea. The early summer evening provided a heavenly light breeze as we laughed. It had been a long time since I enjoyed my porch. Linda returned to the kitchen for more iced tea. The door was closed because the air conditioner had just been turned on for the long summer season. I did not hear the phone.

She returned to the porch laughing heartily. "You just received the strangest call. Some man said, 'Hey, darling, are you ready to work'?" My heart almost stopped. Frank insisted that we act as though our relationship was amorous at all times. He now called me "darling" and "love" often. We laughed at the strange call. Linda stated that he hung up quickly when she told him he had the wrong number. Suddenly, she looked serious, "You aren't seeing someone, are you, Cat? Are you having an affair?" She looked shocked that I would not have shared such news.

"You know better than that, Linda. I tell you everything." She smiled. I felt sick because now the lies started.

25

MRS. JONES

I slept well that night even though I knew what awaited me the next day. I just didn't expect the phone to ring at 6:30 a.m. Frank was an exercise fanatic. He started each day in his private workout room at his home. He described his obsession in great detail. Then he ran for over an hour before reporting to his "office."

The onslaught of words, which I expected from him, began. "Cat, what were you thinking? You made me look like a fool. How dare you make a mistake like that? You may have compromised the entire mission. Years of preparation flushed down the toilet because you have friends over. What happened to your solitary life, which you talked about since college? I always thought that you were a little strange. At least you have been consistent until last night, except for the time that all three of them showed up when you first moved in. Now I have to file an incident report on this lapse. I don't file incident reports, Cat. Mistakes are not tolerated on my team. Are you following me?"

I was holding the phone inches from my ear so that his shouting didn't puncture the membrane of my ear. "Frank, come on, even for you, this is ridiculous. Linda is not suspicious, although you didn't have to slam the phone in her ear. You know, ears are sensitive. For example, my left ear is hurting about now." I hoped that he would get the humor but knew better.

"How many times must we go over this? We don't care about your feelings. Just do as you are told." I said the last words along with him.

"You really blew it, Cat. They finally gave the meat of your assignment, but now, who knows? They don't tolerate mistakes. You had the opportunity to make a name for yourself, but now, who knows?" With that, the line went dead.

The once beautiful day now did not appear so rosy. It amazed me that they knew such details about me. I concluded that once I became accepted as part of the team, whatever that was, I would be dropped from scrutiny. Wrong again.

What did he mean that the work done for years had been flushed down the toilet? I was only a "man magnet." Why would work involving me last for years? Slowly, I arose from my once peaceful bed, my head reeling from "TMI." I showered and dressed for the day.

As I started to the kitchen for a cup of caffeine, the phone rang again. I considered letting it ring. Frank's outbursts were sometimes exhausting. Instead of Frank, it delighted me to hear Ginger's voice. She started calling me each week to give me an update on Max and Natalie.

"Max is really looking forward to spending time with you in Eufaula this summer. They both send their love." Max and Natalie were growing up way too quickly. At that moment, I realized that I had worked with the group for over a year now. Time flies when you are having fun, but working with Frank did not seem like a great deal of fun at the moment.

My conversation with Ginger helped put things in perspective. Certainly, I knew no additional details about the "organization" or "group." Linda did not suspect anything at all. I believed Rhonda may be a little more of a problem, yet they never mentioned the fact that Rhonda seemed suspicions. I missed my eccentric friend. Life was full with visits to and from my other friends, Nat and Ginger. Ginger loved Eufaula. She sometimes came with the children for visits without Nat. We liked to walk the children around the block. Secretly, she dreamed of owning a cottage by the lake for summers but was afraid to broach the subject. He did not like Ginger to be gone from him. Funny, they reminded me of Mom and Dad. I was the only weird one in the family. Even Frank thought that I was "a little strange." Maybe coming from him, that was a compliment.

The morning was beautiful. The day was not steamy. Many people were walking around the block just enjoying the day. I watched with happiness as Jean and Albert came walking up to the porch holding hands. Theirs remained a love story from heaven. When he looked at her, I could see love in his eyes. Why some people enjoyed a love like that while others never felt love seemed unfair. The time slowly rolled past, not yet flying, but I knew my biological clock was ticking. The years took their toll. Lines and wrinkles now screamed each morning from their hideouts around my eyes and mouth. Yes, my solitary life continued to be cherished, but sometimes in the middle of the night or when I saw love shinning in the eyes of one of my friends, I considered the happiness I experienced when I thought that Jim really loved me. Pathetic comparing that charade to real love.

After a brief chat with Jean and Albert, I returned to my studio. The gallery remained an extreme success. Jill and Albert ran it now. Occasionally, I dropped by to check on things. When I did, it felt like someone else owned it. Sometimes, I experienced difficulty believing I started such a thriving enterprise. If I listened to Frank for long, I was convinced that I was totally inept.

The day passed quietly. All through those hours, I wondered what instructions from Frank awaited me. Was my time with him really over for such a small infraction? It became apparent that my role was more important than he admitted. The thought of really doing something important was exhilarating.

Jean and Albert left a little earlier to enjoy the cool evening. I didn't mind. They both worked hard. I enjoyed Jean's homemade chicken pot pie. The ringing of the phone caused disquiet in my heart. As I answered it, I knew that it would be Frank.

"Look, Cat, just calling to tell you that everything is fine. In fact, I was chided for being so hard on you." Did they report every word to each other?

"The group says that you are still with us. I've got to tell you that I am really excited over this opportunity. I am pretty important. My people always excel. I know that you won't disappoint. Cat, I've been a little hard on you. I'm sorry."

It was difficult to believe that Frank, "super-agent," just apologized to a mere "man magnet." Could my rating in this crazy group be higher than I had been led to believe? Anyway, I appreciated the apology but knew better than tell him how I felt. Then, "we don't care about your feelings. Do only as you are told," would follow. Instead, I said nothing, waiting for instructions.

"Cat, we worked out a foolproof plan for the future. You should be able to entertain friends without feeling on edge that they may answer the phone. You know, those things happen." His pause made me question if this was really Frank. Maybe this was a test from the group to see if I was sharp enough to recognize his voice.

"Anyway, are you following me, Cat?" I waited. He knew that I was.

"The procedure will continue as follows: when the phone rings, the caller will ask if this is Mrs. Jones. If it is you, give the last four digits of your social security number. If not, no worries, our caller will say wrong number. Cat, are you following me."

This was like a group of kids playing a game. I loved the intrigue, so I complimented them on the brilliance of the plan. In the future, each phone call with Frank began with the words, "Mrs. Jones?" Since only Frank phoned me, my social security number probably wouldn't be needed.

Then Frank explained that a package would arrive tomorrow. "This is it, Cat. This is our time. You can't know the importance of this mission. I don't think that I have ever been so excited. I knew the first time I laid eyes on you that, well, never mind. Just want to say that I am very happy to finally be working with you. See you soon." The line went dead as it always did with Frank. There were a million questions that I wanted to ask. Truly, I was programmed to know that my feelings were not important. The only important thing was for me to do as told.

Entering my softly lighted studio, the sun was now shining on the back of the house. I turned up Pavarotti and painted for over two hours. Whatever lay ahead, my life was now exciting. My friends thought that I led a boring, predictable life. If they only knew. Years later, I would remember that very moment if only I had known.

26

THE DRESS

The morning after Frank's call, the same scenario, which I became accustomed to expect, occurred. It was always the same courier. We never spoke. He smiled, nodded, then handed me the box. I carried the nondescript package to my bedroom immediately where it was opened. Then I destroyed the box as instructed. Inside the box were layers of tissue paper. Next was a large envelope with instructions for the following day with reservations. Following that would be an incredible gown or dress with heels. Beneath that, carefully wrapped laid the jewelry in velvet boxes. Finally, there was an empty envelope for return of the instructions, as well as receipts and reservation stubs from my job. When the courier arrived the next day, he carried a new box with a different address. He waited outside my door while I quickly placed everything back in the new box in the same order that it had been removed. Special tape for sealing the box also was provided. Even the procedure for taping the box had a distinct system. Carefully, I handed the box back to the courier. He smiled, nodded, and left. The entire procedure was mysterious but intriguing. I loved it. With excitement, I waited during the night for the chimes of the doorbell the next morning. Sleep was difficult on those nights.

This particular morning carried more of a shiver as I opened the door. Frank insisted that this was important. The same courier smiled, nodded, then handed me the box. Immediately, I carried it upstairs to my room. I tore the box apart, cutting the address from the carton. Then I cut it into smaller pieces. As I opened the new box, I noticed that there was more tissue paper than usual. Opening layer after layer of the delicate gray paper, my breath was taken away as I saw the dress. Without a doubt, I had never seen anything so beautiful in my life.

Glistening in the morning light the most gorgeous red dress. The color was Japanese red. I happened to love red. It was my favorite color. As I lifted the dress from the box, the small beads, which were hand sewn to the fabric, caught the light, reflecting rays in bright small bands. It was so exquisite that I literally lost my breath for a second. Also enclosed were stiletto heels in neutral beige with the same small hand-sewn beads as the dress. The workmanship of both was impeccable. I could not imagine the hours and cost involved. I couldn't help myself. I had to try it on. As I pulled the dress gently over my head, it immediately fell into place. All of the beads made the fabric seem heavy. The dress fit perfectly. If it had been one-eighth of an inch smaller, I would not have been able to breathe. It fit like a glove.

The ensembles sent to me were never vulgar. Although they were formfitting, they were classy and stylish. This neckline was lower than the others but still not overly. When I turned to the mirror, I cried. In that moment, I realized that was my reference point. Never would I look that beautiful again. I longed to take a picture but knew that I agreed never to do such. Standing before me was a woman whom I would never forget. This was the best that I had or would ever look. The heels and jewelry were perfect. Whatever was expected of me tomorrow, I would dazzle as I performed it. The day was filled with anxiety as I tried to appear normal to Jean and Albert. Early in my job, the courier waited until my staff left for the day, but lately that had changed. I suspected that they did not see Albert and Jean as a problem. Once again, I explained to my dear staff that Rhonda was in crisis. They never questioned me but sadly nodded as though they longed to tell me perhaps my friend was overly dramatic.

Retreating to my studio, I thought what a perfect candidate I was for this job. My lifestyle allowed me to do whatever they needed without raising questions. I longed to hear the door close quietly behind Jean as she left for the day. Perhaps Frank would phone. I hoped that he might give me more details, although I knew that was not procedure. Soon enough, Jean and Albert left. From my bedroom window, I watched them walk arm in arm to their old Volvo.

I ran down to the kitchen, I was starving. In all of the excitement, I had not eaten since early morning. Gently simmering was a large pot of my favorite soup. The fragrance from the ginger squash was heavenly. Quickly, I ladled a large bowl, adding a dollop of sour cream. A large glass of Cabernet seemed the perfect companion. Usually, I would eat on the porch, but tonight, I longed to be safe. The next few days may be difficult. I planned an early evening. After my meal, I noticed a bundle covered in tin foil. Neatly wrapped were homemade ginger snaps. Jean was brilliant. I couldn't have planned a more perfect meal. Usually, the meals in Washington were heavy, so this was a nice way to launch my job.

After soaking in a warm bubble bath, I lounged in my room for a while. Then with great care, I packed for the standard two-day assignment. Sometimes, I finished in one day, but I was told to always pack for two. When my task was completed, I sat my bags by the door for my driver tomorrow. Suddenly, I felt exhausted. As I climbed into bed, I noticed that it was only 8 p.m. but didn't care. I turned off the light and fell into a deep sleep, which was not what I expected.

The next morning, I was awakened by the alarm. Quickly, I arose and dressed for the day in a business suit. Soon enough, the driver arrived. He carried my bags downstairs. We were off. I never saw anyone at the airport whom I knew, which suited me. I did not feel like small talk on these days.

When I arrived in Washington, it surprised me to see a driver waiting. He held the placard with my name high. Frank had not mentioned this but had told me once that some of the group were provided with a driver. I had concluded that "man magnets" were not. Feeling very special, I held my hand up and was whisked away.

Long ago, I had ridden in limousines. The petition between me and the driver was tightly drawn. In a playful manner, I picked up the phone to hear the dial tone. There was no one for me to phone. Inside a closed panel, I found a bottle of what smelled like bourbon. Nestled in their places were two crystal glasses. *What changed my status?* I wondered. Why all of the sudden luxury? I had not even done anything yet.

The driver escorted me to the front desk. A handsome young man smiled at me pleasantly. Usually, the clerk barely looked at me. This time, he was falling all over himself to be of assistance. The bellhop then escorted me to one of the highest rooms. When he opened the door, I gasped. I was standing in a very regal suite. Had there been some sort of mistake? Maybe I had been given Frank's accommodations.

When I opened the door into the bedroom, there sat Frank at a desk on the telephone. The bellboy smiled at me as he carried my hanging bag and case into the closet. Frank stood, walked toward me, and kissed me right in the mouth. Not a peck but a tongue inserted sloppy kiss. I smiled as I gushed, "Hello, darling, I have missed you so much." Then I grabbed him, passionately kissing him. He pulled away from me with a flabbergasted look. The young bellman rushed from the room.

"Frank, what the heck are you doing in my room?"

"This is our room, darling. Rather nice, wouldn't you agree?" His eyes gleamed that devilish look.

"Since our affair has gone on for so long, I am more comfortable with treating you as if you are my wife, darling. We both know that I am leaving Jenny soon. Oh, I have missed you." He walked to a cabinet and turned on classical rock at a very loud volume. I expected security to knock down our door demanding quiet but remembered we must be stationed in one of their best suites.

Frank grabbed me. He threw me on the bed. To my surprise, he climbed on top of me. I became so dumbfounded that I didn't move. He placed his mouth on my ear, "Cat, from now on, the group wants us to appear as a couple. We need to always be together. Your reaction to me earlier was exactly what they want. That was brilliant. The group will be impressed. Our room is clean, but we need to always be careful. Are you following me, Cat?" I nodded.

The rest of the day, Frank wrote on all sorts of forms. I brought a book, so I quietly sat in the corner as I read Grisham's latest. Exactly at six thirty, Frank startled me by almost yelling, "Let's get ready. We should go on down to the bar for a drink. What do you say, gorgeous?"

Running to his side, I almost knocked him over as I loudly stated, "This is our time. Anything that you want, my angel." Frank put his finger in his mouth as if he was trying to vomit. I smiled. This was fun.

After I showered, there was a knock at the door. My hairdresser arrived. She carried a picture of a hairstyle, which she had never styled for me. It was an elaborate French twist with diamond pins. When she finished, I walked back to our room. Soon applying my makeup, the tension mounted. The shower was running as Frank also prepared. Gently, I pulled the red dress over my hair. I had become an expert at this. I noted that not a hair was pulled out of place. The shoes and jewelry had just been added when Frank walked out with a towel around himself. I turned. He threw his hands up in the air, which allowed the towel to fall. There he stood in all of his glory. He was a good-looking man.

"Cat, I have never in my life seen anyone as beautiful as you look tonight." When he realized his mistake, he merely smiled as he picked up the towel. I thought of the song, "Lady in Red." I did a small bow. He was beaming.

From the time that we left our room until we were seated at a table in the bar, it seemed that everyone whom we passed, turned and stared. Not just the men but the women as well. My mother always said it was easy to impress a man; just show cleavage, but when you impressed other women, that was something indeed. I must have been something.

The principal event was some sort of state dinner with dignitaries coming from all over the world. The ballroom of the Willard was conveniently chosen. After our drinks, we walked to the nearby room, which was already crowded. Frank whispered, "You know the drill. Work the room and smile."

Upon entering, I kissed him passionately. The gasps from several local women were audible. I hoped that I wasn't overplaying my role because even old Frank was perspiring. Not me, I was cool as could be. Working the room, I double kissed everyone that I knew and some that I didn't. The men were drooling. I had been instructed to pick up a glass from the tray and moisten my lips but never drink. Then I would walk to another part of the room and sit the glass down. This repeated all through the night. If anyone watched, they would assume that I was becoming highly inebriated. That was never the case. The music played a little too loudly but created festiveness. Soon enough, my lover, Frank, returned.

"Okay Cat, show time. Your target is that dark-skinned man over there in the tux. Your assignment is to get him to notice you. You should remind him of someone from his past, if you can get his attention. Since he lost her, he is not interested in emotional involvement. He is a cold one." Then he walked off.

Now I perspired. I walked closely to the man, even rubbing against him slightly. He merely nodded. Immediately, he returned to conversation with an older gentleman. I had no clue what to do. Then I noticed an ice sculpture positioned behind my target. It was small so my plan should work. Walking slowly to the buffet table, I saw Frank watching with interest. I picked up a plate while I seemed to be surveying the food. Making a point of stopping by the sculpture, I turned to my left, adding a small canapé to my plate. Then I quickly turned. I knocked the ice sculpture off the pedestal.

As I watched it fall, I made an effort to catch it. This allowed me to fall. There I was in my gorgeous gown, lying on the floor atop the mound of ice. Everyone turned to look. No one moved for the longest time. My eyes met those of the target. He was indeed handsome. He looked at me with compassion. I moaned how sorry I was to be such a klutz. To my absolute disbelief, he walked slowly to me, helping me gently from the floor.

His accent was heavy. I guessed Saudi. "Miss, are you injured?" He seemed innocent. I felt very guilty until I happened to see Frank standing behind the table. If he could have, he would have danced. All of the disappointments I had caused him were erased at that moment. The target could not take his eyes from me. He seemed genuinely surprised as though he recognized me. Gently, he brushed the ice from my shoulders. Then good old Frank came rushing to my aide.

"Oh my darling, are you hurt?" He was definitely overplaying his role. We hurried as he wrapped his jacket around me. "Let's find our host. We need to get you back to the room. What a traumatic thing to have happened." He held his hand out to the target.

"Very nice to see you again. I would love to introduce you to my love, but we need to get her back to the room. We hope to see you sometime in the future." With that, we exited the room.

Frank did not speak until we were safely back in the room. Then he grabbed me as he planted a big kiss on my cheek. "You were brilliant. Many from the group were there. You passed the test with flying colors. Welcome to the group."

Instead of going to bed, I was whisked out the back door into an awaiting car. We were driven to a restaurant. As we entered a private room in the back, everyone stood and applauded. I recognized some of the faces. The applause went on for a very long time. There were toasts welcoming me to "the group." Now I could enjoy the evening.

27

NOT WHAT I EXPECTED

Frank and I really did enjoy the evening. We wallowed in the limelight. He looked so pleased with me. I was thrilled. Not sure of what I had done, nonetheless, I enjoyed the respect. We both drank too much that evening. All the way back to the hotel, we gabbed about one thing then another. I loved having a driver. Frank told me "get used to it." Jim was now my driver as well as Frank's. Always charming, I enjoyed Jim. We told him to keep the partition down on the way back to the hotel. I got the feeling that was unusual.

When we arrived back at our room, Frank reiterated how proud he was of me. He kissed me lightly on the cheek—the kiss given to a best friend or sister. He called "dibs" on the bathroom. That was fine with me. I wanted to enjoy the way that I looked one more time. When he came into the room from his shower, he didn't even look at me. He entered the other room. I heard him pulling out the sofa sleeper. He made his bed. There were no other sounds.

The next morning, I slept much later than usual. When I knocked on his door, he was already gone. I took my time dressing for the day then ordered room service. Just as I completed my morning paper and breakfast, Frank entered.

It was business as usual. No more gloating over our huge success of the night before. "Well, the group seems to think that we won't hear from the target for a few weeks. He will need time to digest what happened. Then determine if it was a set up. Yes, he is a cool operator." I thought of the song by Sade. The song's description seemed perfect for this man.

"Does the target have a name?" I asked innocently.

"Now, Cat, I am proud to tell you that you have been promoted. Please do not think you are an agent. You are not nor will you ever be such. Are you following me?" I merely nodded.

"Anyway, your little promotion does provide a few perks such as Jim, the driver. You will also have a suite waiting now. There will be a small increase in your pay, which is already very generous for someone of your limited statue. Are you following me?"

Nothing could dim my shine. I received a promotion, as well as the respect of my peers. That was priceless to me. I nodded again, waiting for Frank to give me instructions for the day.

Immediately, he continued, "That being said, you are free to return to Eufaula. If the target phones requesting to see you again, we will contact you. Are you following me?"

"Frank, I follow but wonder why the target would phone to see me. He thinks that you and I are so in love." I already knew that he would remind me to, "do as you are told and do not ask questions. Are you following me?"

Instead, he surprised me by adding, "The target knows Washington. Everyone in this town is fickle. If most single women think they can climb the ladder or get a better deal, they will take it. Are you following me?"

No longer did Frank's questions provoke me. I found them comforting. "What do you mean, 'get a better deal?' You are a pretty good deal if you ask me."

"Cat, I mean money. If they can get someone with more money, that means higher social status. Are you following me?"

"Yes, but what about love?" I felt like an innocent child from the look that he gave me.

"Love, what is that? Doesn't exist in Washington society, not unless it is one of the few couples who hang in there through the years because they really do love each other. That is few and far between though, if you ask me." He smiled.

"Now, go on home. You were excellent last night. The reservations are made. Jim arrives in one hour to pick you up. That should allow you plenty of time to paint when you get home. Are you following me?"

Smiling as I nodded my response, I started to pack. Frank returned to whatever he did all through the day as he pored over papers. Gently, I removed the beautiful dress and wrapped it in tissue. Lovingly I placed it in the bottom of my bag with the shoes and jewelry. It only took me a few moments to pack. Frank said I should always carry a book. Now, I sat reading Jeffrey Archer's latest, which was difficult to put down. As the plot thickened in my book, I forgot about Frank, the target, or the group. The phone softy rang.

Frank looked surprised as he nodded to me. The excitement in his voice was apparent. "You have got to be kidding. Are you kidding me? You have got to be kidding. Are you kidding me?" He smiled and stared at me. Now what?

After hanging up the phone, he turned with a foolish grin. "Forget Eufaula, Cat. We are going to the International Marina here in Washington. It seems that the target phoned my office, talked with your ex-lover Jim, not the driver, but my coworker."

"Frank, I know who my ex is although I don't really think he was an ex-anything. Remember, I was told that he was merely testing me to see if I was good enough to sleep with the target." I laughed.

"I'm really glad that you brought that up, Cat. You see, what we now want is for you to take the stakes a little higher. Your assignment, should you take it." He smiled. I felt like an agent in *Mission Impossible*.

"Anyway, we want you to sleep with him. In fact, we want you to make him fall in love with you. Are you following me?"

"Are you kidding me?" I guessed that he had said it so much that I couldn't help myself.

"Cat, why do you always question me? Just do as you are told. You can never go wrong if you do as you are told in spite of your exalted status. Are you following me?"

That was it. He was starting to annoy me. One could only be around Frank for about a day without his becoming extremely annoying. Still, I smiled and nodded as was expected.

"I am following you. Do you mind if I ask what the game plan is now? I mean why are we meeting him at the marina?"

"We are meeting him at the marina because he just called someone whom he believes to be my good buddy to inquire how serious you and are in our little love affair. Good ole Jim explained that although I seemed to be madly in love with you, I really love my wife. Sadly, he explained that I will never leave her. You are in it for the ride, so to speak." He smiled.

"All of that is fine, but why the marina?" I still did not know how the lies were mounting.

"Because good ole Jim explained that you, Cat, are an avid sailor. There is not much that you like more than a big ole yacht and spending time on the water. Except for a good time. Are you following me?" He smiled devilishly.

"Well, you guys just messed up. I share my mother's disdain for boats. That was about the only thing that Mom and Dad argued over. I actually thought that they may separate when they were younger. Each weekend, he wanted to sail. My mom hated it, so do I. You may have assumed that because of my dad's love for boats, which I'm sure you discovered, that I would also. I hate boats. Don't know a thing about them. Don't want to either. Are you following me?" I couldn't resist.

Just at that moment, there was a knock on the door. Frank smiled. This was not good. I knew him well enough to read his looks. He was enjoying something.

When he returned, he carried a rather large box with a bright red ribbon. It reminded me of the red dress, which I wore last night. The box appeared to weigh a great deal. "This is for you, Cat. Compliments of the group. We hope that you enjoy it."

He walked back to the desk and turned with a large smile. I opened the box with disdain.

"You have got to be kidding me. Chapman's? Frank, I can't do this. I hate to disclose it. I get seasick in a fierce way. I'm sure that the target or my new love interest or whatever I am supposed to call him will lose all interest when I throw up all over his fancy yacht." The thing that I hated most in the world would now be my latest assignment. Sailing had not been on my agenda for years. My goal was to keep it that way.

"Read the book, Cat. We are sure that you know a lot more about boating than you pretend. You could not possibly have spent as much time as you did with you father without soaking up some info. We also know that you do not get seasick, although that was a good try. Now if you had been forthcoming with us, you would have been able to read your little fiction book for a few hours. Now read Chapman's. There is a page in the front of the book, which tells you which chapters you need to know by 2 p.m. You have a few hours. I must go to the office. Have fun, Cat. Are you following me?"

He left with that huge smile. I opened the dreaded Chapman's, which Dad insisted that Mom, Nat, and I study. I had just learned to never lie to the organization.

28

I MET FARID

I spent the next two hours reading Chapmans. I already knew pretty much everything, which I read by heart. Any boating enthusiast knows that Chapmans is required reading. Dad kept several copies. You could find them on the boat or on a shelf in his room. Actually, I was an avid sailor. I had grown up spending treasured moments with Dad on our boat. That was not counting all of the Caribbean sails on chartered vessels. Yes, the organization was pretty smart. I would never lie to them again. I don't know why I lied at all except that I was in a panic. It would have been nice to have time to think about how I was going to play my target. Was I actually thinking like that? What happened to my honest natural self? Something happened to me since becoming part of the group. Now, I was lying just as they did. Still I hoped that the group didn't think less of me. Maybe I had hurt my standing by getting caught in a lie. Now I had so much more to consider. If only I could put Chapmans down, giving some thought as to how I was going to make a man like this fall in love with me. Instead of thinking, I did as I was told. Just as it had been drilled into my mind. "Act, don't react." I could hear Frank's banter and his anger as those words were repeated to me for years. It never entered my mind that I was being brainwashed. No, not me. I was just enjoying playing a game.

The required chapters were finished as I realized that I only had a business pants suit, which I was wearing. What was I supposed to wear to dazzle on his yacht? I could picture the opulence of his boat. Dad would have hated the vessel, which I pictured in my mind. He hated ornate yachts.

Now I panicked again. Should I call Frank on his cell, which was something I had been told was only for an emergency? Since my promotion, the pressure had increased. I would surely be held to a higher standard. As I reasoned the pros and cons, I paced back in forth by the window. Our room faced the busy street below.

Standing there in my panic, I saw Jim, the driver pull in front. Frank exited with a large box. I would just bet that the boys had come through. Yes, they were good. I should just learn to trust them.

Frank entered with his big smile handing me the box. "Cat, we are amazed. You are really professional. I'll just bet that you considered calling me on my cell. That is something that you were instructed to use only in emergencies. Am I correct?" I smiled back and nodded.

"You are getting it now. That is a great example of 'do as you are told.' Really good job. Here is your reward. This one is on us. You can keep this ensemble. I'll bet that you can't wait to sail. We know that you love it." With those words, he handed me the box. As he closed his door, I knew that he would be changing for our assignment.

Butterflies filled my stomach. I felt as though there was a lump in my throat. As I opened the box, I was pleased to see Purple Label Ralph Lauren white linen shorts, which were lined, as well as a simple blue tee. At the bottom of the box was a pair of dark-blue Todd drivers. It seemed the perfect outfit, which would provide nonslip shoes, as well as comfortable attire without seeming as if I was trying very hard. In no time, Frank and I were both changed and on our way to the marina.

He was good at driving quickly as he maneuvered through the heavy traffic. The marina was located downtown. It was easy to see the Washington Monument as we drove. Washington was an interesting place.

Walking down the boardwalk, we searched for the name that we had been given. Frank advised me to keep my eyes peeled for a boat named *Sanaa* which was an Arabic name meaning, brilliance. It was a female name. I wondered if this was the woman who my target lost. A million questions filled my mind. Most of all, I hoped that I would be successful in fulfilling my mission. My quest to be respected as part of the team had become important. I wasn't sure why really. Certainly, everyone was nice enough, but I had no friendships in the organization except for Frank, Jenny, and Barrington whom I had become certain was a player in all of this. Was it my desire to please Frank, which had become so important, or was it payback for Jim and the chauvinistic way, which he had treated me? It just wasn't clear to me, but I did desire to understand my motivation. How far would I go to please them? Still, without questioning my motives, I did as I was told.

As we walked in the heat of the day, there was a pleasant breeze, which would make being on the water nice. Frank explained that the vessel would probably be Italian and very ornate. That made me think of my father. He always had been a purist about his boats. He despised anything garish on the water.

"A sailboat should be white with dark-blue waterline trim. There is no point in adding a bunch of stupid décor!" He had been adamant about his standards. Never did he change throughout his life and procession of over twelve different boats of various sizes. Also he stressed that a boat need not be huge to be seaworthy. It was interesting to see the choice someone made in purchasing their boat. I believed that it said much about their personality.

"Oh my word, look at that boat. There she is. There is *Sanaa*." I excitedly pointed to a very large vessel. It was apparent why that name was chosen. She was brilliant. Frank said she was called a mega yacht. Italian, she filled her slip at one hundred forty feet. Sleek and gorgeous, she was beyond words. Dad would have hated it for another reason. He preferred sailboats. He disliked powerboats, but I was impressed.

Suddenly, from nowhere, the target, casually walked toward us. What was it with all of these men and their sparkling teeth? I rubbed my tongue over my "not so pearly ones." My handsome target could not take his eyes off me. I relaxed a little. This seemed easy now. I could do this.

"So nice of you both to join me in a little boating today. Nice day for it wouldn't you agree?" Again, his eyes were locked on me. Suddenly, I felt inept and foolish. Who was I trying to impress? This sheik or whatever he was would not be impressed with someone so simple.

Feeling out of my league, I found it impossible to speak. I mumbled, "Yeah, nice enough." Frank glared at me. There was instant rapport between the two men. I wondered if Frank should stop trying to be his best friend. Wouldn't that make it harder for my sailor to "put the moves on me" if he double-crossed his buddy? Still, Frank was the agent. I still felt like merely the "man magnet."

"Please, come aboard." Our host was most gracious. Frank introduced us at last. The handsome Saudi was named Farid. He was beautiful. *Sanaa* was beautiful as well. He gave us the tour. It was impressive. Much too quickly, we were underway. Farid's captain powered us gracefully from the slip. We glided effortlessly across the water.

"I so enjoy the Capital Yacht Club. This deep draft of eighteen to twenty-two feet allows entry to be easy and enjoyable. Of course the location right in the center of your Capitol is convenient. I enjoy America immensely." He looked at me. Did he think that I might be easy and enjoyable? I hoped so. That should make it easy for me to get him interested in at least spending some time with me. Maybe that would allow me to complete my assignment, quickly advancing on to some larger and more important one.

I complimented him on the beauty of his boat and the fact that she was indeed brilliant as her name implied. Farid smiled with pleasure to know that I had done a little homework on him.

"Sanaa was my most beautiful wife. We were married for over twelve years until she died suddenly in child birth. I lost my only son and my beloved wife as well. My boats will always be named after my beloved. In her honor, I also have my other Sanaa. She is a Ferretti 230." Again, the smile. I gulped. Was it he or the boat that caused such a reaction?

Being with Farid was extremely pleasant. We talked while laughing often. Frank sat like a sullen statue in the back of the boat. Now he was behaving just as I would imagine. Appearing to be the jealous boyfriend may cause Farid to react to his antagonistic behavior.

"Darling, isn't Farid's boat just perfect? We could never afford anything like this, could we?" Frank simply glared at us and shook his head. The day was really becoming fun. I enjoyed being superior to Frank. Now I felt completely relaxed. Farid was a true gentleman. I could get accustomed to his company.

On this day of bright dark-blue sky covered with puffy white marshmallow clouds, I felt free as I felt when I was a child. It surprised me to discover that I did indeed love the gift of boating. The light Southern breeze allowed us to glide smoothly across the waters. Occasionally a wave crested. Farid took the helm. He was in his element. The captain excused himself as the three of us laughed like old friends. The Potomac was beautiful. We were in good company as we soared past beautiful sailing boats, as well as other powerboats. Farid explained to me that he loved sailing, but Sanaa had not felt comfortable, so they seldom sailed together.

My handsome host was attired in all-white which only accentuated his dark hair and skin. He glowed in the light. His smile dazzled. It was difficult for me not to stare. Still, I played him like a pro. I could feel the beginning interest pique to much more. Lightly, he would touch my hand. Those touches sent fire down to my soul. Was I playing him, or was he the pro? Wishing only that I could be given more information, I knew better than to ask. Now it no longer mattered. I knew that my feelings for him were too strong to go back to merely playing the game. This was more. I desired to have a romantic relationship even if it wasn't real. What was wrong with me? Did I have no respect for myself?

Our time together flew past. Frank continued to glare, refusing to speak. This suited Farid and me just fine. Conversation flowed freely between us. The sparkle in his eyes told me that he did indeed find me interesting, worth the pursuit. Twilight was near. We sailed back to the yacht club.

Frank finally excused himself. He played his role so well. I wondered if there may be some real jealousy. As he exited below, Farid put his hand on my arm.

"Cat, why are you with a married man? That isn't right, you know. I realize that I barely know you, but you are so much more than that." I needed to respond quickly.

"I have lost someone that I love as well. You see, I don't want to love again. It seemed easier to just have a good time. I know that Frank loves his wife, Jenny, so do I. We are all friends. Honestly, I know that my behavior is pathetic and immoral, but I am so lonely. At night, I long to be held, caressed. I miss Luke so much."

"I know just what you mean. You see, I too have sworn to the sacred memory of Sanaa that I will never marry again. There will be no more children from my loins. I believe that she should be the only one to bear my children. My future holds no joy only a few pleasant afternoons such as this. In fact, Cat, why don't you consider spending your time with me? I am not involved with anyone since the loss of Sanaa so long ago. We could enjoy our lives together without feeling as if we betrayed memories of those whom we loved. The only ones that we could ever love, right?" He smiled again.

Just at that moment, I heard Frank begin his ascent up the ladder to the stern. I looked into Farid's eyes. I sold my soul. The future for me would become the happiest in my life, but the price that I would pay for that brief happiness would consume me. Frank's head appeared. He continued his pouting as before.

"Cat, we should go. Nice of you to ask us to join you, Farid. I'm sure that we shall see you around." He smiled a very insincere smile.

"Sorry, Frank, but I'm spending the rest of this day with Farid." I could not take my eyes off Farid. His look was that of victor as he smiled an asinine smile at Frank. Good ole Frank played it like the pro, which he was. He argued. He cajoled, but with great fanfare, he accepted his loss with the winning of the prize to Farid.

Farid grabbed me. He kissed me passionately on the mouth as he whispered, "Catherine, you will never regret this. I will make you the happiest woman on earth."

Frank angrily walked off the dock. He turned and yelled, "You will regret this, Cat." I smiled at my new love as my assent into the game was sealed.

29

MY FIRST DATE WITH FARID

Out of nowhere, a beautiful young woman appeared. She was dressed in very short pants with a sheer blouse, all in white. It was apparent that she was one of the crew. Carrying a platter of fresh fruit with yogurt and crackers, she politely asked me if I wanted a drink. Her manner was friendly but professional. We smiled as I realized that it was cocktail hour.

I wasn't sure if Farid would consider drinking, so I stalled. I pretended trying to make a choice. He immediately asked for a glass of pinot grigio, which I seconded. An incredible sound system filled the air with Frank Sinatra singing with the Tommy Dorsey Band. To my surprise, Farid held out his hands and pulled me gently to my feet. We danced. He was the most incredible dancer whom I ever accompanied. We glided as best we could in boat shoes together as though we had danced hundreds of times. The music kept playing. We kept dancing. The wind increased, which was perfect. I did not want this time to ever end. Could this be real? Would we actually find happiness even though it had all started as a lie? One day, would I confess to him the truth about this silly organization? Would I apologize for being so foolish? Would he love me just as he had loved his "most beautiful wife?" I so wanted him to love me.

For some reason, as we danced, I could see my father's face and hear his voice. It was as if I were a child as he reprimanded me, "Now see here, Cat, your impetuousness will be your downfall." Would this impetuous behavior with Farid be my downfall? Suddenly, I turned quickly just as the wind blew hard behind me. Farid held me firmly and smiled.

"It is just the wind, Catherine, my love." He kissed me lightly as a chill spread from the base of my back to my knees. I shivered slightly.

"What is this? Are you chilled, darling?" I shook my head as tears slid down my face. I knew this was a terrible mistake. It would only end in disaster. I felt unable to end it.

Right on cue, the music changed from Frank to the Moody Blues, which was one of my favorite groups. This music was more to listen and ponder instead of dance. As the orchestra's haunting notes filled the air, I collapsed on the seat at the stern. Farid, who had no idea what was going on in my head, sat down beside me with a large smile. I was physically shaken, unable to speak.

"I understand. They are so wonderful, right? That is the cause of your emotion, my love?" I only nodded as I held him tightly,

"Well, I have learned something very important today. You react strongly with emotion to this most lovely music." He tenderly held me as the words from song after song echoed across the waters. It was magical. Eventually, I determined that my father's warnings had always been rebuked by me. Why start listening now? We sipped our wine and ate the delicious fruit. Large strawberries dipped in tangy Greek yogurt with the wine. Farid suddenly rang a small bell.

Another member of the crew appeared, this time a handsome young man with the same white shorts but a shirt with braided gold. His shirt bore navy-blue epaulets on the shoulder. Farid nodded.

"Humphreys, bring us the best champagne instead of this very nice wine." Immediately, Humphreys disappeared. Soon he returned with a silver tray holding two champagne glasses. Several small linen cocktail napkins with a tasteful Sanaa embroidered on the front, laid to the side. Immediately behind him appeared the young woman with a bottle of chilled champagne carried in a teak champagne holder. All was quickly set by Farid who smiled again.

He poured two glasses of the French champagne whose bottle I recognized as something my mother loved. We touched our glasses as our eyes met. Over an hour passed as we sat sipping our glass of champagne, not a word was spoken. Suddenly, Farid leaned into my side. Pulling me gently toward him, he kissed me. This was a different kiss. I could feel the desire. Clinging to him, I returned his kiss just as passionately. Quickly, he pulled away with a sad, foreboding look.

"Catherine, I need to move very slowly. There is much for me to consider. I must be sure that you are real. It would be too much for me to lose another love. Do you understand? You see, I feel much more for you too quickly. Sanaa and I were promised to each other. For years, we only passed each other. When the time came for us to be joined, we barely knew each other. Yet I loved her with a love that is hard to describe. Only if you have experienced such a love would you understand. Do you understand?"

The lies just tumbled from my mouth as I looked him directly in the eyes. "Yes, I do understand. My love for Luke was such. His love for me as well. I miss him terribly." Tears streamed down my face not for the loss of love but for yet another lie. Farid only held me. I smelled the salt on his shirt with a very light scent, which was so clean. Feeling dirty and false, I continued to cry.

"There, my love, have a good cry. I can't tell you the number of times that I have wept for my loss. Sometimes, I think that I can't cry again, but I hear a song or return to a place, the grief wells up inside. Never will I fault you for your tears over your love. Let us never be jealous of each other's lost loves. Is that a promise? Our first promise, correct?" He smiled.

Finally, the tears stopped. I felt as if my heart would break. Still, I remembered Frank's words, "We don't care about your feelings. Just do as you are told." Now I had someone who did care about my feelings. Someone who cared for me. It was all very confusing. I managed to continue my lies, "I promise, but you know that I will always love Luke." He nodded.

"Now that we have shared something so vital of ourselves, let us have dinner. Do you enjoy lamb?" Actually, I had never eaten much lamb. My father loved it, but my mother did not. My mother ruled our house, so I had mostly seen my father enjoy it at different restaurants.

Easily, I lied, "I just love lamb. It is one of my favorites."

"I knew that we would be together when I saw you that night. Remember?" Again, the dazzling smile of love. Before I could answer, the sliders at the stern opened to reveal a huge dining table extraordinarily set for two with Versace china. The entire setting something from a magazine. There were long white tapered candles. The massive silver salt and pepper shakers with matching napkin rings only added to the splendor. He escorted me to the table. As he pulled my chair to seat me, he kissed me again.

"Our first of many dinners together, my love." He seated me. Carefully, he sat down beside me. Magically, two members of the crew arrived with another bottle of the champagne and appetizers. Each morsel only titillated my palate for another. Much too quickly, the plates were removed. The meal continued. Whoever the chef was on this yacht, he knew lamb. It was delicious. Yes, this was a lie, which I could honor. We laughed. Kissing each other frequently, we relinquished tales of our childhood. I was beginning to understand him. He had been very Westernized. Much of his time as a child spent in London, as well as the Far East. His tales were something from a book as he described, not meaning to boast, his elaborate childhood and education. His family was loving and supportive. We had both been blessed with successful parents who loved us.

Soon yet another course, then we were escorted by a member of the crew inside the main salon. Waiting for us was another platter. This was covered in a sinful dessert of meringue and fruit. Hot coffee was carefully poured into Versace cups. Earlier, I had thought that I could not eat another bite, but I found myself indulging in several cups of coffee and two servings of the light sugary concoction.

Soon, Farid yawned, and I knew that it was decision time. Obviously, he expected me to stay the night, but should I? Trying to decide what Frank would want me to do, my mind was hurling different scenarios of possibilities when he gently said, "My love, you know that I would love for you to stay. It pains me to send you home alone, but that is the way. We will be together soon. Yes."

This was perfect. Yes, nice and easy would allow me to plot my strategy, which might save me from a costly mistake. This man had a sixth sense. It amazed me that I had been able to keep him from becoming suspicious tonight, but I knew that it was only a matter of time. He would certainly investigate my past. Would there be trails of Frank, Jim, and Barrington? I could only continue the masquerade.

Before I knew what was happening, I found myself in a chauffeured car. I turned to see Farid standing in front of his yacht as he happily waved good-bye. I was escorted to my room at the hotel. Not a word was spoken. The escort nodded then was gone.

Entering the suite, I noticed that everything "Frank" was removed. Thinking that I would be flooded with melancholy, I was surprised to find myself feeling giddy. Once again, I felt like a schoolgirl with her first crush. Did he love me? Tomorrow, I would return to my home in Eufaula. The plane ticket for tomorrow's exit was lying on the table under the lamp. Glorious Eufaula, my home, and friends awaited. I only hoped that I would never hear from Frank and the organization again. I was finished with them, however, just beginning with Farid at least, I hoped.

30

EUFAULA AT LAST

The next afternoon, I arrived home without any trouble. Peace awaited me at my sanctuary. Upon entering, I found Jean and Albert sitting in the kitchen.

"Where have you been? We have been so concerned. You haven't answered your phone for two days. Rhonda phoned. She seemed very confused about your being there, although she did finally admit that you were. Each time we called, she stated you couldn't come to the phone. She called yesterday saying that you had left. Nat and Ginger have phoned several times. He is running for the House or Senate or some such big deal. Margie phoned as did Linda. We were discussing phoning the police. Are you well?" Their worried faces and distraught manner made me laugh.

"Please, don't ever phone the police when I am gone. You must promise." They looked at each other in confusion. Still, they shook their heads in agreement. "You know Rhonda gets things confused. Barrington keeps her too busy for her own good. She did finally admit that I was there, right? So you see, nothing to worry over. That crazy Jim has been trying to contact me. She was trying to protect me. I'll phone everyone right now. How about a 'welcome home' hug?" Oh, how easily the lies came to me now, almost second nature.

They looked confused, but each hugged me. The house looked as though I never left except for the yard, which looked even more incredible. Albert was the best gardener on the planet. He just didn't look the part of a gardener. Handsome and rugged, yet he spoke with knowledge on many different subjects. I never found him without answers.

Albert returned to the yard. Jean started a hearty stew. After putting the few clothes away, I went into my studio. The painting I had been working on before my trip waited eagerly for completion at the easel. I took a picture of my favorite location on the lake. Then I transformed it into a lifelike rendition on the canvas. I turned on Pavarotti. Finally, I began to paint. Thoughts of Farid filled my mind. So deeply did I miss him. What was he doing right now, and did he think of me? Would I ever see him again? Just at that moment, I heard the phone. Running into the hall, I heard Jean say, "There is no Mrs. Jones residing here, good-bye." She returned to the preparation of the stew seemingly without suspicion. I ran to my room. Turning on the fan in the bathroom and the radio by my bed, I phoned Frank. He answered immediately.

"Good going, old girl. We are proud of you. You couldn't have played it any better. You are a pro, Cat." His voice sounded cocky, which irritated me.

"Now, see here, Frank. This has to end. My feelings for Farid are real. I want out." To my surprise, Frank laughed.

"Oh, your feelings are real, are they? Sort of like your feelings for old Jim? Remember the one who made a fool of you? Catherine, you are so out of your league that it is shameful. Your brother, who is about to become a member of Congress, would be very disappointed. Your gallery, which is doing so well, would be shut down. Farid would be told about your association with a group watching him. Your little nephew, well, who knows when he may have an accident? What were you saying about being 'out?'"

I fell onto the bed. Sickness flooded my body. What in the world was I involved in?

"Frank, please tell me these are idle threats."

"These are not idle threats. We see everything that you do, Cat. Rhonda was covering for you because she was instructed to cover your butt, Cat."

"Do you mean that Rhonda is also involved?"

"No, she is married to one of us, you knew that. You figured out a great deal as anyone with intelligence would, but you haven't touched the tip of things nor will you ever. There is no 'getting out.' Not now, not ever."

The room was spinning. I slammed the phone into the cradle. Then I cried in hysteria. My family was threatened. Everything paled in comparison to possible harm of my nephew. *Farid, what have I done?* At that moment, I became aware that there was no going back. Quickly, I phoned Nat and Ginger. He answered, sounding innocent. I could not control myself, "Nat, are the children all right?"

Sounding most surprised, he assured me that things could not be better. He was amazed at how his run in the House had fallen into place.

"It is as if someone is staging everything. I had no idea I weld this sort of power. Ginger is president of the Junior League. Can you believe all of this?" Yes, I could but denied any idea that this was happening. I promised to visit soon. Then I phoned Rhonda. She chastised me for not contacting her sooner, instructing me that in the future, I should let her know if I needed her to give me an alibi.

"But, Cat, why do you need an alibi? You live alone and have no one to worry over you." Well, that was an encouragement. I assured her that it was nothing. I would probably need her to cover for me in the future.

"I'll just bet that you are involved with another married man. Cat, when will you learn?" I could not handle her innocence.

Hastily, I made an excuse for needing to shorten the call. Then I phoned Linda and Margie. Linda was not home, but Margie, just like Rhonda, went on about her life. Things seemed so normal and happy. I remembered having a similar life before becoming involved in the dangerous mess I now found myself.

My thoughts turned to Farid. They were devious. Frank probably would tell him about the truth just to keep me in line. After a long cry, I took a hot shower as though the soap and heat would remove the crime of my sordid life. Then I went downstairs to find Jean and Albert gone for the day. The chasm between us was penetrable to me now. Surely, they knew that something wasn't right. Maybe the group even contacted them. At any time, they may resign from my employment. What a mess I created by my impetuousness. Then I remembered dancing with Farid and hearing my father's voice chiding me for such reckless behavior that day.

Had I actually felt happy and loved in Farid's arms? I longed to see him and to have him hold me and comfort my fears. Yet I knew that anyone whom I drew into my hell would be in danger. I put the bowl away, refrigerating the stew. Nausea overcame me. I was unable to eat. With a heavy heart, I slowly walked upstairs. This was not the time for the intrusion of the telephone. It was Jill. Life for her was happy. She informed me that a strange man visited the studio about three days ago. He purchased all of the major paintings.

"We are almost cleaned out. Can you believe it? We made so much money. The studio is thriving. Can you come tomorrow? We need to decide, which artists you want to fund. Funny thing, it was mostly your paintings that the man purchased. He said he was a friend but wouldn't give a name. He said that you would know. Do you know who he is?"

"Yes, I know. That is great news. I'll be in tomorrow. Great work, Jill. I guess I need to take more trips." She continued with the latest news in Eufaula. However, she ended by saying that dear Mr. Greene had a fatal accident. It seemed that after leaving the studio one day, he had driven into the lake. No one could understand how it happened. Maybe he had a heart attack. An autopsy was pending. I knew how it happened. He paid a price for being my friend. Friend to the liar could be fatal. I was no longer surprised by what they did. Feeling numb and scared, I realized that I was just a pawn in a very dangerous world.

I went to bed as soon as the shower was completed. I dreamed of Frank and Farid. They seemed to be connected in my terrifying hell. The Willard Hotel was comforting in my dream until I heard him banging on my door. I yelled, "Go away, Frank." Over and over, he banged on my door until I awakened. Then I was aware that there was someone at the front door. Trepidation filled my soul. I calmly picked up my gun. I walked to the door. I could see the shadow of a man. Lifting the curtain covering the door's window, I saw him. This could not be happening. I opened the door, falling into the arms of my love.

31

OUR FATE IS SEALED

As I opened the door, Farid staggered inside. I could see the fire in his eyes. His face was hot. He grabbed me. "Catherine, I tried so hard not to do this. I know as do you that we are acting foolishly as children. Rushing a relationship is a grave mistake. Still, as foolish as it may be, please forgive me. I must have you. My time without you has been miserable. Each moment, you are in the back of my mind. Truly, this is more than just lust, although I will admit that is a large part. This is not a one-night stand. I don't do that. Since the death of Sanaa, I have not had another woman. There were plenty of opportunities, but I was never tempted. At least not until you came into my life." He grabbed me, kissing me very roughly. This was a side that I had not seen. I wondered, did he kiss his precious Sanaa in such a way, or was it because I was not as treasured? Of course, I did nothing. I returned the passion. Not because of the organization but because I cared for him.

After a long passionate kiss, he released me. "Catherine, I can see that you feel the same. Obviously, we know where this is going. Are you all right with this?" I was confused. He must know that I wanted him. Then he explained that he was referring to my strong feelings for Luke. I felt sickened. Without missing a beat, I looked sadly at him as I pledged my love to poor dead Luke, but that I was ready to move forward. Would the lies never cease?

"Good, good, but there are a few things that you need to know. I conducted an investigation on you. Not just on you but everyone in your life. This may sound strange. Someone in my standing must. You see, I am related to the royal line. My life is dangerous. There are things that I will never be able to explain. What I am asking is that you trust me. You must never question me about where I go or my actions. Sanaa could never do that. The only source of contention between us were her unending questions. She believed that if I loved her enough, I could tell her everything. That is not the way. Can you accept this? Are you prepared to live in such a way? I may be gone days, weeks, or even months without correspondence. Can you agree to this?" The passion burned in his eyes, yet he had the consideration to think of me. He cared of my feelings unlike the organizations' chiding that my feelings were unimportant.

I ached for him. I would have promised him most anything. I agreed that his request was acceptable. It did not even seem odd at that moment. Therefore, I wholeheartedly agreed.

"The other thing that I must explain is that you will never meet my family. The reason is they will not approve. It is not of you that they will object but to your nationality. Do you understand that, and can you accept that you will never be my wife? It does not mean that I will love you less, but you will never know the family support, which Sanaa was given. You will be as Americans call, 'the step child.'" Sympathetically, he looked into my eyes. Trying to hide the ecstatic feelings of not having to be drawn into his family, I sadly nodded. The lies were becoming easier each day. I had thought that he would want me to return with him to Saudi Arabia. I did not want that. Since 911, I had a disdain for the Muslim people. I knew there were good people, but it was hard for me to forget what happened. In the beginning of this assignment, I struggled with the fact that I had to pretend to love someone whom I considered the enemy. He changed my mind.

Farid, gently lifted my chin and smiled. "I am sorry, little one. I come with so many exclusions. Please know that I will make it up to you. Instead of Saudi, we will visit the home in Bali. You will love it. We shall go there soon. Are there any items that you need to discuss with me?"

Desperately, I wanted to yell, "Do you mean that you did an investigation and didn't find connections to a secret organization?" That gave me hope. I only wanted to be loved. That was all. With those thoughts, I nodded that there was nothing to discuss on my part.

Suddenly, he grabbed me with brute force and carried me to the bed. He dropped me and started to undress. This was not what I wanted.

"Farid, please, not so quickly. I want to remember this for the rest of my life. Can't we go slowly?" He was shaking.

"Do you know how long it has been since I was loved? I don't think that I can go slowly. Please, I promise to make this up as well, but right now, please?" Again I agreed to his request. Yet I slowly undressed him. Then he did the same. Now he was moving slower. Gently, he carried me again to bed. This time, he lovingly deposited me between the sheets as though I may break. Gently, he laid on top of me. Slowly sweet kisses lovingly covered me from face to feet. Now I begged him to hurry. He smiled as he must have thought of Luke and the time since I too had known love. I wondered why he didn't question the fact that there was no Luke in my past, but right now, it didn't matter. We made love all during the night. *Unbelievable* was the only word. We came together as if we were virgins. It thrilled me to find that he was a little awkward. I would have thought that he would be smoother. Later, he explained that Sanaa did not enjoy lovemaking. He must have really loved her. That would not be the case with me. I would be the lady in public but not in his bed.

The next morning, we were awakened by Jean and Albert's arrival. Farid looked startled. "You did not tell me that you had staff arriving. My bodyguard is downstairs. They are probably confused. He carries a gun."

I jumped from the bed. Covering myself, I ran into the kitchen. Jean looked pale. "Miss Catherine, are you well? There was a man guarding the door. He asked us many questions. He would not let us enter. We rang the bell and knocked. You are a light sleeper. Why didn't you hear?"

"Jean, all is well. I have a lover. He is very important. That is his bodyguard. I am so sorry to have startled you. Farid will be with me often now." Jean did not approve, I could tell. She nodded as a loyal staff member would. Then she turned to her duties. I returned to the room to hear the shower running.

"Catherine, join me. What a great shower." Of course, I entered the shower with my handsome lover. He washed my back and hair. He would not allow me to do the same.

"You my queen will be paid back every day of your life for all of the concessions, which you have so graciously given." After dressing, we both went downstairs. I introduced him to Jean. He requested eggs and tomatoes with toast. Jean appeared friendly but guarded toward him. After eating, I felt awkward. What now? It was great in the bed, but how did we spend our days? I was at a loss.

Instinctively, I walked to my studio. He followed. Opening the door to the bright room, I lovingly looked at my current painting. Farid whistled. He assured me that I was a very talented artist.

"You know, I once painted. It has been years, but I would love to try my hand. Do you have an extra easel? Would I, how do you say 'cramp your style?'" I smiled. It had always been my dream to have a partner who enjoyed art. Removing another easel and board, I put the can of brushes within his reach. Pavarotti was turned up. He smiled. We painted. Without talk, we just painted. Occasionally, he would squeeze my hand. The light in his eyes could not lie. He was happy, content. His art was exquisite. The touch of his brush was heavy. The paints, which he used, were bright and bold. The heaviness of his brush created deep marks, which were beautiful to me. My touch was light and more concise. We were complete opposites in our approach.

Jean knocked softly on the door. "Miss Catherine, I did not call you to lunch. I heard the music and did not want to interfere. The day is gone. Albert and I are leaving, but your steaks are prepared with baked potatoes and salad. There is a raspberry torte. I hope this is acceptable, Mr. Farid. Good-bye. See you tomorrow." Lightly her steps eased away.

Farid and I looked at each other with laughter as children who have been slightly scolded by their parent. We washed the brushes heading for the kitchen.

"I am starving. After we eat, there is something else for which I starve. Do you?" I nodded at him with happiness.

32

SO THIS IS NORMAL?

Our days together were as Pavarotti's music—smooth and soothing feelings surrounded indescribable joy. Sometimes at night, I would awaken wondering if we were moving too quickly. The episode with Jim remained painful, this too, felt surreal. We were behaving as a married couple, but I wanted it to be real. Even if we could never be married, I would give up almost anything to be with him. Was my pattern of behavior so obvious? Could there really be experts out there who could follow your actions as a child determining the choices you would make as an adult? How had I become so entrenched with a group of people who were able to stage my life? It didn't seem possible, yet I knew in my heart that there was a sinister presence in my life. Although the bells and whistles were ringing, I ignored them all, just as my mentors knew that I would.

A few mornings later, we were enjoying breakfast on the front porch as we read the morning paper. I was a speed reader. I found a particular article intriguing. I heard myself scream as I read that Mr. Greene's death was not the result of a heart attack. The case had been closed for lack of evidence. My hands started to shake. The truth was known to me. I knew Frank was involved. This was a message. Did Farid have knowledge? Was he part of this dangerous group? Paranoia encased my mind as a tomb.

"What is it darling? You look as if you have seen a ghost." I felt ill. Things began to spin around me. Farid helped me to my room. I could not stop shaking. He wet a washcloth and put it on my head.

"Catherine, please, what is this about?" The sincerity in his eyes erased my doubts. He was not Jim. I refused to believe that he could be involved. In fact, I may be placing him in danger. So I told him about Mr. Greene. He had no knowledge of him but promised to look into it. Again, a similarity to Frank who seemed capable of finding out anything. I slept all day. When I awakened, the room was dark. The house was ghostly quiet. Had Farid left? I ran down the stairs. There he sat in the darkness with a small reading lamp. He was busy at work on his computer.

"Well, there is my girl. You can't keep a good woman down, right, darling?" He seemed happy to have me by his side. I fell into his outstretched arms as a child might find solace in a parent. He kissed my head. We sat down on the sofa. He covered me with a blanket. After kissing me again, he left the room and returned soon with dinner.

"That Jean is a pretty good cook. I hope that you don't mind, but I have already eaten. It is something called mac and cheese with bacon bits. Jean says that is comforting food for you." I smiled. His misuse of the English language delighted my heart. I hungrily consumed with gusto Jean's pasta with a small salad and glass of wine. Then Farid left again. Soon he returned with more bowls.

"More of Jean's comforting food. This is really good. It is apple cobble." He smiled as he handed me a rather large bowl covered in vanilla ice cream. I noticed that he also had served himself another.

"Catherine, I have never been so happy. Honestly, I am content. However, I feel that it is time to expose you to my world. Instead of such a long trip to Bali, I want to take you for about two weeks to my home in Abaco, Bahamas. Let's leave in two days. Can you be ready?" He looked into my eyes. I saw my future there. Two days later, we flew in his private plane to one of his many homes. Mr. Greene's untimely death was forgotten for the moment. I would always think of him and miss his friendship. Had he died because of me? I did not believe in coincidences, so I had my answer. Someday, I would have the facts.

33

FARID AND SANAA'S HOME

As we flew over the pristine turquoise waters of the islands of the Bahamas, I already felt at home in Farid's private plane. Would I fit into his world of extreme wealth, or would he discover that I was not the interesting person that he thought? Would memories of Sanaa, his "most beautiful wife" overcome him, forcing any feelings of me from his heart? These ideas whirled through my mind.

Soon we landed. Things seemed typical of most of the islands. Farid's driver promptly appeared. We were loaded into his car. The intensity of the heat made my nervous condition even more perilous. This just did not seem right. Once again, this was another mistake on my part. Eufaula pulled at my heart. Home, I longed for home. Fighting back the tears, I ignored my heart. Trying to put on a tough armor, I smiled at Farid's comments. I was unable to hear him due to the rush of blood through my head.

Suddenly, we turned into a paved courtyard behind a white stucco wall. Standing in the center a lovely fountain welcomed us. The sound of water trickling over the stones was calming. The name on the wall was FarSan. It seemed an odd name. Farid's island home was lovely. It was not grandiose as I imagined but lovely. The entire outside was white stucco with a gleaming blue barrel cement roofing tile covered in a shiny glaze. The estate consisted of the main house with a smaller guest cottage. All of these effects gave a Moorish quality to the home.

As we entered, I commented on the strange name. Farid explained that he and Sanaa had fallen in love with the home due to the simplicity. They had taken the first part of his name with the first part of hers. The result was "FarSan." *Oh great*, I thought, *this should be interesting*. Her presence would be everywhere. I didn't stand a chance. We had made no plans, so I didn't know how long I would be here, but from the way things were going, probably, not very long.

The stark bright exterior soon was replaced with a darkened interior. Each of the rooms were large with a broad hall. The floor sparkled with glazed blue-and-white tiles. Most of the furniture seemed oversized and dark. We followed the stairs up to a large balcony from which there was a dark hall. I followed my host with sadness. The darkness inside was gloomy. All of this created a feeling of foreboding. Why would Sanaa create such an environment for her husband? As Farid opened the door into the master bedroom, I gasped. At last, light flooded through the windows. The walls glistened brightly white with cobalt-blue trim. Here, the furniture was light, whimsical. Sanaa's playfulness was apparent. Over their bed hung her portrait. Standing there, looking at his former love, I felt as if I was trespassing. She was stunning. The portrait was her standing in a garden. Her dark hair was cut into a bob. Large dark eyes glowed with health and light. The effect was mesmerizing. It was difficult for me to look at him. I saw no similarities between us. She was beyond beautiful.

Moments passed as we stood speechless before his love. Her presence filled the room. I was an interloper, a fake. Yet I could not stop staring at her face. She was younger than I. Her smile was slight. Yes, she knew that she was a beautiful woman. My demeanor fell as the moments passed.

Farid put his arms around me, pulling me close. "I never thought I would ever bring another woman here. Forgive me, I should have chosen another room for us. We shall move down the hall. There are plenty of rooms." Then I spied through the arched doorway leading into another room—her studio. The easel was graced with one of her paintings. Slowly, I walked as though drawn by a magnet. Yes, it was the magnet of creativity that drew me to her. There was the painting she painted before her death. Odd, I thought that she painted a child in a bassinet sitting in the garden. Alone, a small hand reached up into the air. Her strokes were magnificent—dainty, perfect small strokes with just the correct amount of paint. The flowers that surrounded the child were all red and white with touches of blue.

Everywhere, there shinned glints of blue. These colors made me think that her heart was here by the water in the glazed blue tiles at their home in Abaco. I longed to know her. She was his love. What other gifts did she possess? No wonder he loved her so deeply. I could feel her touching my heart. She was not jealous. No, she longed for Farid to be happy. It was as if she was telling me to love him. Make him happy. My presence in his life was blessed. Turning to him, I looked into the same dark eyes, which she possessed. His eyes also shined at me. This was meant to be. Not as Jim's scam but as a real love. If he loved me, it would be real. That was her message. All fears left as I hugged him tightly.

"I will love you. Yes, she would want us to love." Farid looked at me with confusion.

"What, my darling? Who would want us to love? I don't understand."

I smiled. I understood his confusion. "It is just that I love you so much. I feel that you should be happy. Will you let me love you? I mean really love you. Not a physical lust but a deep and abiding love such as you shared with that beautiful woman who graced your life? Of course, I realize that I can never compete with her. I don't want that." A small smile crossed his lips. He understood. Nothing more was spoken.

Quickly, we changed into our swimsuits. The waters were heavenly. No matter how deeply we walked into the turquoise bath, I could see the bottom covered with the white sand. The sand was soft as sugar. Farid gently hugged me. Lately, it seemed that our passion had changed into a quietness, a softness of touch and feelings. This felt more natural to me as things should be.

Our days were surrounded in Pavarotti—our reference to peacefulness. Time passed slowly as we shared long walks. Sunsets on the other side of the island found us holding hands as we sat on a blanket by the water. Sanaa was never mentioned. We never changed rooms. It was as though instead of becoming a wedge, she was the glue that held us. I understood. Farid appreciated that I respected with deep admiration the woman whom he loved. Perhaps she was watching us. Could she respect me as well? I could only hope.

Everything about this time was perfect except at the end. I would awaken discovering Farid gone from the bed. Several times, I walked to the end of the hall. I could hear voices speaking in an Arabic language. Often, the conversation seemed heated. Anger was apparent. These events repeated themselves night after night. Farid's earlier warning to me not to meddle, not to question came to mind. So I never mentioned waking to find him gone. He did not know that I heard the angry voices. That even once, I had seen the group of dark men dressed as Westerners. They were not. The clothes that they wore were very expensive. These men could pass as well-heeled Europeans. They were not. What was going on? I could only wonder. I felt an evil feeling. Each morning, I told myself that I overreacted as a silly woman. Sanaa questioned him. He told me that was the only source of contention. I would be more supportive than she. No, I would not speak of it unless he did. He never did.

Our love seemed to grow. His laughter was spontaneous. No more did he mention his wife. He doted on me. Several times, he presented me with staggering gifts of jewelry. Promises of trips to London and Bali abided. Our love was growing. Only the nights, when did he sleep? Only brief moments did he rest. Where did these strange men come from? Where did they go? Never, did I see them during our days. I was never introduced to them. It seemed that they were phantoms of my imagination. They were not.

One morning, he announced that he needed to return me to Eufaula. It was necessary that he leave for a while. He would return to my home as soon as possible. Dutiful love that I was, I never asked a single question.

34

CONFUSION

The plane ride from the Bahamas to Birmingham proved different than the one as we arrived. Farid barely looked at me. He appeared pensive, distant. There were no touches or kisses, no smiles or looks of love. Dr. Jekyll and Mr. Hyde was the only description. Tenseness filled the plane. When we finally arrived in Birmingham, he walked me onto the tarmac. "You will be driven from here back to Eufaula. I am in a hurry. Business you know." With a quick kiss and nod, he was gone. The car ride was uneventful. The driver never looked at me either. Besides my analogy to Jekyll and Hyde, I thought of the same feelings of confusion and chaos, which surrounded most of my episodes with Frank. Speaking of whom, I had received no calls. That suited me fine. Truly, I hoped that I would never be faced with him again but knew that to be untrue.

As I approached the house, it was midmorning. The summer intense heat baked the ground. Humidity caused trouble breathing. For some unknown reason, I decided to stop by Albert's green house. It had been several months since I was last there. As I approached, I admired all of his work. The yard was a masterpiece. How did he do it? Suddenly, I heard his voice speaking in fluent French. This was unbelievable to me. How could a simple farmer/landscaper be so fluent? This was not an elementary level as I spoke but spoken through years of use and training. I stopped in the doorway unable to move. He was laughing, appearing very happy. His speech was so advanced that I could not understand a word. Frozen, I listened in fascination. When he finally noticed me, he smiled. Quickly, he ended the call. Calmly walking toward me as though this was an everyday occurrence. Whose gardener didn't speak French, he seemed to say as he walked confidently my way.

"Albert, I didn't know that you were fluent in French. That is amazing. Where did you learn to speak like that?"

"Oh, I speak several languages. I teach myself on Rosetta Stone. They make it easy, you know."

"Well, I don't think so. You see, I also speak French and have visited there several times. The way that you speak is greatly accelerated." He only smiled.

"Welcome home, Miss Catherine. We have really missed you."

Now, unknowingly, I had learned several things from my experiences with Frank and the group. One of those morsels of information was that you never react. Always, you act, which to me in this situation meant that I would watch and learn. I did not press him further. The flag had been raised. I knew that he realized there was now a trust issue, which was heartbreaking to me. I was surrounded in lies and deceit. I had thought that the only reliable people in my life besides Nat and Ginger were Albert and Jean.

The lies were unfinished because Albert then sheepishly said, "Look, Miss Catherine, I have a friend in Paris. It is no big deal. I mean, it is not an affair but just a friendship. Jean doesn't know, so if you don't mind not mentioning it to her." That was the worst thing that he could say. I questioned his sincerity. If he was having any sort of relationship behind Jean's back, he was not whom I thought. This was extreme betrayal. I was disappointed. Nodding, I could only grimace. Then I walked inside as though

I was carrying the world's lies on my back. My entire life had developed into a lie.

As I entered the house, I smelled the heavenly scent of Jean's vegetable stew, a perfect meal for later this evening. Jean popped out of the kitchen with her freshly scrubbed glow. My heart felt sad that she trusted Albert so much. She would be brokenhearted to know that he was a liar as every man seemed to be. Even Farid had disappointed me. What was going on here?

Jean hugged me as she welcomed me home. I almost ran up the stairs. My sanctuary of the bright-yellow room called to me. Even there, I was saddened to see Farid's latest rendering of art. He had painted a bright scene of Lake Eufaula. It was glorious. The trees were all in bloom. In the center of the painting was a delightful ketch. She was sailing with two people aboard. The faces were faded. It was impossible distinguishing identity. You could see the boat zipping over the waters right in tune with the wind. For several moments, I stared with fascination. *This would bring a nice penny at Carnegie Hall*, I thought. As I continued to stare, I knew that I had to own that one. I would pay whatever price he set.

Seeing the painting only made me miss him more. Yes, I loved him in spite of all of the baggage. In fact, I couldn't imagine my life without him now. As the phone began its shrill sound, I ran for it. Could this possibly be Farid? No, I was delighted but a little disappointed to hear Ginger's soft croon. She went on and on about the children, all of the little things that children do. At that moment, I realized how tired I was from all of the drama of late. Albert's little secret shocked and saddened me.

When she finally completed her news, I walked to my easel. Carefully, I studied the painting that I had been working before the trip. Ah, yes, I remembered now the painting. It was my beautiful home. The house was indeed famous, so I decided that any number of patrons to the gallery would desire it. Carefully, I picked up a brush, but my heart just wasn't there. I knew better than to paint when I felt uninspired. I washed the brush and was tidying up the room when there was a gentle knock. I opened the door to see Jean.

"Miss Catherine, would you mind terribly if we leave a little early today? We have some friends coming for dinner. If it is not acceptable, we understand." Jean and Albert were such hard workers that even though I was upset with him, I quickly agreed that they should leave now. Soon, I heard the door quietly close behind them.

Once again, the intrusive ring of the phone shattered any peace. I was shocked to hear as I answered, "Mrs. Jones?"

"Oh, no Frank, not you. I just can't deal with your nonsense today."

"Right, Cat, now we are 'nonsense?'"

"Frank, please, this just isn't a good time."

"Well, you see, Cat, we don't care whether it is a good or bad time for you. For the billionth time, your feelings don't matter. Are you following me, Cat?" There was no point in protesting. I quietly listened as he praised me for the great way that things were going. The group couldn't be any more delighted. They thought that I had Farid just where "we" wanted him. He pumped me for information. Since, I didn't have anything important to report, I merely told him about Farid's latest personality change. I added the men who came and went in the night. If this was important, he made no sign of interest. When I finished relaying anything that I thought was important, I hastily added, "My gardener speaks French."

To my surprise, this got his attention. "Repeat, please." So I reiterated my latest info that Albert was fluent in French. This was added as a joke. It was meant to show how absurd I thought all of this.

"Catherine, very good. You never seem to stop surprising me. This is indeed noteworthy. Thank you for adding that. Well, got to go. Good-bye, Mrs. Jones." The line went dead.

After finishing a large bowl of stew on the front porch, I caught up on all of my past due issues of newspapers. I went inside, discovering a bite of dessert. Jean did not disappoint. Banana pudding waited all warm on the sideboard. Generously, I served myself a large portion.

Later that night, as I read my current Grisham, the phone rang. No one spoke. This was repeated three or four times. Odd, I thought that no one was on the line. Then I thought of Farid. Could he possibly be in danger, trying to contact me from a distant location? Those thoughts added to all of the sugar, which I digested, made for a sleepless night. My dreams of Frank, Farid, and now Albert were all intertwined. Chaos shrouded my once peaceful life.

35

FARID RETURNS

The weeks seem to move slowly without Farid. I wondered if Sanaa endured the sleepless nights and loneliness that loving him entailed. Trying to appear busy, I spent more time at the studio with Jill. Things were thriving there. About three weeks dragged past when one morning as I entered Carnegie Hall, Jill came rushing toward me.

"I am so glad that you have finally come!" She appeared flushed and breathless. Surprised, I explained that actually I had been in attendance more often than usual since my return.

"No, you don't understand. It has been exactly three days since you were here." It seemed like only yesterday to me. Apparently, I was in more of a haze than I realized. She went on to explain that there was an order from London for all of my paintings. Once again, we were without any of mine. It seemed that all of Farid's were also ordered. She and Albert packed and sent them yesterday. Albert seemed to be avoiding me, so I had not been given that news. Was the group once again trying to threaten me? This did not make sense. I had done everything that they demanded. Confusion, always confusion when they were in my life.

Jill continued to emphasize that I must paint more. "What is wrong with you? You have been back now for over three weeks.

Usually, you have several by now." She smiled as if I should magically produce as many as needed. Halfheartedly, I assured her that I would get right on it. So I departed for home not knowing how I would paint when I felt so uninspired. There were plenty of other artist's works, which equaled or were better than mine. Someone insisted that they must be mine and Farid's. Farid was a fast painter and could complete his paintings much quicker. Then I realized that no one even knew of his work. That was no one except the group. Consumed in the latest disaster, I stumbled to my car.

As I approached my car parked on the street in front of the studio, desperation filled my heart. What if something had happened to Farid? I even contemplated contacting the group. They were aware of everything, which occurred in my life. My instructions were never to contact them. Going home was not an appealing idea. It was hard for me to face Albert. This was the time of day that he would be working in the back of the house. I would have to face him as I parked in the garage. All at once, I thought of the painting that Farid completed before we left for the Bahamas—the pretty little ketch sailing on the lake. Never had I spent much time there.

As I drove, I found myself heading not toward home but the lake. Yes, this was a great idea. Summer was winding down. Fall would arrive soon. Autumn had always been my favorite time of the year. The sky seemed bluer, the clouds were higher, scents were sharper, and colors brighter. Yes, I should spend more time at the lake. Lakeside had never played much into my life, but with the benefit of living in a lake town, it just made sense.

Lake Eufaula or Lake George as it was also called induced the idea for colorful happy paintings. Without Farid, I felt so uninspired. Perhaps I could gain momentum for painting again. As I approached the lake, I remembered Jean mentioned that it was the bass fishing capital of the world or some such tidbit. Never had I fished, but I loved being by the water. Hastily, I found a parking lot. Selecting a spot across from a marina, I spread a blanket that I always carried in the car.

Dazed, I sat in the sun until it became overpowering. I moved to the shade. Jean's comments about the lake kept coming to my mind. I remembered a time when being around the two of them had been so happy. Now I avoided Albert, as well as Jean. It felt deceitful being around her as she beamed over Albert, her love. He was probably correct; his friend in France was just that, a friend, but I had already caught him in a lie over the fluency of his French. How could I believe him about his relationship with a woman whom he phoned in a location that far away?

Still, I thought of Jean's details about the lake. It comprised over forty-five thousand acres on the Chattahoochee River gracefully spread between Alabama and Georgia. Comprising over six-hundred forty miles of shoreline, this was a very sizeable lake. Some areas contained depths over ninety-six feet. Boating abounded as I noticed today. There was plenty of powerboating as one might expect. I also thrilled to watch sailboats skimmer past. Why had I never considered purchasing a sailboat? That would certainly add inspiration to my life especially with long periods of life without Farid. Contemplating how I would go about locating the right vessel made me sleepy. I laid down on my blanket to think. Soon, the temperature seemed chillier, so I covered myself with part of the blanket. This was a wonderful escape. I soaked up the fresh air. In a few moments, sleep seduced me.

When I awakened, the sky had turned dark. The temperature was cooler. Rain was on the horizon. Jean and Albert should be gone for the day. Much to my displeasure, I decided to head back home. I became aware of a great deal of ruckus across the water by the marina. Sitting up to see what was the cause, I became enthralled in what was taking place.

A small group of dark Cadillacs arrived. There were six to eight men mulling around on the hill by the boat ramp. A man standing near me explained that he had just come from that side.

"There is some nonsense about an important sheik. I doubt that there is a sheik in Eufaula. Crazy darn notion if you ask me. Some people will believe anything." He smiled and walked away.

Now they really had my attention. Soon, another car arrived—a Land Rover. All of the vehicles shined in the small amount of remaining light. The men in that car took forever to leave the privacy of their auto. Still, I watched with both dread and fascination. It had to be Farid. What were the chances that another sheik would be here? Yet it could not be. Farid would have phoned me. Why would he appear with an entourage at the lake? I determined not to leave until I saw who this important person creating such fanfare might be.

It seemed that over an hour passed, I could not be sure. I watched fearful that darkness would descend before they appeared. All at once, another truck appeared. This was a large truck, which hauled a boat on a hitch. The truck expertly backed a very pretty boat into the water. She was a ketch and sparkled with the last rays of sun for this day. As beautiful as she was, I soon peeled my eyes off her onto the woman who proudly climbed out of the vehicle.

She was as beautiful as the perky ketch. Long flowing auburn hair shined even deeper than the dark wood of the old boat. Someone had done an incredible job of restoring the wood of that sailboat. That woman also spent a great deal of time on her appearance. The lady was much younger than me and knew of the beauty, which she possessed. She appeared confident strutting among the men. It was all so fascinating. I noticed a small group of people to my right. All of them seemed glued to the scene playing before us. Slowly, I walked over to them. They explained that Cassidy was a local. She and her husband owned a boat repair shop.

"They are as good as they come when restoring old boats. Just look at that beauty." All of the heads turned to watch the scene. I wondered if they meant the boat or the woman. Her figure was stunning. Not an eye could turn away.

The boat was now in the water when the door of the Land Rover opened. To my absolute shock, who should appear but Farid? I could not believe it. All of the men gathered around him. I recognized his laugh and his voice. Anger overcame me. To make things much worse, Cassidy ran over to him and threw her arms around his neck. He picked her up, swinging her around. She was so small that she looked like a doll, a beautiful doll, in his arms.

I was determined to see this through even though I felt nauseated. The men all entered the boat including Farid. Cassidy unhooked her. One of the men started the engine of the beautiful ketch. Cassidy yelled, "See you tomorrow, Farid."

All of the men were laughing unnecessarily loudly. Farid yelled back, "Yes, tomorrow, Cassidy. Thank you for a wonderful experience!" More laughter as the men hit him on the back.

They motored out of sight. Cassidy left. I was left with a broken heart. Literally, I felt ill, unable to move. Could anything else go wrong? What would I do now? How in the world could I go forth without him? He had been my world. Even though it had started as a game, he was my love.

I struggled up from the blanket. My face was covered in tears. Thank goodness for the darkness, which now enthralled us all. Farid and his entourage were almost out of sight. What had he done to us?

36

ALL IS WELL

Tears were pouring out of my eyes in about the same way that the rains were descending from the clouds. The heavens opened. The deluge of rain was horrific. It was a miracle that I arrived safely at home due to the rain and my tears. I walked slowly from the car. There was no need to hurry. Nothing mattered to me anymore, not since seeing Farid and Cassidy. What I didn't understand was why in my town? This place meant nothing to him. It was as though everyone was intentionally trying to hurt me. I felt as though I couldn't take being used anymore. Since Jim, not the driver but Frank's friend, I felt abused and scorned.

As I entered the kitchen, the smells from Jean's dinner were wonderful, but I couldn't eat. Without looking inside the warm neatly wrapped package, which contained my dinner, I pushed it inside the refrigerator. My sobs were borderline hysteria now. As I turned out the lights, I noticed a large platter of rich chocolate brownies. Jean knew they were my favorite. Hers were the best ever. She used only the finest chocolate, which made a huge difference. Not tonight, not even Jean's brownies could be "comforting food." I thought of Farid with longing and disappointment. Climbing the stairs, I heard the phone ringing. Even after what I had seen tonight, I couldn't help myself. The thought that it may be Farid made me run to the shrieking black box. I answered it with hope.

"Mrs. Jones?" It was Frank. The tears increased if that was possible.

"Cat, are you all right?" I couldn't bear to tell him about Farid. He would have laughed, reminding me that he could have told me this would happen.

"Frank, I am fine. I need to go." Perhaps he was shocked at my voice because to my amazement, he did not hassle or probe me. The line went dead. Such "courteous" behavior from the group never shocked me anymore. I sat down on the bed and looked at a small photo, which Farid had given me. He was sitting in a large chair in a lavish home. His good looks always caused me to smile.

Even as I showered, I continued to sob. My heart was broken, never to be repaired. Not ever did I want to have another relationship. Since childhood, my desire for a solitary life may have been based on the fact that unbeknownst to me, I was not capable of being in a proper relationship. I had all the pain that I could take. Finding a bottle of sleeping pills, I took two. Sleep was all that could save me from the anguish.

Almost as soon as my head touched the pillow, I fell into a deep but troubled sleep. Dreams of horror ran through my head. Thoughts of Frank, Albert, and Farid were all jumbled together. I could hear Frank calling my name. It felt as if he was touching me. Anger flooded my heart. Thrashing and punching into the air, I wanted to hurt him as he had hurt me. To my amazement, someone put their hand over my mouth. A strong body fell heavily on top of me. I awakened to find that I was not dreaming. This was actually occurring. Someone from the group must have broken inside. They were here to hurt me. I hit even harder. Then the pressure was removed, as well as the hand. The light quickly came on. As I opened my eyes, there stood Farid. He looked shocked.

"Catherine, what is wrong with you? What sort of welcome is this?" He was standing by the bed, looking at me in disbelief. I jumped from the bed.

"Who do you think you are? Why would you try to discredit me here in Eufaula? Please go back to Cassidy or whoever she is. How did you get into my house?" He sat heavily on the bed in disbelief, explaining that I had given him a key to the house before leaving for the Bahamas. I did recall that incident.

"How did you know about Cassidy?" He seemed confused.

"I witnessed the entire sordid display today. It seemed that I was heartbroken at the long absence. I went to the lake to find solace. What I found was watching as you lifted that woman and whirled her around. I agreed to your demands, but it seems that you could carry on like that anywhere in the world. Why here?"

Farid fell over on the bed in laughter. He was laughing so hard that tears were rolling down his face. Each time that he almost stopped, he would look at me and start again. Now he was pointing at me as if I were the village idiot. Anger consumed me again. At least I had expected some morose.

"Catherine, this is all so absurd. I have returned with love and longing. It is understandable that you may be upset with my long absence, but I am back now. Please, stop and think. Do you really think that I would come here and carry on as you have suggested? If you think that, you do not know me. I promised you that I will never hurt you. Death would be easier for me than to ever create pain. The scene that you witnessed has a happy explanation. Will you agree to wait until morning for my explanation? I am famished. As I passed through the kitchen, the scents were succulent. Knowing how upset you are, I bet that you haven't eaten either. You sit right here. I will be back in a few moments." He walked nimbly from the room.

Not knowing whether to laugh or cry, I rubbed my eyes. The phone rang once again. Who else but dear ole Frank?

"Mrs. Jones? Look, Cat, I am worried about you. Has something gone wrong with the target? Have you messed this assignment up?" It had been a long time since he had referred to Farid as "the target." I no longer cared to play his game.

"No, I haven't. He is downstairs. Would you care to speak to him?" The line went dead. Someone should teach him that it was simple courtesy to say good-bye and not to slam the phone.

Farid soon entered with a large tray. There were two plates of chicken piccata with two small salads, as well as two glasses of wine. He sat the tray on a table in the corner by the window. I noticed a large plate piled with brownies.

My eyes were so swollen that I could barely open them. Farid helped me to my seat. Gently, he kissed my puffy face.

"Oh my darling, what have I done to you? Is being with me too hard for you? My desire is to bring you joy not destroy you. Tell me what I can do?" I could not help it. Lately, I cried so much that again the deluge of tears.

"It is that I love you so much. I was doing all right until I saw you with that woman. You seemed to enjoy her company. For many days, I had tried to find joy in my life without you, but that never occurred. Then, there you were laughing with your entourage of men who seemed to applaud your relationship with this stranger. How could you be so happy without me while I ached for your return? Happiness surrounded you. Desperation ate at me. That woman seemed to delight you, I could not understand."

Farid knelt beside my chair. "Catherine, you are suffering from a lack of trust. Someone hurt you pretty badly, haven't they?" Like a child, I nodded. Talking about Jim, the slime bag, I did not want to go there.

"Well, we are all hurt by someone. Now, you have a man who loves you and will never intentionally hurt you. You are transferring old feelings and experiences onto us. That is not healthy." Why was everyone else so much smarter than me?

"How do you know these things?" I could barely speak.

"Because psychology was one of several majors in university. It comes down to trust. Can you find it in your heart to believe that unlike whoever hurt you, I will not? I am incapable of hurting you, ever."

As I looked into his eyes, I knew that he was right. If I was unable to trust him, we would be happy when he was with me, but the moment that he left me, the doubts would start.

"I think that I can but am not sure. All that I can promise is that I will do my best." He squeezed my hand.

"I have something for you. If you wake up during the night, look at what I am about to give you, believing that this is my promise to you. Quickly, he left the room. Soon he returned, carrying the painting of the sailboat. Odd that the very idea that prompted all of this was his gift to me now.

"Farid, I love that painting. I was going to ask if I could purchase it." He smiled.

"No, my darling, you can't purchase it because it was always meant as a gift. I am home now. We are going to have some wonderful times. Tomorrow, everything will be clear. In a few days, we will take another trip. Does this please you?" I fell into his arms. All energy was gone from my body. He held me gently. We completed our dinner in silence. My eyes were severely swollen. My appetite had returned. I was even able to eat two of the large chocolate bars, which were filled with pecans. Before he carried the tray downstairs, he helped me to bed, placing cool compresses over my eyes. Soon he was back, gently holding me throughout the night. I did awaken once and looked at the image that he had so lovely painted. He sat it on a small easel by the bed. Then he opened the shutters so that the light from the street was shining directly on the painting. It was beautiful. The water glistened in the soft streetlight. Yes, Farid loved me. It was essential that I forget what Jim and Frank had drilled into my head. If I was unable, my relationship with the man that I loved would never be as fulfilling as I believed he desired.

37

CAT'S CATCH

Farid could not believe that most of the swelling had dissipated from my eyes. God blessed me with a body capable of healing much more rapidly than most. My mental state also healed. Farid's presence by my side was all that mattered to me. For the longest time, we simply hugged, looking into each other's eyes. Not a word was spoken. We tried to understand the very soul of each other. Filled with love and a little shame for not trusting, I pledged in my heart never to doubt him. All of the brainwashing from Frank created a person incapable of trust.

"Do as you are told. Act, don't react. No one cares about your feelings. Are you following me?" I hated all of those nasty phrases. Years of frequent repetition had changed me. Now I had no self-confidence. After Frank's barrage that no one cared about my feelings. How could anyone love me? I longed to share my history with Frank to Farid but could not.

Finally, Farid spoke gently, "Catherine, I placed such a burden on you. I am aware of that. You are younger than me. Even though you think that you are tough and worldly, there is much that you do not understand. Love is the most important asset I offer. All that I am capable of loving, I give to you. Beyond that, can anyone ask for more? Please try to trust me. It is absolutely necessary that I make these trips or I would not. They are not enjoyable to me. Now, let us see what the day offers?" He smiled that dazzling smile.

We bounded out of bed. Immediately the shower accompanied by his song, which I did not understand since it sounded Arabic, blessed my day. Quickly, I dressed as I headed downstairs. When he entered the kitchen, he nodded courteously to Jean. She wasn't buying anything that he offered. It appeared necessary that I speak to her about her attitude toward him, but not now. Now, I only wanted to enjoy whatever time remained with him.

After breakfast, we walked outside. The Land Rover, which I had seen yesterday, was sitting in the drive. His bodyguard looked cozy by the front door. Farid opened the door to his car, helping me inside.

"Catherine, just remember that those times when I am no longer by your side, I will make up for my lapses when I return. Just like I am about to do. You are going to be a very happy young woman soon." Lightly, he kissed my lips.

To my amazement, he drove toward Lake Eufaula. Arriving soon at the marina, I followed him down one of the boardwalks. Docked in a convenient slip, sat the beautiful ketch, which I had seen yesterday. To my surprise, there Cassidy sat on the stern of the boat.

Farid looked irritated as he mumbled, "Now, what is she doing here? She was excused yesterday and paid for her services." I wondered to what services he was referring but kept my silence.

"Well, Mrs. Cassidy, what a surprise. Where is your husband? You did not need to come here again. Since you have, let me introduce my love, Catherine." She extended her hand with a gnarly look. I accepted her handshake with an innocent smile.

"My, my so this is the Catherine? She is just as lovely as I would expect. I so enjoyed the time working on our project." She made sure to emphasize *our* as she stood closely to Farid. Again, I smiled. He loved me, and I would not play her games.

"If you don't mind, Mrs. Cassidy, my time with Catherine is short. There remains a great deal for us to accomplish. Please excuse us. Thank you again for coming all of the way out here, but it was not necessary."

Mrs. Cassidy's big smile turned downward. She did not look happy. Again she snarled at me, which was greeted by my big smile. "Well, you sure are different from yesterday. When you were with your male friends, you were more fun." With that pouty statement, she rubbed up against him.

The irritation on Farid's face was obvious. "Mrs. Cassidy, you don't know me. Our time together besides the briefness to which you refer yesterday has always been in the presence of your husband. Is that not correct?" That did it. She walked away.

"Whatever!" She yelled as she walked away. Her head was down as she refused to look at us. I couldn't help but laugh out loud. He was brilliant. He pulled me closely, "You don't ever need to worry about me. Catherine, I am pleased to present you with the keys to your beautiful new ketch. Mr. and Mrs. Cassidy have worked for weeks refinishing your most beautiful boat. That painting, which I gave you last night, was to introduce you to your new ketch. Months ago, I decided that during times when I am gone, especially this fall, you may enjoy sailing on this lovely lake. Your keys, my love." He handed me a large floater key bob.

I could not believe that this was my boat. My mouth opened wide. This had been my thought, but I had no idea how to make it happen.

"Now, the other surprise is the name. Since Cassidy has turned the boat around, you can't see it. So we'll have to wait till we return."

Gladly, I powered out after Farid loosened the lines. The wind was blowing briskly from the north. The Carolina-blue sky with the trees radiating the sun created a perfect day for sailing. The water was slightly choppy by lake standards but placid to those who had sailed on the fearless ocean. I wondered about the name of the boat. He told me that all of his boats must be named after "his most wonderful wife, Sanaa." That was fine. My boat would be called, *Sanaa.*

Soon, all thoughts turned to the wind, the current, adjusting sails. Farid laughed as we were on a reach with the rail of the boat almost touching the water.

"Cat, you are different from Sanaa. I love sailing with you. In fact, there is nothing that I don't treasure." Then he walked toward me. "I love everything about you," he yelled to the wind.

The boat glided easily over the small waves. I usually only sailed sloops, yet the speed and agility of this vessel were appealing. Finally, I turned the boat over to Farid so that I could check out the accommodations down below. She was beautifully fitted. Her diesel Volvo engine purred. The Cassidy's skilled hands lovingly perfected any abuse to the wood of the hull. All sanding and refinishing were impeccable. I owed a visit to their boat yard and a great deal of appreciation for the beauty, which they had bestowed on my aging treasure. Her beauty reminded me of a gorgeous aging woman whom time had stripped of her glow. Yet after the skills of a fine surgeon, some of that beauty was resurrected. My old vessel glowed again with such perfection. Yes, my boat sparkled as brilliantly as those dedicated to Sanaa.

We sailed for hours. I was not disappointed when Farid suggested we turn around. The lake proved confusing due to the vast size. Farid helped me find my way back. Eventually, we saw the welcomed sign of the marina. I felt exhausted after my day yesterday combined with the sun and vigorous sailing of today. Now I was eager to snuggle in Farid's arms. I longed to see Sanaa's name on the stern.

As we made our way back to the berth, I backed into the slip with skill. Farid looked impressed. Once we were there, I couldn't contain myself, so I jumped onto the dock. I ran to the stern of the boat. I squealed when I saw the golden words *Cat's Catch.*

"Oh, Farid, she is named for me." I was so happy. Surely, he loved me in the same way that he had loved Sanaa.

"Yes, darling. This is your boat. All of the other boats were my boats. Remember, I said all of my boats would be named for Sanaa, but I never said that your boats would. Do you understand the significance of *Cat's Catch*?

I wasn't sure that I did. As I pondered what he meant, he lovingly pulled me to his side. "You see, Catherine, I am your 'catch.'" I laughed, I felt as if my heart would burst. Yes, he was my catch.

38

FARCAT

Weeks flew past now that Farid was home. Soon enough, even Jean smiled laughingly in his presence. Yes, it was very difficult not to like him. The strange thing was his relationship with Albert. Once I introduced him, they were as brothers. This really pleased me. Albert must have many friends, but my love had none here. A male friend should bring much joy. They puttered in the yard. Now it was they who argued over the location of new paintings. Finally, I explained my displeasure toward Albert's overheard phone call and his explanation of a female friend in Paris.

Laughing cordially at my anger, he smiled. "Cat, that is not your concern. You liked him fine until he displeased you. What does that say about your friendship? If I displease you, will you exile me?" He hugged me.

"Men are not so quick to look for faults in each other. You must believe that he is capable of doing the correct thing for I believe that he is. Albert is an outstanding person. What would you do without him and Jean in your life? You better consider these things before you start harboring negative feelings toward him. Come on, Cat, lighten up a little. I am here to protect you." He lightly kissed me before running back to the greenhouse and his new friend.

Farid and I painted copious amounts of new paintings. They were sitting all over the studio. Albert really needed to load them and deliver them to the gallery. I walked to the backyard delighted with the cooler air. Seasons would soon change from fall to winter. The cold weather did not bother me as long as Farid stayed near, keeping me warm.

As I entered the little greenhouse, Albert and Farid stood together, speaking in fluent French. This shocked me. Loudly clearing my voice, neither seemed in the least startled to see me.

"Ah, Cat, now please don't be angry. I have told Albert of your revelation and concerns over his hidden talent for the French language. I miss not being able to speak one of the seven languages that I speak. Not using them constantly may hinder my ability to be fluent, you see."

"You speak seven different languages? Why would anyone need to be fluent in so many?" It seemed odd to me.

"You have to realize that because of where I was born and my education, it is very necessary that I speak many different languages. I would like to understand more, but it becomes difficult as one ages." I noticed the gray in his hair, which I had never seemed to notice before. My handsome man was aging nicely.

"Look, Farid, you and Albert need to deliver some of our paintings to the gallery. Jill is expecting them." No longer did it seem important that Albert conversed with a French girl. Farid was correct; it wasn't my concern. Both men looked pleased that I had not pressed Albert's earlier episode. Albert punched Farid lightly on the arm as they rapidly walked off together. Arm in arm, they continued to speak French. Life always presented surprises when Farid was present.

As they entered the house, they continued to laugh, speaking in French. I ran behind to witness Jean's reaction. She never even turned from her station at the counter. "Jean, does it not surprise you that Albert is so fluent in French?" I asked. To my amazement, she replied to me in French. Her mastery of the dialect was so far above my rudimentary level that I was unable to follow her. Laughing, she denied any shock at Albert's skill.

"Oh, Catherine, you decided that we had not been properly educated. However, that is not the case. We have traveled all over the world. We fluently speak several different languages."

"You learned through Rosetta Stone?" I inquired. The surprise came when unlike what Albert told me earlier, she explained that they enrolled in university for several years.

"I don't understand, Jean. Why would you and Albert need to know other languages?" She smiled. Then she explained that Albert possessed a genius IQ, which did not surprise me.

"Why not? You see, I feared that he would become bored with me. When he expressed interest that I learn a new skill, I became apprehensive. Never would I desire to hold him back. It surprised me greatly to learn that I was very good in other languages. The university explained that I had aptitude for quickly developing my language skills, so I was hooked." She returned to her latest soup.

My suspicious nature caused me apprehensive that I had caught them both in a discrepancy. Had Frank created this uneasiness in me? I considered what Farid said about men not being so critical. I decided to give them all a break and keep out of it. Farid was home. He would protect and guide me.

Time quickly flew. Farid never mentioned leaving. As Thanksgiving approached, I had not made a single plan. One day, as we painted in the sunny yellow room, Farid said, "Catherine, let's take a little trip. Go pack your bags. We are going to spend Thanksgiving and Christmas in Europe. Hurry on, pack but not too heavily. You won't need a great deal of clothes. Just some jeans and sweaters, as well as a warm coat."

"Don't we need plane reservations?" I was unprepared.

"Darling, the plane can be ready and waiting in Birmingham by the time that we have our driver. Now hurry on. Shall I inform Jean and Albert they will be celebrating these events without us?"

"What about Nat and Ginger? I so wanted you to meet them and the children." Again he smiled.

"Are you afraid that we can't after the first of the year? Don't be so rigid, Catherine. Come on, go with the flowing as it goes." The smile that always won.

I wanted to tell him that it was "Go with the flow" but decided that I liked the *flowing* better.

Loving a sheik had its perks, I thought. As I looked around the studio before leaving, I noticed that all of the paintings had been delivered to the gallery. We had a few new ones but only two. Farid had become so involved with Albert that now he and Albert met with Jill on all gallery things. I was demoted to merely a slaving artist expected to turn out one masterpiece after the other, while they enjoyed the gallery. Yet, I didn't mind. I was doing what I loved most, and the two men were really enjoying themselves.

Quickly, I packed. As I began carrying luggage down to the door, Farid yelled at me. "You stop right now. You are not to lift another piece of luggage. We don't do that. Since we pay people to help us that is not in your job discipleship." I could only smile. His mind was so advanced. Occasional mistakes made him seem human, not so perfect. His slip was usually better than the correct work. *Job discipleship* seemed much better than *job description*. I loved that man.

When we arrived in Birmingham, the private jet sat on the tarmac ready to fly. We were cleared for takeoff. I didn't ask where we were bound. For once, Frank's drillings were in line with Farid's. "Do as you are told." However, instructions from this man were considerate and loving.

Always I read as we flew. He did some mysterious research on his computer. I was never allowed access to his work, nor did I care. It would probably be in another language, which made me feel inadequate, so why bother? Hours past as we flew in silence. That was one of the things that I loved—not feeling like we needed to entertain each other. The silence was golden to me.

As we descended to land, I recognized Heathrow airport in London. I enjoyed London. Definitely, I felt delighted to be here. Never had I spent a holiday here though. Usually the summers were for visiting. There was a light snowfall, which excited me. Grateful for Farid's reminder to pack a warm coat, I kissed him on the cheek, but he barely noticed. He seemed miles away with his pensive and uptight look.

"Don't tell me, I think that I suspect there may be some business involved in this trip?" I smiled. He looked at me so sadly but nodded.

"Yes, you are right. I should have come alone, but I could not leave you during such a special time. You need me to be with you. Your melancholy would only be exaggerated if you were alone during these times. Please be patient with me. The days are yours, but the nights are filled with meetings and plans. Of course, I can't explain, but you will be delighted by my Christmas present for you." He squeezed my hand.

"Farid, I have nothing to give you for Christmas." He nodded. "You are my gift. I want nothing more, my darling. Your happiness is paramount. If you are happy than I need only that." He kissed my hand as he sadly looked out the window. What did he see? I could only wonder. Was his statement about my melancholy really about his? I wondered further if he suffered the same depression, which I encountered when we were not together. These business trips, he must hate whatever he did. Was he being forced to do something that displeased him? Something that caused him tremendous pain? I would always think of that moment and those questions. At the time, I merely wiped the thought away because I wanted to have fun. I desired to enjoy each moment. If I had asked him then why he was in such pain, could I have changed what was about to happen? For the rest of my time on earth, I could only wonder and pray for forgiveness.

After clearing immigration and customs, we were picked up by yet another private driver. He was a charming man named

Eugene. Eugene was quick-witted and extremely funny. In no time, he seemed to have Farid laughing. The apparent depression brushed aside, at least for a while.

Eugene expertly maneuvered the busy London streets. Snow covering the old streets was appealing. Making our way to the London flat, I was impressed with the premiere location within the Mayfair District. Surprising was the modern architecture. I loved the fact that it was very close to Hyde Park. For a moment, I thought of Dr. Jekyll/Mr. Hyde. Farid's name in Arabic meant "unique." That described him completely. I shuddered to think that we were so near Hyde Park. Was he Mr. Hyde, or was I being silly? Still, I brushed aside such thoughts. He now seemed more relaxed as he laughed at the chauffeur's latest brash remark. Eugene assisted us with our luggage.

The private elevator or lift delivered us safely to the penthouse. Surrounded by bright sunny views overlooking the park on one side and Mayfair on the other, the views were the best in London. *Perfect* described this special home. Everything in the apartment was white. The floors were shiny white marble. The kitchen was painted stark white. White cabinets, appliances, even the flowers were white. Never had I seen so many white orchids. Modern decorum supplied the four bedrooms. Beds draped in white duvets provided a peaceful feeling. Massive amounts of white instead of appearing sterile became "our winter retreat." Doctor Zivago's Laura played in my head. Being surrounded by the illusion of snow only encouraged me to hold my love closer. Our "winter wonderland' situated on the twelfth floor of an upscale building delivered a punch to the senses. We were about to have a wonderful time.

We quickly unpacked, pulling on our warm scarves and coats. We both arrived attired in designer jeans with sweaters, so we were ready to walk. Farid told me funny stories about different episodes concerning him and Sanaa. I noticed several photos scattered around the apartment but no large portraits as I had seen in the Bahamas. We walked for a very long time. We stopped once for tea and scone, but the coldness was starting to bother me a little.

As we began our walk for home, he asked if I enjoyed pub food. I had to laugh because I loved the British pubs. Margie and I visited London on our sophomore year. There, we enjoyed the locals whom we met at various restaurants. Then Rhonda and I visited London and several pubs where we shared a pint or three with several of London's best. I couldn't remember any of the names. That seemed like such a long time ago.

As we passed a red door, Farid steered me inside. "Catherine, meet my pub." He said that as though I was being introduced to a person. As we entered, there was a round of applause. It seemed that Farid spent most evenings here when he was in London. Shepherds Tavern was a very friendly place. Farid introduced me to most of the patrons. It was warm, and I loved being able to watch the pedestrians hurrying past. We had a delicious meal. Naturally, I had to eat fish and chips, which did not disappoint. Not a fancy place as I would have thought but just a good-natured fun establishment. We spent many a happy evening staying warm with ale and laughter.

As we returned home, my sense of direction caused me to realize that we had taken a detour. Farid again steered me into the doorway of a closed building, which provided a buffer from the wind.

"Catherine, I have such a surprise for you. Truly, I meant to save this until Christmas, but I just can't. This is your Christmas present." I was unable to follow what he meant. We were standing in the doorway of some sort of business, which was closed and unlighted. I looked at him in confusion. Handing me another set of keys, he nudged me toward the door.

"Merry, Merry Christmas, my love. Go ahead, unlock the door." Before I did so, I walked a few feet into the empty street. It was now late on a Thursday. We were not on a major street, just out of the busy section. The sign over the building was beautifully rendered in small gold letters, FarCat.

"Farid, what is FarCat? I don't understand."

Again he smiled as if he enjoyed explaining everything to me. "Catherine, remember the Bahamas house, FarSan? Well, this is you and me. Not a house but a business. My way of providing for you. Welcome to your Carnegie Hall of London. This is another art gallery. Think of the fun that you will have hanging your art and that of others. Instead of remaining in Eufaula all winter, you can come here and sale art. Art is so important to you. That and helping other artists. Come inside, my darling."

My hands trembled as I opened the door. I recalled telling Rhonda when we were here that I would have a gallery here someday. It sounded silly, even impossible then. Could this really be mine? As we entered, Farid switched on the lights. Everything was modern and shiny white. It reminded me of his penthouse. It could not have been more different from Carnegie Hall, but I loved it. To my amazement, hanging on the walls was our art—all of the paintings that had been displayed in Carnegie Hall but sold to a London buyer.

"Do you mean that you ordered our paintings so that you could show them here? Why would you do that? It must have cost a pretty penny. You could have just told me, and we could have transferred them."

"True, but then I couldn't see the look on your face. This is priceless, my love. Plus we helped the gallery there, which benefits so many. We must keep both galleries thriving and successful. Do you like?" I was so shocked that I literally sat down on the floor. Of course, the floors were so shiny that I could have eaten from them. Never in my life had I witnessed such love and concern. How could I have ever doubted or questioned him? My parents shared true love, but this person seemed capable of understanding my deepest desires. Farid brought a chair and helped me sit. Then he disappeared briefly. Returning with two glasses of champagne, he toasted our new enterprise. "To you, Catherine, my love and to FarCat, our love."

Sometimes, it felt as if we were one person, enjoying so much our love of sailing, painting, Europe, and the islands. It was as if we were meant to be together. The hours passed. We sat basking in the soft light. Farid kept refilling our glasses until I wasn't sure if I could walk back. He offered to call Eugene, but I wanted to stroll around the other businesses surrounding ours. It was very late by the time that we made our way back home. The weather turned cold and windy. Snow continued to fall softly. Streetlights made the scene surreal like something from a romance long ago.

Our time in London rates as one of the happiest in our lives together. Yes, I loved the Bahamas. I had grown up spending summers in the islands. Here, I desired to learn and appreciate so much. Just spending days in FarCat produced excitement as I met kind and gracious people. Days were beyond wonderful, but the nights were frightening to me. Again, Farid would go to bed with me, but I would awaken during the night to find him gone. Once more, I would hear heavy accents with angry tones. Sometimes things would escalate to yelling. There may be violent arguing. The next morning, Farid seemed sad. It would take a long time for his happiness to return. It always did return.

Before the time that it would have been Thanksgiving, he took me to the Brown's Hotel for a special dinner. We checked into one of their suites. He told me that he spent many weeks here. The hotel graced London for one hundred and seventy-five years, a five-star, newly renovated hotel, which was a legend in London. High teas here were famous. That night, Thanksgiving for Americans, we enjoyed our lovely accommodations. Eventually, there was a soft rap. Farid opened the door to room service. He arranged for the kitchen to prepare turkey, dressing, sweet potato casserole, and cranberry sauce, all of the usual. As I enjoyed the most delicious Thanksgiving meal of my life, he picked at his. Obviously, he did not appreciate our traditional feast. Still, it meant so much to me that he had gone to all of the trouble of providing my accustomed tradition.

The Brown's Hotel was notorious for catering to their guests. I was impressed. Watching my Arabic lover, I thought how easily we crossed custom barriers. If only citizens of the world would attempt to understand the differences, would it be possible that our world could be a peaceful place? On that night of Thanksgiving, I never bowed to grace. I didn't want to cause discomfort for my love, so I denied my beliefs. Not considering that doing what was right for me may open a door for discussion, my decision was to keep the door closed.

The next day as I prepared to return to the gallery, Farid asked me to sit with him. As we watched the courtyard out of our window, he explained that it was necessary for him to leave right away. I was to remain at the Brown's until he returned. Of course, I did not understand, but he sternly reminded me of my promise not to question. One of his bodyguards would be stationed by my door. This made no sense. When he was preparing for one of these business meetings, he could behave irrationally. He was angry and on edge. I learned better than to test him. I was further instructed that I was not to return to the gallery until he returned.

"They know that you will be there, Catherine. I must consider your safety. Please don't argue. Eugene will arrive later with some of your things. If you lack anything, you can shop, but only if accompanied by our guard. The hotel has a library of sorts. Help yourself to all of the books you want. I know how much you love to read. This is not such a bad place to celebrate Christmas, is it?"

"Farid, do you mean that you will not return until after Christmas? That is weeks. What am I to do?"

"Catherine, please, use your imagination. You have been provided everything. I don't even know if I will be back for New Year. Please, I need for you to be strong. Be everything that Sanaa was not. I must go. I love you." With that, he walked away.

I learned from this experience that I was a survivor. Each day, I slept as long as I desired. Sometimes, I never left the room instead, calling room service. I read for hours. Lunch in the dining room of the Brown's was sometimes frequented. I would see celebrities entering the hotel. The guard accompanied me for walks. Ian was funny and very thoughtful. Often, he brought me flowers so that my room was gayer. High teas were wonderful. Soon I didn't mind being alone. In fact, I felt like a queen. Long afternoon naps were frequently indulged. Dinners were enjoyed in the dining room. Ian would wave from his post by the door as he read the paper like an ancient patron. He always walked me from my room to wherever I was going. Often, I would enjoy a cocktail in the lobby as I watched weary travelers checking in from exotic places.

Christmas came and went without so much as a phone call, but I was no longer sad. I knew that he would return. When he did, my life would begin. It would be grand. Ian and I became great friends. We started our own private book club. Each book that I read, I would pass on to him. Lively discussions were held in the entertaining section of the suite. I did not expect Farid to return for New Year. No mind, I planned a wonderful evening.

Often, I checked in with Jean and Albert, who had taken care of Cat's Catch. She was safely winterized as was I. They sent their love. Christmas for them was spent at my house. They had hoped that I would return. My gifts waited. That made me think of the sailboat painting. Out of all of the wonderful things, which Farid had done for me, that was most precious. I remembered him telling me that should I ever not have him; I was to cling to that painting. He had not signed it, which I thought odd. Then he explained that I must never reveal that he painted it. It was to be a painting, which I purchased as a gift for him. All of that made no sense when he was telling me, but later, it was chilling. Before we left for this trip, he had framed it himself as he gently chided, "Remember Catherine, should anything happen to me, think of this painting." All of these warnings seemed frivolous at the time. Old age would be the time for morose discussions, not youth.

New Year's evening found me decked out in a bright-red satin gown. Ian and I shopped all over London to find just the right one. Red seemed appropriate since that was the dress that had captivated Farid. My day had been wonderful. Heartily enjoying dinner in the dining room with the patrons, some of them permanently resided here. I made several friends among them. We laughed our way into the lobby so that we might observe weary traveler's arrivals. As we enjoyed glasses of champagne before the magical hour of midnight, we were blowing little horns and making fools of ourselves. I felt someone very cold encapsulate me within their arms. Ian was standing over in the corner, smiling. As I whirled around, there stood my love. He seemed to have aged years. His hair was grayer than when he left. The tiredness was all over his face. His eyes were swollen, almost closed from lack of sleep.

As everyone yelled Happy New Year, he collapsed against me. Ian rushed to my side. We carried him to the room. Ian undressed him. I quickly undressed to assume my place beside him. The next day, nothing was mentioned. We returned to the penthouse. One more month, we resided there. He never left my side. FarCat was exceeding his expectations not because of monetary rewards but so many struggling artisans were assisted. Once again, many new artists were added to our rostrum. Our love changed again. Connections were deeper, conversation quieter, love unfathomable.

39

THE CHANGE IN FARID

We had been back in the penthouse almost one month when I returned from a visit at FarCat. I had not seen Farid for several hours. As I entered, he sat by the window staring out at the winter day. He did not hear me enter, which was unusual. Since New Year's Day, there was a decline in his health. No longer as robust as earlier, his energy level seemed abated. Still, I attributed that to age. Yet on this day, I really looked at him. I became mortified. His attributes were old, tired. That dazzling smile now was just a glint. Eyes, which previously glowed, lost their shine. He turned. His look was one of foreboding. He sadly nodded in my direction. Why had I not been aware of his ghostly appearance? Suddenly, I recalled the past energetic charges toward me when I entered. Now, only sadness. He quietly asked, "Can we go home now, Catherine?"

Shocked by his question, I was confused. This was his home. Not sure what he meant, I was careful not to upset him. Lately, he easily got tired, then he became confused with rambling confrontations. "Darling, we are home. This is one of your homes, remember?" His strange behavior was frightening me.

"Farid, should we see a doctor?" He shook his head.

"I don't want to see anyone but you, Cat. I want to go home. You know, our real house. The beautiful one that we both love. The house in Eufaula." His smile was that of a wounded child.

"Yes, of course. We will get you home today. I will take care of everything."

"Good, I'm going back to bed so that I will be rested for the trip." He walked away a little bent over. When had all of this occurred? Had I been so involved in having fun and feeling important at the art gallery that I had ignored him?

All of the plans were completed. Soon enough, we cleared the proper agencies and were on our way. He held my hand almost all of the way home. Occasionally, he would awaken. Sadly, he would smile.

"I love you, Catherine."

Once when he had said this, I replied, "I love you too, Farid." He sadly smiled. "No, I really love you."

What did that mean? He knew surely after all of this time that I loved him. It made me sad to hear that statement. He just wasn't himself. When we finally reached home, even I was exhausted. The day spent, darkness surrounded us. He was incapable of making any decisions. It was as if he had made all of the choices that his mind was capable of delivering. What sort of major decisions had he made lately? It must have been his last business trip, which tired him so.

I phoned ahead so that Albert would be at the house to assist me in getting him safely up the stairs. Farid's face came to life when he saw Albert. He made a few weak jabs at humor. Albert looked at me questioningly. All that I could do was shrug since I had no idea what had happened.

As we helped him to bed, I asked Albert if he thought we should take him to the hospital. Farid started to shake.

"No hospitals, Cat. I already told you. If you even try to take me to the police or hospital, I will leave. You will never see me again. Do you understand?" Never had he been so angry at me.

He was terrifying when he was angry. His face became darker, his eyes filled with strong emotion.

"Farid, darling, I think something terrible happened to you. It is as though your mind can't deal with something. You must understand that I will not take you to the hospital, but you seem to need help. Why in this world would I take you to the police?"

He began swearing, raving in a language, which I didn't understand. Albert answered him in the Middle Eastern dialect. They seemed angry as they looked at me. Not only did I feel shocked but very frightened. Once I thought Farid was going to hit Albert. Instead, he shuffled away. Then spinning around, he began a verbal assault on Albert. A barrage of anger unlike anything I ever witnessed in my life rained from my gentle love. "The Dr. Jekyll /Mr. Hyde" analogy was correct.

When we got him up the stairs, Farid walked ahead of us. Slamming the door, I heard the lock. Albert and I faced each other. "Albert, please tell me what is happening? Is this my dear Farid? I don't know him." I pointed to the locked room.

"Catherine, please forget this happened. He is tired. His body needs rest, that's all."

"No, Albert, we had one month doing only that. He had more than enough rest to recover from his business trip. Barely did he leave the penthouse in London. He sat by the window, appearing paranoid. I really didn't think much of it until now. How can you speak Middle Eastern? What was that language?"

Albert turned pale. His face covered with perspiration. These reactions were more than a result of carrying Farid up the stairs.

"If you love that man, forget this ever happened. What he is experiencing is post-traumatic stress. Do you understand?"

"Of course, I am not an idiot. I know what post-traumatic stress, is but what would bring it on?"

"Catherine, Farid and I often talked. He once told me about the difference between you and Sanaa. I am aware of the love he possessed for his first wife. Also, he told me of the deep love for you. One of the things that he needed so vitally, Sanaa could not provide. It amazed him that you tried so hard to be all that he needed, all that she was not. I believe that you made a promise to him never to question him. As you see, our friendship was more than you may have thought. I care deeply for both of you. This is one of those vital moments when you must respect that promise. If you don't, your world will change but not in a good way. It will become hell for you and for us all. Please, just give him time. If he doesn't recover soon, I will get him back to Saudi. Now you must trust me."

Having no idea what any of that meant or what had happened to Farid, I only knew that I *had* made a promise and a covenant with Farid. Although we weren't married, in my heart we were. I pledged to Albert my silence.

For about two weeks, I tiptoed around Farid. He barely spoke to me. I thought he was angry because I had insisted that he needed help. Farid compared to Frank in that he was powerful. He resented advice from a woman.

Weeks passed. One day, I entered the bedroom to find him gone. Albert was not to be found either. Jean seemed pensive, troubled during this time. She barely spoke. Running through the house, I burst into my studio to find Farid standing behind his easel. He smiled that smile. I ran to him as he happily painted. He appeared lighthearted again. Almost knocking him over due to his recent weight loss, I hugged him tightly.

"Catherine, where have you been all of this time? I have missed you. It is wonderful to have you back. We really need to produce some art for these two galleries. Yes? Come on, get your brush. Let's paint all day. Why don't you give Albert and Jean the day off? We'll have dinner downtown at that great restaurant at which you sometimes treat me. Do you still have those coupons, which Ronda and Margie gave you?"

Unbelievable to me was the fact that his mind seemed sharp. His eyes shined with light and intelligence. I did not know what happened, but he was back with me. That was all that mattered.

40

JOYFUL LIVING

My love returned from a dark place. He appeared to be his old self for about three months. Without reason, he experienced extreme forgetfulness and paranoia. Never again did he react in the angry way, which had occurred with Albert. During the "abnormal" periods, he behaved like a child. His smile seemed a little goofy. He looked as if he lost his intelligence. Those periods were random, not lasting very long.

February turned to March. The beautiful spring season was once again upon us. Farid and I busied ourselves with *Cat's Catch*. We had her overhauled. Her wood once again sparkled, thanks to the loving hands of the Cassidy's. Farid did not understand my reluctance to be in her presence, but I thoroughly liked her husband. I felt sorry for him. Did he know of his wife's attraction to Farid? It was not my concern. I was relieved when our trips to the boat yard were complete. *Cat's Catch* lazily bobbed in her slip.

That summer was unforgettable. Almost daily, we put our painting on hold. Long rides in the boat exploring Lake George brought us great joy. Sunsets holding hands as we toasted another perfect day with a glass of champagne or wine. Often, Jean would pack delicious picnics for us. We found areas that were wild. There we could sunbath nude or skinny dip. Our love secured, no more drama. Farid's laugh and smile were vital to me. It gave me joy seeing him laugh heartily at some ridiculous thing, which I did just to make him laugh. He would fall over onto the ground or blanket holding his stomach, just laughing. Laughter and hugs, day after day—that is what I remember of those idyllic spring days. Foolish behavior did not keep me from imitating some scene from a favorite movie. Farid loved Western movies. My ridiculous banter was greeted with belly laughs. Life was back on track. Anything that made him happy pleased me as well. I treasured the end of each day together. Often, we sat on a blanket, holding hands as we sipped a glass of cold champagne totally enthralled in the reds and oranges of a spectacular sunset. What more could we want? Life was a dream of perfection. If only it could have remained.

Spring turned into summer quickly. We held a summer reception at Carnegie Hall. This time, not only were Jill, Jean, and Albert by my side but my most handsome love. Farid dazzled all of the locals. Many seemed impressed having a sheik in the small town. Everyone seemed to know him. He was welcomed and encouraged to join all activities. The reception with him was the largest and most successful financially that we ever witnessed. We featured five different artists. Farid and I hung many of our favorite pieces. No painting ever compared with the beautiful one, which Farid had given me of what I now realized as *Cat's Catch*. Often, I thought of what he told me that evening. There was something almost cryptic about his statements. What was it? What secret did it hold? I questioned him one evening as we enjoyed a fresh tomato salad from Albert's garden.

"Catherine, I really don't want to talk about that painting. You see, that is for you when I am gone. Thinking of your life without me is difficult. Please do not discuss this again. It is important that you merely file in the back of your mind that as far as anyone else is concerned, you purchased that one for me. Really, I tried to paint as a stranger, but that is difficult. What you need to tuck in the recesses of your mind is that if I am suddenly gone, there is a message for you in the painting. This is so important. Listen most carefully to my words. There is a message in the painting but only if I am suddenly gone. I am referring to an unnatural death. Do you understand? Don't concentrate on this, or it will cause you to do something foolish like pry with it before you should. That would be fatal. Just let it go for now. You are a brilliant person. You will figure it out."

Nathaniel had been labeled "brilliant." He impressed Farid. My baby brother was turning the political world upside down. Possibly, he had his eye on the governorship of New York. At one time, I felt silly contemplating such a thing but no more. His family developed into a storybook image of elegance and beauty. Ginger was now sophisticated, but she never forgot her roots, nor did she forget that kindness would remain the essential element to any politicians hope for a long future. She became the perfect mate for my gorgeous brother. They aged beautifully together.

When we visited them for the first time, that look Nat emitted when he entered the room noticing my dark friend caused me to laugh. Farid looked at me with the same humor. No longer did it cause me a feeling of discomfort to wonder at the reactions of others to us. I simply did not care anymore. Farid never had. Still, Nathaniel and Ginger welcomed us into their home. At the end of our time, they genuinely had fallen in love with the Middle Eastern–man who adored their sister. The children were drawn to him. He played basketball, badly, with them. Funny stories at night before bedtime resulted in belly laughs at this unusual man.

Nat hired a professional photographer to take photos of our family. One in particular graces my bedside table. We stand on the grand staircase. Nathaniel is standing at the top in the spot of importance. Next is Ginger surrounded by the two children. Farid insisted that I stand closest to Ginger so that he was lowest of importance. The amazing thing is that your eyes go automatically to Farid. His presence commands respect in that photo as in life. There's something special about him that we could not understand. The camera was his friend. Always, I hold that photo to my heart. That was another treasured memory.

Once we returned to Eufaula, summer slipped past. Much too quickly, we were again speaking of Thanksgiving and Christmas. Albert, Jean, and I made extensive plans for decorating and inviting Nat's family, as well as Margie, John, Rhonda, Barrington, Linda, and Sam. That should be a real celebration. I hoped this would please Farid. He entered the room as we laughed about how much wit Rhonda would bring to our party. She loved lavish large events. Farid shook his head at me.

"Catherine, plans already have been set for some time. I hide a surprise for you. There is still one more home, which you haven't seen. There is a special reason that I have never shared this with you. The place that we will visit soon is one that holds my heart. It is the sort of place that is like sailing, you know? You either love it or you hate it. There is no middle ground. If you react the way that I hope, you will experience something unforgettable. Sanaa never understood. She only went with me once. That was cause for disappointment. Even though she assured me that she loved it there with longings to return, I never took her again. You cannot fake your feelings for this place. You must be forthright when we go there. I will know if you pretend. The place is that special. If you don't love it, please say so. I will know. If you do, we will spend the happiest times in our life there. If not, you will never be asked to join me there again. Cancel all plans. We have a trip of the hearts waiting for us." He smiled.

"Farid, I will gladly cancel my plans, but may I ask where this special place is? I know that we can't visit your home in Saudi. I know that you mentioned early in our relationship that you own a home in Bali. Is that the place?"

He turned and kissed me softly. "Bali, yes, that is the place. I think of it as the closest thing to heaven. You will see." The joy in his eyes increased my desire to visit.

41

I LOVE LA

Although my body and heart ached to remain home for Thanksgiving and Christmas, I could not disappoint Farid. In my mind, I became bewitched by the festive mood of poinsettias, paper whites, and amaryllis filling the house. There would have been a fire in each of the fireplaces. Live trees would fill the house with the aroma of pine. Yes, it would have been grand. I knew that Farid would have treasured the moments. Instead, we were on our way for three nights in Los Angeles.

Both Farid and I loved LA. He had business to conduct, not overnight but a few meetings. I'm not sure why, but I always stayed at the Century City Plaza Hotel. I enjoyed going over to Century City. Of course, I visited Rodeo Drive where I had my hair styled by the experts. Farid commented in a disappointed way as he did when he didn't get his way that he always stayed at the Beverly Wilshire. It didn't really matter to me. We were together and that was the important thing.

One afternoon I decided in the middle of the day that I wanted a martini. I never had a cocktail in the middle of the day, nor did Farid, but it just seemed festive. We entered Harry's bar. As we sat at the bar enjoying the delightful bartender, I was shocked by the rudeness of some of the patrons.

Victor, the bartender, was extremely nice looking. Farid and I found him engaging and interesting. There sat a group of ladies who appeared to have enjoyed one too many drinks. They were loudly treating him in a patronizing manner. He, on the other hand, remained kind and attentive to their needs. Things got worse. I could not sit by and watch the abuse. I questioned Victor as to why they would behave so badly. He insisted that he did not know them, but each Wednesday, they appeared treating him the same. I excused myself to go to the ladies' room. As I passed them, I told them that I found their behavior rude. The leader told me to mind my own business. When I passed their table from the restroom, she asked me to sit down.

"I like you." She smiled at me.

"Well, I would like you as well if you were not so rude to my new friend. Victor is a remarkable person. Perhaps you should try to get to know him."

To my surprise, this difficult person agreed. "I am sorry that I was so hard on him. He did not deserve such combative behavior. In the future, I will be nicer, I promise."

When I returned to the bar, Victor seemed impressed that I had tried to help someone whom I barely knew. When Farid and I left, we promised to return to Harry's on our next trip to Los Angeles. For some reason, I mentioned where we were staying.

Upon our return to the room, it surprised us to hear the soft ringing of the phone. After all, no one knew of our location but Jean and Albert. A brief pang of remorse that something may be wrong at home erased the lightheartedness. I was delighted to hear Victor.

"You sure made a difference. Those ladies came over and apologized to me. You see, I am only helping the owner of the bar who is a good friend. I would like to do something nice for you in return for your kindness. Is there anywhere that you would like to visit? Maybe a restaurant or place that you may need help in obtaining last-minute reservations? I can't guarantee anything, but I am from LA and have a few connections." Thinking quickly, I remembered reading about the Magic Castle. Farid would enjoy dining there then catching an act. I read that it could be difficult getting last-minute reservations. When I told him, he laughed.

"Well, I can probably handle that. I will call you right back." We hung up. Just as I started to undress for a shower, the phone rang again. There was my new friend happily explaining that arrangements were complete. He gave me the secret code to get inside.

The day was almost gone. Dinner hour approached. We rushed to reach our reservations for dinner and show. Approaching the front door of the establishment, I felt foolish. My instructions as I reached the front door were to repeat magic words. Looking around me, I saw a few stars, which added to my feeling of foolishness. After all, I barely knew Victor. He may be playing a joke on me. Farid would not understand if everyone started laughing at me. Still, I believed in Victor. Somewhat confidently, I walked to the closed door, uttering the secret phrase. Happily, the large doors opened. We entered.

The entire evening was great fun. Dinner was most enjoyable which set the stage for the magic show that followed. To our good fortune, the magician was one of the most respected in the country. As we walked through the large bar for one last time, someone called my name. I kept walking; there are a great many Catherines. Suddenly, someone put their hand on my shoulder. I turned to see Victor. Not the bartender in white jacket as before but someone who looked like a movie star. He was dressed in designer best and glowed.

"Did you enjoy your evening, Catherine and Farid?" His contagious smile warmed our hearts. Thank you, Catherine, for defending a stranger." That was one of those moments when I was certain that I did the correct thing. We encountered someone whom we would never forget. Yes, I love LA.

42

THE REST OF THE TRIP

Farid attended a few meetings. We ate heavy dinners at some of the best restaurants. Farid agreed to go on a tour of the star's homes. Who knows if we really saw the correct homes, but it was fun. We went to places that I had not visited in years, promising to take the scenic drive from Seattle to L.A. someday soon. We laughed as he told me funny stories about his college days from his one year at Berkeley.

"That place was just too far out for me," he fondly disclosed. After three days, I thought how happy I would be to return to Eufaula. Instead, we had a long flight facing us.

Soon enough, we were flying high in the sky over LA. I lovingly touched the window of the plane. Our next stop was Hawaii. We had both visited there several times, but one never tires of the beauty awaiting. Farid had taken care of all of the plans.

Our time in Hawaii would be four days. We arrived on the big island. The hotel was beautiful. Immediately, we changed clothes and headed for the ocean. The waters of Hawaii are all shades of blue. The deep blues will never leave your memory. Although this was not my favorite island, we enjoyed our time. There were some great shops in the hotel. Farid excused himself to find a gift for me. Naturally, I had to find something for the "man who had everything." At last, I purchased a lovely gold key chain. I thought that since he had so many homes, he could always use another chain on which to hang his many keys. It was pretty with a palm tree containing a large green emerald in the center of the leaves.

When we returned to our room, I couldn't wait to exchange gifts. He refused to give me mine until we reached "our home in Bali." Since I did not have much self-control, I thrust my small gift out to him.

"Are you sure that you don't want to wait until I give you my purchase?" I assured him that I couldn't possibly wait for his gift scheduled for our arrival in Bali. So he gently removed the heavy green wrapping paper. There was joy in his eyes as he took some of the keys from his heavy key ring attaching them to my gift.

"Well, this allows me to bestow another gift to you. Here are the keys to all of the homes except the home in Bali. If anything should ever happen to me, I promised my mother that it would be hers. I hope that you aren't disappointed."

"Farid, are you sure? You are giving me the penthouse in London and the home in the Bahamas? The key ring, which contained these keys, was very heavy ornate gold. My simple gift was small in comparison.

"Please give me the key ring back."

He looked confused. "Now, Catherine, you can't take a gift back. I love this beautiful palm tree." He reluctantly handed the keys and ring back. The emerald on the leaves shined in the light of the window. Carefully, I removed a spare key to my Eufaula home, adding it to his assortment of keys. He smiled. Since it was repetitious, he already had been given a key, I had to give him something more.

"Farid, your generosity is extraordinary. Honestly, I can't accept all of this. You have already bestowed *Cat's Catch* and FarCat. Besides, I would feel funny going to your homes without you."

Lovingly, he held my head in his strong hands. "Listen to me. You have made me happier than I ever dreamed. I wish that I could give you the Bali home. It is the best, but I made a promise years ago to my mother. When she visited there, she cried at the serenity and beauty. After we discovered that Sanaa did not understand, mother requested to purchase it from me. I promised upon my death, it would be hers. I would never go back on a promise, so I hope that you understand. You will have a great life flying to our homes. Yes?"

"Farid, lately, you have mentioned several times what is to occur when you are gone. Do you have some sort of premonition? I don't understand this obsession."

He sadly smiled. "Yes, I do know that my time with you is short. All of this must be discussed. All of the arrangements are made. Just promise me that you will love me and never doubt my love or the person that I am."

We exchanged tears as we kissed each other. I could not imagine my life without him, hoping that he was wrong about his feelings. The emotion of that evening was so strong that neither of us were hungry for dinner. We ate a small salad and slept in each other's arms.

The next day, we left for my favorite island of Kauai. Majesty surrounds this beautiful place. Frequent bouts of rain, for it is known as the "Rain Island," result in posh greenness. The gardens flourish large bright flowers. Even the birds are spectacular. Blue water soothes the stress as soft beaches wait to be explored. Oh, I enjoyed breathtaking sights awaiting beyond each bend. We spent two nights finally leaving reluctantly. I wondered if Bali could really be more magical.

Soon enough, it was time to wrap up our Hawaii time. We spent the last day on Maui—the surfer's dream place. The waves crashed dramatically as we stood on a high bluff, imagining surfers who realized their dream of "catching a wave." We thrilled at the architecture of magnificent homes as we rode around the island.

"Farid, just leave me here. Send me lots of money." I played with his hair.

"Catherine, I will never leave you for long if I can help it, but I plan on leaving you with enough money." He smiled. What he had given me was more than money. At last, I had known love, real love as Linda and Sammy, Margie and John, and Rhonda and Barrington. Someone really loved me.

The excitement was building as we made our way to our last stop before finally visiting Farid's magical island. What a trip we enjoyed. How could things possibly be better than all of this?

Our last stop was Guam. It was lovely, but we were only there for one night. That wasn't enough time to really explore. We were both tired from all that we enjoyed. The flying was wearing on me now. Sadly, I announced that I just couldn't go anymore even though it had been great fun.

"Well, that is why I scheduled only one night. You would wear me out dragging me to every tourist stop. I hoped that with one night, you may want to rest before we arrive home. Don't forget that I have a few years on you."

Sadly, we spent our only night in our room with a current movie and room service. Farid wanted an early start so that we could arrive in Bali before sunset. We enjoyed a great dinner sleeping late the next morning. I was awakened by the sound of panic.

"Quickly, Catherine, wake up. We have slept for over ten hours. Is this normal? I hope that we don't develop bed boils." That one took me a few minutes to figure.

"Farid, you mean bedsores, don't you?" He shook his head. He was certain that they were "bed boils." We rushed down to a breakfast buffet. I would need to get down to some extreme exercise when we finally arrived on the dreamy "Bali high."

43

COME AWAY

Bali Hai may call you, any night, any day. In your heart,
you'll hear it call you. Come Away, Come Away.

—Rodgers and Hammerstein, *South Pacific*

Excitement was penetrable the next day in the plane. Farid was
all smiles, happy to share his beloved island. I had not done any
homework and had no idea what to expect. The only thing that
I knew was the beautiful music from South Pacific. A smile
came as I remembered being about eight years old as I danced
in yet another ballet recital. That particular recital centered on
the music from South Pacific. Never did I dream that someday, I
would be visiting this faraway island with the man of my dreams.
Remembering the soft lilac tights and stretchy leotards, which
were trimmed in shinning green beads, I laughed out loud.

"Ah, you are under the Balinese spell even before arrival. This
is a good sign." Farid gently squeezed my hand.

"I am remembering dancing to South Pacific as a small girl
of about eight. The haunting music to 'Bali Hai' never leaves one,
does it?"

"No, my darling, it does not. Nor does the serenity of the
island. Although there have been some terrorist attacks, they are
rare. The island is safe besides some of the typical scams, which

you see everywhere. Have you ever visited the Pacific islands besides Hawaii?"

"Never, although I have dreamed of Bali and Tahiti since South Pacific. Do the island winds really whisper, 'Come away?'" It was a foolish question, but I was becoming so enamored with the mystery of this island paradise that it seemed possible.

"You will have to listen for yourself. Perhaps you will hear the beckoning call of this most special place. If you hear it, you will never be the same." He smiled. Farid continued by warning me that unfortunately this time of the year, between December and March, I should expect much rain due to monsoon season. It mainly meant high humidity with heavy frequent showers. "Don't worry, it is not as threatening as it may sound," he assured me.

I questioned him about the house, but he would only reply, "Wait and see for yourself." Always with a smile, his love for this place was evident. We spoke little, burying our heads in books. Although we had brought a great deal of art supplies, Farid assured me that the arts abounded in Bali. We would not have a problem finding adequate replacements for tubes of paint and canvasses. According to him, there were an abundance of galleries and studios.

The flight was tiring. We both wanted to arrive finally partaking of the charms awaiting us. Unfortunately, the airport was not a good start. Honestly, this could be said of any airport in the Atlantic or Pacific islands. Ngurah Rai International airport was no different. Farid warned me not to allow an official-looking custodian to carry my bags. No harm would come, but even if they just picked it up, they would demand payment. So we stood with our two bags, each waiting for the driver. No surprise, "You are in the islands, mon, so chill," Farid stated this in his best islandy voice, which was not very good. Chill we did for almost an hour. Although it was interesting, I thought how I would chide such behavior but not Farid. He smiled and joked with some of the locals. Very little upset him in everyday occurrences. It was those dreaded business trips that seemed to cause him trouble.

Eventually, "Bob" the driver arrived. This was, of course, not his real name, but he liked to be called that. He was jovial, but who wouldn't be in this paradise? He kissed my hand as Farid scolded him for being so sophisticated.

"Bob, you will ruin her. Now, she will expect European behavior from everyone."

"Now, Mr. Farid, you know that I love the ladies. She is exceptional, but I'm sure that you know it." Farid only smiled. We drove around the town in the expert hands of our driver. I noticed that pedestrians put their lives in jeopardy as they walked over streets, which were uneven and narrow. No matter what Farid said, I would not be walking there. It looked like a storm drain to me.

Shortly, things improved greatly as we moved away from the airport. Bob was humming a lovely tune. "Do you know 'Bali Hai'?" I innocently questioned.

"Bali, what?" I was shocked that he did not know one of the loveliest tunes in the movies.

"That was a little before his time, Cat." Farid covered his mouth with his hand to avoid laughing. No matter to me, no one would spoil this time that we had together. Farid explained that we would remain through the New Year. The custom for this Hindu holiday named, *Nyepi*, was to be silent. Most everyone, even tourists, remained in their home or hotel room for that day. I liked the idea of silence in this electronic/television-addicted age. He also told me tidbits of information such as not to drink the tap water anywhere. It seemed that bottled water, Aqua, was profuse.

There was an active volcano on the island, mighty Mount Agung. It all sounded like a scene from a movie, but where was his house? I couldn't wait to walk on the grounds. My body ached from travel even though we had a nice rest in Guam. Could this really be my life? Jet-setting with a handsome, romantic foreign man? My mother would be shocked. My grandfather would remind me of my impetuousness. Again, I smiled. Maybe Bali did have powers to conjure up guarded and precious memories. I hummed 'Bali Hai' as Farid and Bob looked at each other in the mirror. When I began to sing, they covered their ears as they were racked in laughter. Somehow, my rendition did not do the song justice. The scenery, however, was doing the sense of sight an incredible justice. Beyond lovely was the only explanation.

We drove for some time when Farid told me that he had a confession. Knowing how much I loved the beach, he used the famous beaches of Bali luring me to his beloved lush landscape. However, unlike the Bahamian home, this home was not on the beach at all but near the mountains. In fact, it was located in the foothills of the smoldering Mount Batur just outside the town of Ubud.

"What, Farid, the mountains and a smoldering one at that?" I had envisioned beaches, white or black sand, it didn't matter but beaches. The mountains, a smoldering one? "What will we do all day?" This was far from my vision of sunny days like those spent in the Bahamas.

"Cat, don't you see the allure? Think of it. We have it all. A gorgeous country home, a London penthouse, a Bahamian beauty right on the beach, and this most beautiful mountain paradise. What is there not to love? I didn't want you to arrive with a preconceived dislike as Sanaa did. You don't even know anything about mountain terrain. Just give it a chance. Yes?"

I had never spent much time in the mountains. I knew Farid well enough to know that if he loved it, so would I. As we continued our drive past Ubud, I felt as a child waiting to unwrap that large gorgeous present at the back under the tree. Bob started to sing again. His voice was melodic, soothing. He lived on the compound with us, which made me feel better about security because he was a strapping young man. That was another uneasy feeling that I possessed. This was a strange and somewhat scary place for me.

I couldn't help but ask, "So this smoldering mountain? Do you mean we live near an active volcano?" He smiled.

"Mount Batur is an active volcano, but don't worry so much, Catherine. Would I put you in harm's way without protection? You know me well enough to know that I would keep you safe at any cost. I do have another surprise. What I haven't told you is that Ubud is located in central Bali, the cultural hub. The known history of Ubud goes back past the eighth century. Your love of architecture will be stimulated as never before. The house, which you are about to see, is one of a kind. The architecture is Balinese, as well as other influences. It will take you weeks of study just to understand all that has been accomplished here. Another added benefit for not being on the beach is that we are located two hundred meters above sea level, so the temperatures are cooler, but the days can still be very warm. You will love the need for a wrap in the evenings but able to lie by the pool in the afternoons. At least we aren't arriving in the depths of the wet season of January and February. We should be gone before the heavy rains begin."

"The days when we paint here, there are so many choices. We will never tire of all of the history and architecture. So many things for us to do in such a short time, my love." The sadness crossed his eyes as he looked into my soul. I did not want the fun to end. I began to sing songs from South Pacific again. Their groans were followed by endless laughter. Just the thing that I needed to hear.

It seemed that we had driven forever. The suspense was almost unbearable. Where was this elusive home? Then we turned onto a winding road leading to the back of the structures. The plants were large and so green. Magical colors of the brightest hues of every color in the spectrum assaulted the senses with beauty. Then I saw it! Unlike anything that I had ever witnessed, the beauty was staggering. It should have people lined up paying to be able to enter. The house was built on a promontory that comprised over four acres with a one hundred eighty foot drop down to the river in the back. The front was accessed from the street by massive brass doors.

The double staircase was comprised of river boulders, which led down to the first floor. There was a clear stream running through the property. This created coolness, and the sound of running water was soothing. His main home contained coconut columns. The rafters were bamboo. Lush vegetation filled the landscape dotted with steps and hand-worked balustrades. There were massive rocks with plants filling each rocky crag. The numerous pergolas were covered in jade vines, adding to the splashes of color.

Carvings were beautifully done. I loved the red, gold, and green paints, which decorated them. There were several homes, all of which contained numerous pavilions. Each in itself would have been stunning, but together, it was overwhelming. It was a maze of steps and greenery everywhere. There were swimming pools, wine cellars, bridges, and palms and bamboos framing each. Again, all of the variances of the deep Indonesian colors were titillating to the senses.

As we walked around the compound, Farid pointed out things that I would have never noticed. There was so much to take in. This was more than I could have dreamed. A separate smaller bungalow with private pool was very appealing to me. The main house with the large reception pavilion was almost frightening. This smaller one was welcoming, almost sensuous. I felt drawn to it. Once again, the colors were intense.

I touched ornate ancient carvings, which appeared to have been from antique *joglos* (houses). It faced rice paddies on one side with a large wraparound veranda overlooking the valley on the other. Farid said that in the mornings, small birds landed on top of the rice. When you looked across the rice paddies, there was an ancient temple. This was supposed to be the guest house, but Farid said this was his favorite part of the compound, so it was here that he stayed on his visits.

"Catherine, we must sleep in later than usual. Then we will have an espresso and start the day with the most incredible view in the world as we gaze across the river into a rainforest. We will never tire of all of the museums and art interests, plus I guarantee that we will paint our best works here at our home." His excitement was contagious.

As I turned to face him, tears of joy caressed my face. "Farid, it exceeds all expectations. I am thrilled to be off the tourist crowded areas, to be surrounded by God's blessings. What can I say? I am speechless."

"I knew that you would be such. What you have finally said is God. I have been meaning to talk with you about Him. You have tiptoed around the thing, which should have been central to you, Catherine. Perhaps you concluded that I am Muslim, but I am not. I have been a Christian for many years. I know Jesus, Catherine. I love Him and am not ashamed to speak of Him. Why have you never? Never did you mention what should be the most important part of your life. Why? Are you ashamed of Him, or were you afraid that you may insult me? What if I did not know Him? Would you not want to have given me the chance to accept Him by telling me of His presence in your life? Did you think that I would love you less?"

He went on to explain that was the only thing about me that he didn't understand. Sanaa had been Muslim. He had told her many times of his beliefs, but she would not hear. That had caused him great pain, but he had loved her so.

Shame faced me because I knew that he was correct. How many times had I tiptoed around the thought that he may be Muslim? What a relief to know that he loved my God, my Jesus. There were no excuses for not being forthright with him. A grave error had been made on my part. God must be shaking his head at me. What a deeper connection we would have shared all of these years. All of the Sundays that I had missed taking Farid to the local church. Once again, I was speechless. He was right; this had created a sort of barrier between us.

We started our time in Bali after getting settled, talking about our very souls and our love for God and the fact that Jesus was the very topic that should have been discussed over the years. Was I so shallow that I would have traded God's love for a few good times? Had I once again sold my soul? Together, we knelt in this foreign bungalow and prayed for forgiveness. The tears that were shed were those of Farid. Tears of sorrow that the love of his life had failed to speak of the essence of life for so many in our country of America, that very country founded on the love of God. Why had I not welcomed the chance to witness to a foreigner whom I suspected of being of a different religion? Did he not deserve the benefit of hearing about my faith and denying it if he wished?

As we sat in the fading sunlight, I felt all mystery in this land of ancient beauty now removed. There was only one God for Farid and me. That bond broke all others. After hours of talk, I felt as if I truly knew this man before me. I knew him in a different light. All suspicions and doubts were laid aside. He was the nature of my grandfather, my father, and my brother. Here was someone whom I understood and could trust. In this land of misty mountains, streams, beaches, bustling cities, sophisticated culture, and endless beauty, I now knew that man whom I had longed to know.

Farid gave me the small box wrapped in golden paper, which he purchased earlier. Inside was a beautiful diamond cross. I would wear it until the day that I died. It represented all the tears and hours of discussion. Together, we would do something that counted in this world, something for our God. I did not understand my reluctance earlier to speak of Him. It had not been shame. Farid was a better person than I. All night, we sat in that spot and talked. We laughed, we cried, we shared our souls. Finally, we bowed and prayed again. Together we watched a brilliant display as the sun rose in this mysterious land. That was the most perfect day in the most perfect place of my time on earth.

44

LUXURIOUS LIVING

Our schedule in paradise became reversed. We had always been early risers, so bedtime was early evening. In paradise, we sat all night talking, which we had never done. After the sun was brightly shinning, we took showers and settled for a day's sleep. Farid was instantly breathing heavily. I knew that he was soundly sleeping. For a long time, I watched him. As he slept, he would frequently smile. Once, he even laughed softly. Lightly, I touched his cheek. Then quietly I left the bed to kneel by the side. Now I was so consumed in lies that I didn't even think about them.

Last night, we bore our souls and prayed for mercy from lies and deceptive behavior on my part. Never did I even consider the lie of lies, not until now. I had not made an attempt to explain that our entire relationship was based on untruths. Frank and his group of cronies had me so enmeshed in their schemes. Why had I not fessed up? Did I think that it would end when I told him about the way we met? What about the fact that there was no Luke whom I still grieved?

Surely, once all of the lies were exposed, he would send me away forever. What bothered me deeply was that I made no effort to be truthful last night. He would never forgive me for acting as though I had relinquished all secrets from the past. As I prayed for strength, I realized that I would suffer the consequences for my betrayal to the man whom I loved. All of this sickened me. Before I awakened him from a sleep of innocence, I went to the toilet and threw up.

"Farid, please wake up. I hate to do this, but I must tell you a few things, which I have kept secret for all of these years together. I'm afraid that you will never feel the same for me. After this, I will fly back home on my own expense. You never have to see my lying face again." Tears once again flowed from my eyes, which were now lined with more wrinkles. No longer the beauty that I had once been, I felt very vulnerable and small.

"What? Catherine, what did you say? I'm sorry, I was soundly asleep. Give me a moment to clear my head of dreams of you. We were walking in the surf of the beach, I guess in the Bahamas, laughing and joking as we always are." He smiled. Then a look of confusion crossed his face. "What were you saying about my changing feelings or some such nonsense? I don't know what you mean. How could I change feelings for you, my darling? We have been together for so very long. What have you done? It cannot be so serious. Yes?" He smiled and tousled my hair.

"I am so afraid. You see, for all of these years, in fact since we began together, I have kept a secret from you. That secret grew into a pack of lies. This will sound unbelievable, but here goes. Before we met, I joined a group. Really, I don't know the name of it or the purpose. Sounds preposterous, I know, but at the time, it seemed challenging and fun. Thinking that I was so beautiful and special, it seemed like a great idea. The promise that I would never be in danger was an enticement. Farid, there was never a Luke. The night that I fell into the ice sculpture, sprawled on the floor, was my opportunity to meet you. It was just a fun game to me. Never did I think that we would fall in love. I am a liar and a deceiver. You would be better off without me."

For several long moments, he just looked at me. Then he rose slowly to a sitting position and smiled. "Catherine, I am a part of something even bigger than yours. You know that? Don't you think that I would know of your involvement? I even told you that I had done an investigation on you. Did you think that I wouldn't find the truth? All of these years, I have waited for you to tell me the truth about two things—your involvement in the organization and your love for God. Here, in this special place of soul searching and truth, you have felt the need to be honest. I love you. Nothing has changed, my darling. I still feel the same but am relieved that you are honest. Really, I almost laughed when you came up with the Luke thing. Did you really think that I didn't know? Now, lie back down. All is well. When I love, Catherine, I do my homework, and I know all of the facts. In love, my heart is strong but my mind stronger." He put his arm around me and pulled me close. Almost instantly, he was back asleep.

I on the other hand, wiped my eyes, hiccupping due to all of the tears and emotions. It seemed forever before I fell into a deep and glorious sleep. Free of lies and deceit, I too slept the sleep of innocence.

When I finally awakened, it was dark outside. I was famished. Farid was still soundly asleep. The sounds of the night were strange. Insect sounds, which I had never heard, filled the air with haunting hisses. Strange birds were calling for their mates. I had my lifelong mate right beside me where he belonged. Soon Farid squeezed my arm.

"I am starving. What about you, my love?" His smile was dazzling even in the dark. He turned on a lamp then he rang a bell. Shortly, one of his staff entered with a large tray. We had moved to a table in the corner. Dinner was served with a large glass of Aqua and red wine from Farid's private collection. The appetizer was a delicious foie gras with hot homemade bread. We had small courses of other scrumptious faire such as tangy chesses, which I had never encountered. The main entrée was *sate-lilit*, which was minced seafood on lemon grass sticks grilled to perfection over charcoal.

Everything was to perfection. Even though the portions were small, I was completely satisfied. Farid made jokes about my confession. I knew that he was trying to soothe me, but I felt like such a deceiver and liar in his presence. Soon enough, dessert was served. It was a homemade orange sherbet with orange zest releasing in our mouths with every bite—refreshing and perfect.

Finally, we carried our glass of *lemoncillo* outside in the gardens. Farid had given me a wrap. It was as he had explained, very cool. We sat in the darkness with soft lanterns lighting the various paths crossing the compound. The effect of the lantern light softly glowing was haunting. We were facing the rainforest in the distance. I was shaking due to the cool temperature and all of the emotion lately. If truth be known, I was also a little afraid. The sounds were all different from nights in Eufaula. Yet I did not miss home. This enchanting place excited me. There was a feeling of intrigue and suspense.

We walked over the flowing stream. I stopped to put my toes in the water but quickly withdrew them. The water was very cold. Farid laughed. He explained that we could set our easels here in the afternoons and cool off easily by submerging our feet in the cold waters. I couldn't wait for tomorrow. All awareness of time dissolved. How long had we been here? I wasn't sure. We said nothing as we strolled the beautiful, peaceful grounds.

When we returned to the room, all traces of dinner were removed. The bedding refreshed. Together, we turned off all of the lights and once again slept for hours.

Upon awaking, I was surprised to see that it was late afternoon. Now I was tired of sleeping. The thought of setting up our easels and painting together thrilled me. Still, I remained quiet until Farid opened his eyes. He laughed to see me wide awake and ready for adventure.

When we walked out into the gardens, our easels were set with tubes of paint and various boar-hair brushes. There was even a large tent by the stream, which sheltered our stations from the hot sun. This was to be the pattern daily. Almost as if able to read our minds, whatever we desired was waiting. I never had to lift a finger in exertion. I felt like royalty but smiled as I realized that Farid was of royal lineage.

We had the most marvelous end to our day. Quietly, we painted together. I was trying to capture the mountain but was really struggling. Plein air art was not my forte. Seldom did I paint outside. I would paint from photographs once I was inside my studio. Never had I realized how difficult it was to capture the light just as it was at a particular time. It was almost impossible for me to do that with oils. Farid was very quick in his strokes so that he could capture the light perfectly. He explained that it was easier to do so with watercolors, but I was not experienced in that medium. Finally, he suggested that I wait on painting the mountain. Instead, he suggested that I concentrate on painting the face of a flower in the light. That I was able to easily complete.

Dinner that night was delicious. We were served *babi guling* roast suckling pig over rice. It was so flavorful that I had a second portion. Farid had assembled such talent in his staff. They were in and out of the room quickly. Never did they speak. They did their jobs to our complete satisfaction. Such were our days and nights in the island of mystery.

45

MY LAST ASSIGNMENT

Our beloved Bali days rushed past. Each one as happy and fulfilling as the day before. Soon, we were back on our schedule of early rising. Mornings we enjoyed an espresso as we watched the birds land in the rice paddies facing our home. They put on quite a show. Then, we enjoyed a wonderful breakfast by the best cook in the world. We rushed downtown where we found treasures galore. Sometimes we enjoyed lunch at one of the many restaurants. I became fixated on *balek betutu*, which was darkened duck topped with herb paste roasted over banana leaves again over charcoal. Often we would be full from dinner the night before so that we would only enjoy a *lawar* Balinese salad with thinly chopped vegetables, minced meat, coconut, and spices. Farid told me that the traditional way included blood mixed into it but assured me that they did not serve that unless requested.

Thanksgiving arrived. I was not disappointed. His cook served a turkey that outdid anything in the states. Dinner was beautifully trimmed complete with all of the extras. I noticed that this year, Farid ate with relish. We were as an old married couple now.

Farid's circle of friends included writers and entrepreneurs. Comprised of four couples with two extra men, they were all highly educated and competitive. This was a successful group of eccentric people. They had accomplished incredible success, more than most people could only dream. We shared dinner almost nightly at each other's home. Enchanted, Farid's home was my favorite, but they were all so beautifully appointed with staff to rival Farid's. Banter from evenings together would sometimes become heated if politics were involved. We seemed well-rounded with strong opinions. Often we played charades or told stories to each other. There were no barriers of pretension between us. Laughter was sincere and spontaneous. These were beautiful people who enjoyed the "good life."

After Thanksgiving, one day, we were painting when out of the blue, Farid asked if I would consider staying on indefinitely in Bali. The other homes were well-staffed as were the two galleries. Actually, the galleries were in much more competent hands with Jill and Farid's friend, Paul. Since I was enjoying myself so much, it seemed like a great idea. All plans of leaving after the New Year were dissolved. We planned to stay until the spirit moved us to return to Eufaula; unsure as to the time.

We decorated the houses for Christmas. Nothing very elaborate. Displaying live trees throughout, it was a challenge varying the theme. We added white lights outside on the balconies sprinkling them through many of the adjoining trees. The result was beautiful and festive. Things could not be happier until one day in Ubud. We had just completed lunch, preparing to head home. Farid received a phone call. While he was talking, I strolled outside to enjoy the cool rainy day. Noticing Frank standing by the side terrified me. He motioned for me to approach. My heart raced, my palms perspired. I couldn't do this anymore.

"Frank, go away. The jig is over. Farid knows everything. I have nothing to lose, so please don't come around me again."

He glared at me angrily. "Fine, Cat, we just have one more assignment. After you complete it, we will leave your life for good."

Thinking that I had finally won my freedom, relief overtook me. "Great, I'll do anything but please leave me alone." I glared back at him.

"Great, no problem, Cat. We want you to kill Farid."

I staggered backward. I thought that I misunderstood him. "What did you say? Kill Farid? Is this some sort of sick joke or test? You must be out of your mind."

Frank explained very calmly that this was the intention from the beginning. Since I possessed constant access, it would be easy for me. Did he not understand that I could never kill anyone especially the man whom I loved?

"Don't be absurd. I will do no such ridiculous thing."

"That is fine also, Cat. Then say good-bye to your brother and family. We will take them all out. This is not a game. Remember Mr. Greene? They will have an accident similar to his. Farid is not the man that you think. In fact, he is a vicious killer. A terrorist whom many have tracked for years. You love your country so much? Well, there is a plan to kill thousands. He is a part of a complicated plot. Cat, he is a con artist of unparalleled precision. Can you really sleep with yourself when they carry out something with no regard to human lives lost? You better think carefully. You following me, Cat?" He strolled away but not before turning to smile at me.

The rest of the day was a blur. My paradise descended into hell. I could not help but think of the many "business meetings." Those meetings were mostly followed by tremors and silence from my love. Had he been involved in something sinister? I never watched the news anymore. Enjoyment of my life seemed a priority. Sure I would have heard about something in my own country, but could he have been a part of something evil in another part of the world?

Again, I felt as if I would be sick. We planned to visit Noel's home for dinner that evening, but I couldn't. I needed to think. I begged Farid to attend without me. Noel was his closest friend. Finally, he agreed. After he left, I phoned home. Things were fine there as well as with Nathaniel. I felt guilty for not calling him earlier. He appeared amazed that I was in Bali but seemed to understand my wanderlust. Our parents also had shared it. After hanging up the phone, I knelt to pray. I knew that there must be a way out of this agony.

My prayers helped, but no answers to my plight were given, not at that time. After taking a sleeping pill, the phone startled me. Thinking that it was Farid, I was outraged to hear Frank. "Mrs. Jones?"

"I don't know what to do. I will not kill him."

"Fine, I'm glad that you phoned your brother. That will be the last time you speak with him." The line went dead. Terrified, I hung up the phone. Farid entered. He seemed festive. Explaining that it wasn't as much fun without me, he busied himself for bed.

He climbed in his spot beside me. I knew what needed to be done. I told him everything. Explaining Frank's role as my contact, as well as Barrington and Jim, he listened with deep intensity. I assumed this was news to him.

"Catherine, just relax. We know all of this. They are an important agency accomplishing tremendous good. A force to reckon with, but our organization is higher, more advanced. There is nothing that you can tell me that will surprise me."

"Did you know that they want me to kill you?" I finally whispered.

He turned ghostly white. I assumed that he did not. Expressing disbelief at such a far out idea, he guaranteed me that they did not have the ability to perform such an action without approval. According to Farid, clearance had not been given. I felt encouraged. One of the staff entered with our nightly glass of Campari. We walked around the gardens. Farid assured me that he would take care of these threats from Frank first thing tomorrow.

"This is all so absurd that I won't even think of it tonight. It only makes me angry." Suddenly, he dropped his glass, staggering slightly.

"I guess that I had more to drink than I realized. I need to lie down." I assisted him back to the bedroom. In just a few moments, he was breathing heavily. I smiled as I thought of Frank finally being put in his place. Just then, the phone rang.

"Mrs. Jones, Farid is out? The gun is under your side of the mattress. He will never know what happened. You will be immediately removed from the scene. All will be well if you do as we say. Nathaniel and family are driving on a little trip as we speak. Their car is bugged. Listen to your precious nephew." Suddenly, I could hear the children laughing as they were all singing. Farid drastically miscalculated this. Dropping the phone, I jumped from the bed. Sure enough, tucked deep into the mattress was a gun with silencer. I picked it up, pointed at his back. One shot, it would all be over. He would never suffer. *Not a bad way to die*, I thought. Perspiration ran down my face. I could not believe that I stood pointing the gun at my love. Falling to my knees, I screamed, "Dear God, I can't. I can't kill him. Please forgive me, Nathaniel."

Hearing a noise behind me, I turned in shock to see my Jean from Eufaula holding a much-larger gun. Two shots were rapidly discharged into the back of Farid. I watched in horror as blood ran from the site. Suddenly, the noise of a helicopter arose from the valley. Jean grabbed me. Pushing at me, she ordered me to run. We ran as deer from the house to the awaiting chopper. I was shaking so badly that I could barely breathe. Once again shocked, I could not believe that my Albert was the pilot. We were up and gone in minutes. Other neighbors had private planes and helicopters, so this would not be suspicious to our friends.

Our friends? What had I caused? For weeks, I would be unable to speak. Now, I listened as Albert explained that he could not reveal details. He and Jean had been part of the plan from the beginning. They were valued members of the organization. Everyone hoped that I would be able to carry out my orders, but just in case, they were backups. He assured me that my family would be fine. They never intended to harm them. As I digested all of this, I thought about my suspicions for Albert. His deep intelligence. An uncanny ability to speak several languages, as well as all of his other talents. He had been aware of everything that I did from the beginning. Jean, dear, placid Jean was an assassin? This seemed ridiculous and impossible to comprehend.

"Is Jill a part also?" I trusted no one. They assured me that she was not. I feared that Jean and Albert may have killed my Mr. Greene as well but knew better than ask. Not another word was spoken. Jean gave me a pill. I would have taken anything to stop the pain. I would never forger seeing his blood freely run out of the two holes in his back.

I was rendered unable to speak until we landed in Birmingham. Albert told me that I would never see him and Jean again. From that point, I would be left alone. It would have been impossible for me to look them in the eyes. When we arrived back home in Eufaula, I staggered inside. Our bedroom remained as we left it except for clean bedding. My painting had been removed. It was the only thing that I could not find. I was heartbroken remembering Farid's warning that the answers would be provided by the painting.

They had taken everything that I loved except for Nat and family. Never did I cry again. Numbness covered me in a blanket. The rest of my days, I would pay for silly actions of my youth. If only I could go back denying Frank's deadly organization from ever entering my life.

Just numbness surrounded when I awakened the next day and each day thereafter. Nothing more was said of Farid. A few weeks later, the deeds to all of the property that he promised arrived. I would call the caretaker of each but could not bring myself to visit. My self-imposed hell seemed only fitting. No more did I paint, although I did enjoy the gallery and the work of others. I knew that God had forgiven me for my impetuousness. My grandfather had been correct. I was foolish beyond what he had suspected of me.

46

THE PAINTING

Years have passed but not a day without aching for Farid. When I look in the mirror, it is not a fifty something that I see but an old woman. Old way beyond my years, it does not matter to me. Beauty is so fleeting. When you are young, you don't expect to be old, not really.

Life goes on. I find joy in the sunset or the face of a child. My new staff are nice enough, but I do not reach out to them. They are workers in my home, nothing more. My friends wonder what happened but no longer ask. Seldom do I see them although I know that I could correct that with a simple phone call. Life passes me just as I desire.

Instead of painting, now I work in the gardens. A part of me actually misses Albert and Jean, or maybe it was the life that I had that I miss. Each day, I touch the spot where the painting sat for so long. In my mind, I go over each detail.

You are very intelligent, Cat, you will figure it out. He had been wrong about two important issues. That cost him his life. Maybe if I trace each stroke in my mind, I may be able to dislodge the secret that the painting held. I am not able to discover the answers. All seems lost.

I hear locals talk when I enter a restaurant or even in the gallery. They discuss my great beauty at one time. "Something happened when she traveled abroad with her lover. He was a sheik you know. They lived here in Eufaula. We hear that he was married back in Saudi Arabia. He wanted to end a long affair with Catherine. They traveled far away so that he could explain things. It must have broken her heart, as well as her body. Look at her. She is almost reclusive. No longer a beauty. It is so sad. After he ended things, she never was the same. He probably returned to his true love, his wife." I smile. They are so wrong. It is almost humorous. I am known as a recluse. Visitors are not welcomed in my home.

Late afternoon on a summer day, the front door chimes. I answer the door with haste. No one would visit me unless they are looking for money. These thoughts pass through my mind as I open the door. The woman standing in front of me is tanned with short, very blonde hair. She is lovely. Wearing designer clothes, her look is familiar. She is not looking for money. I am sure that I know her. A few moment pass as we stare at each other.

"Catherine, it is I. It is Jean. Time is of the essence, so I must be speedy. Here is a package for you. I removed it long ago from your bedroom. I think that it may be the answer that you have longed to discover. I wish you well, Catherine. Good-bye." She walks quickly away as she looks over her shoulder.

Locking the door, I carry the brown-paper package upstairs. I know what it contains. My hands shake as I remove the wrapping. There sparkling as it did long ago is the painting. I can't cry. I have longed to be able to do so. Perhaps the tears will release some of the pain and confusion in my heart, my mind. For hours, I study it. Nothing comes to mind. Jean was heroic in her actions. She hid it from the organization. But why? Did she know that Farid was innocent, but she had to do her job? More questions assail me without answers.

I lovingly turn the painting over, a thought comes to mind. *Farid made the frame.* He covered the back professionally with heavy brown paper. With a letter opener, I remove the stiff cover from the back. Something falls to the floor. It is a letter from Farid. My heart skips a beat.

Dear Catherine, if you are reading this, I am gone. Possibly, they even convinced you to end my life. Regardless of how it occurred, I know that you have assumed responsibility for my death. Do not blame yourself. That is an order! We were both involved in things beyond our control. My regret is that we were unable to grow old together. I hope that you are painting and sailing *Cat's Catch*. All of the things that I gave you were for you to enjoy as you age since I can't be a part of your life. I will try to explain what happened, but I can't give details. You understand.

Catherine, your organization was important but not the highest. I was involved in something that few knew existed. Unfortunately, there was a problem of communication between the two factions. I understand both sides, how they think. If only they had not been so arrogant, they could have kept many of us safe. The behavior from your group is predictable. Shamefully, I can imagine the lies, which they have told. They must cover their mistakes. I was not a terrorist, so forget that statement. My job was to work with terrorists. That is why I would be upset on return from my "business trips." I witnessed horrible things by people with no regard for life or faith. My death was necessary to protect a small group of people who keep the world safe from those who spew lies and death.

Don't morn for me any longer. It is time to enjoy your remaining days. Travel, my love. Visit London and the Bahamas. Now you know why I could not leave the Bali home to you. It would prove extremely dangerous, even now. I never really thought that they would act with such abandonment of rules by killing me. It could have been prevented. I did not understand how out of control they had become. Most of all, don't forget your faith, not ever. My most important gift was reminding you of our God. Please never leave him from your life again. Don't let them win, Catherine. Do something of importance. You will know how to help. Remember to enjoy your life. Until you cross the final river, I wait for you with opened arms, my love.

Farid

Now, I could cry. Restricted tears could not be controlled. I cried as a young girl cries for a love that never existed or the loss of a friend who was never such. The innocence stripped from me is released in tears. My nights freed of the terrible images, which wrecked my sleep.

Friends, now I surround myself with Linda, Sammy, Margie, John, and Rhonda. Rhonda never mentions Barrington, which is well with me. My house staff now are my friends. I opened the door of my life to them. They are as wonderful as I once thought Albert and Jean. I purchase a new wardrobe of the latest styles. My hair is the latest cut. I spend time going between London and the Bahamas. Life is good. I know that Farid would approve. I paint. Each home has two easels sat side by side. My French easel and Farid's favored metal Italian one greet me each day. The paintings that he was working remain on his easel as he left them. He continues to paint beside me, at least in my mind.

Most importantly, my God will never be ignored. My foundation, in Farid's name, reaches people of all faiths, just as Jesus never pushed himself on anyone, nor do we. With biblical instruction, we teach all who are interested about our God. They need to know that he doesn't force anyone to accept him. The choice is theirs. Faith is a gift not for everyone. Yet those who understand are the blessed. Changes will occur in those lives. Those who believe, understand what the faithless can never grasp. Many have been reached. Farid would be happy to learn Muslims have joined. This is my quest, my gift to an extraordinary man, my love.

Life is happy once again. Each night, I look at the painting. Gratitude fills me that Farid loved me so much. Even in death, he reached out to me. Bali? I long to return but don't think that I ever will. The pain would be more than I could bear. I don't need places to remind me of Farid. He lives in my heart. Still, on misty, rainy nights, the winds blow hauntingly as that magical place soars in my mind. Eerie voices seem to whisper, "Come away. Come away!"